a girl's best friend

kristin billerbeck

a girl's best friend

BOOK II: *spa girls* COLLECTION

kristin billerbeck

INTEGRITY®
PUBLISHERS
Nashville

A GIRL'S BEST FRIEND

Published by Integrity Publishers, a division of Integrity Media, Inc., 5250 Virginia Way, Suite 110, Brentwood, TN 37027.

HELPING PEOPLE WORLDWIDE EXPERIENCE the MANIFEST PRESENCE of GOD.

Published in association with Yates & Yates, LLP, Attorneys and Literary Agents, Orange, CA.

Unless otherwise noted all Scripture quotations are taken from the King James Version. Public domain.

Scripture quotations marked (NIV) are taken from The Holy Bible, New International Version® (NIV®). Copyright © 1973, 1978, 1984 by International Bible Society. Used by permission of Zondervan. All rights reserved.

Cover Design: Brand Navigation, LLC/www.brandnavigation.com
Interior Design: Sharon Collins/Artichoke Design, Franklin, TN

Library of Congress Cataloging-in-Publication Data

Billerbeck, Kristin.

 A girl's best friend / by Kristin Billerbeck.

     p. cm. -- (Spa Girls collection)

 Summary: "Second in the Spa Girls series focuses on Morgan, who seems to have it all, but her etiquette-controlled, well-sculpted life has left her without an identity to call her own"—Provided by publisher.

 ISBN-13: 978-1-59145-329-1
 ISBN-10: 1-59145-329-1 (pbk.)

 1. Socialites--Fiction. 2. Rich people--Fiction. 3. San Francisco (Calif.)--Fiction. I. Title. II. Series.

 PS3602.I44G57 2006

 813'.54--dc22

                                                    2005030300

Printed in the United States of America
06 07 08 09 10 CHG 9 8 7 6 5 4 3 2

Dedication

To Jeffrey Yao, who keeps my handbag "issue" from becoming one, and to his wife, my great friend, Jackie Yao. She is my voice of reason, the antonym of me, and I'm so thrilled we're friends. One can't replace a friend who's willing to meet you at Pho Hoa every time you're in town, nor one who tells you that you are incredibly wrong when you are. With all the college degrees between them, you'd think they'd be smart enough not to hang out with me. Love you guys!

Acknowledgments

Once again, I must thank my posse of support: My critique group of Colleen Coble, Denise Hunter, and Diann Hunt. My agent, Jeana Ledbetter. The entire Integrity team. And special thanks to Leslie Peterson for editing this manuscript.

"I am come that they might have life, and that they might have it more abundantly."

John 10:10

chapter 1

There are plenty of fish in the sea. But really, there's not. It's not just our imaginations. It would be great if decent men were as plentiful as jumping salmon in a rushing river, but they aren't. For every Mr. Darcy (and he's married, incidentally) there are a hundred Mr. Wickhams. Or in more contemporary terms, for every one of Colin Firth, there are several thousand Hugh Grants. The odds are against us. But what can I say—I'm a romantic, and I can't abandon the fantasy of Prince Charming altogether. What girl with a heart can? I mean, I'm not asking to feed the five thousand; I just want one good fish!

I should give up the dream. Especially now, when common sense dictates that anyone possessing an IQ might want to take serious stock. If I were in battle, the general would yell, "Retreat! Retreat, stupid!"

I did graduate from college—a good one in fact, so I definitely know better. I read that women's brains have their neurons more tightly packed than men's, and consequently we process things faster. Apparently, I'm currently experiencing a bad circuit. Or complete and utter synapse failure. I'm not quite sure which.

I scan the newspaper's headline again and then clasp my

eyes shut, hoping when I open them this will be all over. But I open one eye slightly, and then the other, and I feel my strength leave me when I catch sight of the words again.

"This is not happening." I slink down into the overstuffed sofa and focus on the chenille texture. I hear myself cry out, though I have nothing left for tears. It's sort of a dry heave of sobs, a pathetic remainder of what was once a full-blown emotional wave. I suppose it is time to be moving on from this existence. It's too much work to cry anymore.

"I hope now you'll listen to your father when he suggests a man. He only has your best interests at heart." Mrs. Henry, our family maid, grabs the newspaper from me and crumples it before shoving it in a black plastic bag. She has always spoken to me like I'm four. But in her defense, I often leave the thinking to those around me. Why be bothered with petty issues like my opinions?

"No, please don't!" I reach out for the paper, and she pulls the bag away. I try to show her my pink, puffy face for a little sympathy, but she just looks away. Mrs. Henry probably wouldn't be moved by the average steamroller.

"Enough. We all make mistakes; now you get over yours."

Mrs. Henry has never had a first name, though she's been a fixture in our home for over twenty years. She dresses like Mrs. Doubtfire, exudes the warmth of a chilled cactus, and is under the distinct impression this is her home. Not ours.

I don't have the strength to fight her today. I allow her to pick up my feet from the coffee table and pluck the graveyard of balled-up Kleenex into her bag, her hand pecking like a determined chicken.

I wish I could just get over it. I'd relish the opportunity, but I'm not made of hearty German stock like Mrs. Henry. I feel everything far too intensely. That's always been my problem: an inordinate amount of emotions and guilt. A powerful combination of fuel to the explosive mental fire.

As Mrs. Henry drops the garbage bag for another task, I pull the newspaper back out and stick it under a decorative pillow. I smile at her when she looks at me and the bag. "The place looks great," I say, feeling a tad guilty. Just a tad. Part of me still wants to run through the house dropping Kleenex like the bread crumbs in "Hansel and Gretel." I am human.

I sneak another look at the picture on the newspaper and my stomach flutters again. I keep waiting for someone to come in laughing and say, "It was all just a joke. You've been punk'd!" But that's not going to happen, and I keep having to stare at his handsome face, trying to reconcile my emotions with what the police have said is the truth.

"There's a new *Chronicle* if you truly want to wallow." Mrs. Henry pulls out the morning newspaper, all crisp and pristine in its fresh round of hatred. On today's front page is the picture of me in a wedding gown, being carried off the fashion show runway.

"Jilted Jewelry Heiress's Lover Jailed," the paper shouts at me in charcoal black.

"He was not my lover!" I say to Mrs. Henry.

"But you are the Jilted Jewelry Heiress?" Mrs. Henry gives her best look of disgust and leaves the room.

It's a good thing there's nothing within reach for handy throwing!

I look at the picture of me, with a wistful smile on my face as I'm literally swept off my feet, and the corners of my mouth actually begin to turn up at the memory. Even with the way this ended, I still feel joy well up inside me like a perfect soap bubble as it lifts to the sky, its slick rainbow sides glistening with color.

Well, more like the oily dregs in a puddle at the gas station, really.

I look at that picture again, and note I look good. I'm happy. Even if it was brief, and a complete mockery of the emotion, it felt good.

Lilly Jacobs, my best friend and fashion designer, had begged me to do her fashion show.

"You'll be the talk of San Francisco!" she claimed.

And wasn't it the truth.

I know people don't generally think of me as shy, but I don't like the limelight. It's been thrust on me daily because of my birth, but I would have been just as happy to be in the back, pinning models and guarding my father's jewelry, which Lilly borrowed for the show. Really, I would have.

But then on that runway, I saw him. Oh, it was such a perfect, incredible moment. His eyes met mine, and everything that had passed between us was said in that moment. *I love you*, my eyes whispered. *There is only our future now.*

Maybe if I hadn't been in the wedding dress . . . But when I'd first looked at myself in the mirror . . . that elegant gown, clinging in all the right places . . . If only I hadn't had that Grace Kelly fantasy, maybe I wouldn't be here now.

However, as it was, I jumped into his arms willingly. "You've come back for me."

"I never would have left, but I had to make something of myself," he said, and we fell into a kiss. A stunning and vibrant kiss that made my body shout with joy.

"I love you, Andy Mattingly."

It was the last thing I said before he whisked me off into the San Francisco sunset.

From there, things got decidedly worse. I started remembering the returned letters, the disconnected phone numbers, the postage due for my "Dear Morgan" letter. Those types of irritating things, like the bad, itchy tag in the back of a new, luxurious silk T-shirt.

"Why didn't you answer my letters?" I demanded.

"I couldn't contact you until I'd made it big, Morgan. You mean too much to me. I had to prove to your father I could provide for you."

Oh, well, okay.

As he whisked me to the waiting limo, I realized his music contract must have come through. I was going to marry a Christian rock star. How cool was that?

Andy Mattingly wears charm like expensive cologne. It clings to him sweetly, masking his motives and blinding me with its intoxicating power. His words are like honey, and when they drizzled over me that day, I became paralyzed in the sticky film. My brain simply shut down and I wanted whatever he said to be true. It was so good, who wouldn't want it to be true?

As we ran onto the street, breaking away from the security guards watching my father's diamond pieces, I thought only briefly about my father's worried face and Lilly's fashion show becoming a spectacle. In my mind, I knew they'd rejoice for me and I sang that old Howard Jones song "No One is to Blame."

Andy Mattingly had rescued me from a life of social drudgery and familial duty. No longer would I have to answer to my father's every whim or parade around in front of San Francisco matrons so they could inspect my father's latest diamond acquisition.

I am free! I thought.

"Where to, Mr. Schwartz?" the limo driver asked.

"Schwartz? You stole Max Schwartz's limo?" I was incredulous.

This should have been my first clue. He had indeed stolen Lilly's boyfriend's waiting limo and I was his accomplice. Not only had I abandoned Lilly, but I'd left her dream night in a shambles. It had been her turn. Her night to shine.

"What was I thinking?" I say aloud, tossing a Kleenex on the floor.

"You were thinking, 'What I really need is a good spa date with my Spa Girls, but I want the big bed at the spa, and this is my chance. Because normally, my life is so perfect. I never get the bed to myself.'"

I look up to see my best friends since college, my Spa Girls: Lilly Jacobs and Dr. Poppy Clayton. Lilly is the designer who got me into this mess. Poppy is the accessory who helped her, convincing me I was the perfect showstopper. Well, if that wasn't the truth. . . .

"You know," I say accusingly to them as they approach. "If I hadn't been in a couture wedding gown during fashion week, my humiliation would have been my own private misery. Perhaps even a figment of my imagination. But no—" I hold up the paper for them to see. "No, being in a wedding gown made me the talk over San Francisco cornflakes. The West's newest, dumbest blonde."

"Get over it," Lilly says, plopping down into a chair and fingering a nearby Lladro figurine. "Life is full of bad surprises. Think of mine when I had to take a cab home that night. I mean, I get a write-up in *Women's Wear Daily*, and I have to take a cab. What a letdown. So are you coming with us to the spa?"

I sit up on the sofa. "Actually, I'm not really up to a spa date. I was thinking about what I was going to do with my life now that I'm a convicted adulterer without so much as a trial." Well, I may not be an adulteress, but I'm certainly guilty of extreme lack of common sense.

Poppy shrugs. "So you can do that at the spa. Ask Lilly— her life was crap a few months ago. The spa helped, right Lilly?"

Lilly purses her lips. "As Poppy so eloquently puts it, yes, my life was . . . less than stellar. The spa and thinking through things definitely helped. Come play with us."

Lilly comes toward me, takes the newspaper from my hands, and gazes at Andy's mug shot. "I gotta say, he's a fine-looking specimen. Even in a mug shot. If it makes you feel any better, I'd have gone willingly, too, Morgan. It's not just that he's handsome; he's got that Tom Cruise charm, the kind that makes you say, 'I know better, but what the heck?'"

"Come on and get ready. What else are you going to do?" Poppy asks.

"The media might follow us," I explain. I seem to have become Madonna overnight, with flashing bulbs and microphones stuffed in my face. It wouldn't have been any big deal if I hadn't been engaged to another man a few months ago. But between one fiancé dying and this one going to jail, I am currently the Black Widow. Or more appropriately, the Spinster of Death.

Poppy shrugs. "So the press will see Lilly trying to sneak pickles and Diet Pepsi into the spa. It's not like we have a lot to hide, Morgan. We're far too boring for that."

"I'm not bringing pickles," Lilly fires back. "Nana made us biscotti. That new boyfriend of hers has her baking."

At this point, my father comes walking into the room carrying a big, silver box. "Hi, girls," he says absently, then bends over an outlet and plugs in the box. It's a sign that reads (in sparkly lights, I might add), "San Francisco's Jeweler. Your Jeweler for Life."

"What are you doing with that, Dad?" I ask, knowing full well I don't want the answer.

"The press is at my door every day hoping to get a glimpse of you, and look at this!" He lifts the newspaper and shakes it. "They don't get the store name when they shoot the shop."

He starts to shake his head. "But this way—" He drops the paper and holds up his index finger. "This way, they can't help but show the shop name. If we're going to get publicity, we should make use of it. Bring all these gossip-mongers into the shop and bam!" He slaps the box. "Before they know it, they're applying for in-store credit."

"Maybe we should just get a sandwich board made and I can walk around Union Square handing out flyers," I suggest.

"Would you do that?" he asks excitedly, then notices my expression. "No, no, of course, you're kidding. She's kidding me, girls. She likes to make fun of her old man." Then he wags his finger at me, though I notice he doesn't relinquish his grip on the tacky sign. In all likelihood, the upscale merchants of Union Square will have his sign down in a week, but he won't care; it will be long enough to serve his purpose. I'm sure he factored all that into the cost.

"You know what they say, Dad. Any publicity is good publicity."

"All my male customers are afraid to come in. They don't want to be caught on the front page of the *Chronicle*. The least we can do is market new business—mine the ore, as it were." Then he drops his head, and his mouth comes open as he pauses.

I love his dramatic pauses; they're meant to give you the impression that he just can't bear to say what he must. Naturally, he always says it, and if there ever is any remorse, I've certainly never seen it.

"You couldn't get into the paper for getting engaged to San Francisco's wealthiest bachelor like Lilly? Lilly, when am I going to see that boy in my store?" He holds up a finger before she can muster an answer, and I give him the look that politely tells him to shut up. Not that he usually listens, but I see him snap his jaw shut, and I feel a wave of relief. "Before you all go running off, I have something for you, Morgan." He opens a velvet box and inside is an extraordinary blue diamond ring. "You need to wear this. We'll get more publicity if you put it on your left hand."

"But that's not going to happen," I tell him.

"Fine, fine. Wear it on your right. But if anyone asks, I am now the purveyor of the best blue diamonds in the United States. That's just a taste. That's three carats, VVS-quality surrounded in platinum. The ring can be designed to their taste."

"Whose taste, Dad? I'm not invited anywhere."

He waves me off. "You will be. Slide it on."

I put the ring on with a big sigh. "Happy?"

"You sure you won't wear it on the left hand? Then, the newspapers would wonder if you were engaged again, and—"

"Dad!"

"All right."

Lilly and Poppy are both staring at my dad with their mouths ready to catch the next fly that passes by. We've all known each other since college, but my dad isn't usually in his sales mode when my friends are around. I guess he's finally decided to tear the veil. All this time, everyone thought I was a princess. Well, even princesses have their calendar of duties.

"I'm concentrating on my business just now, Mr. Malliard, but when the time comes, you'll know." Lilly winks at my dad.

"I don't understand this generation. Businesses, spa trips … Whatever happened to good, old-fashioned getting married and having babies?"

Silence.

"So, Morgan," Lilly finally says through the icy stillness. "The spa?"

"I'll pack my bags," I say hastily as I reach for the newspaper in Lilly's hands and head to my bedroom.

Once inside, I let out a deep breath and slide to the floor on the Iranian carpet my father paid a fortune for. ("Six hundred knots per inch!" he boasted.) I lift the paper and look at Andy's picture one last time. I keep thinking that with just one more glance, I'll have the answers I need. But they aren't there. Not before. Not now.

Sure, there were signs he was slick like a water slide, but truthfully, I loved his quiet bravado and mistakenly took it for the nerve he'd need to face music rejection in Nashville. I pictured him standing up to the country version of Simon Cowell, and my heart clenched for him under such pressure. I was thankful for his solid personality and Bond-like arrogance.

What a putz!

Gazing around my professionally decorated room, I stare at all the "homey" touches given by the designer to generate the impression of warmth and comfort. In reality, someone could rip a picture out of *Architectural Digest* and it would feel more like home than this. I have lived my entire life like a piece of exquisite sculpture, careful not to disturb my surroundings or move from my appointed spot. I'm just one more piece of furniture.

I know my friends are waiting, but I suddenly feel like there's so much to be gleaned from this bedroom. So much about me that I need to understand before I venture out into the world again. I pull myself off the floor and cross the room to the oversized, arched window. It's a gorgeous day. Sun beams into the room, and I can see clear to the Marin Headlands. One thing about San Francisco's fog, when it's gone, the view is unparalleled. No one has a truer appreciation for a clear view than a San Franciscan who generally spends her days buried in a misty gray world. At least, the beginning and the end of the day are spent in soggy bookends of clouds.

From my window, I can observe the litany of city traffic below: the cable cars, the ferries on the Bay, even the halted cars lined up on the Golden Gate Bridge. I wonder how many of those people read the *Chronicle* this morning. I wonder how many know me only as the Jilted Jewelry Heiress.

As I look across the water to Alcatraz, it suddenly dawns on me that the jail I've created for myself is probably harder to escape than that jutting hard rock in the middle of the frigid San Francisco Bay. Mine has Richard Malliard as the warden.

I've waited up here on Russian Hill, hoping for Prince Charming to rescue me. And when I finally let down my hair, I placed it smack in the hands of a con artist. What I'm seeing for the first time in my bedroom, with the absence of anything I'd really call my own without the decorator's help, is that I have no idea who I am. I'm not interesting enough to rescue is the sad fact of the matter, and I have made my own bed.

Okay, not technically speaking—Mrs. Henry actually makes my bed. But my mental bed? That's all mine. A tangled mass of 600-thread-count Egyptian cotton sheets that no one wants to bother straightening. The thing is if I don't do it, no one will.

I stuff the newspaper into my desk drawer and pull out my designer luggage before realizing this is part of the problem. I hate this luggage. My father bought it in Paris, hoping to impress someone, I suppose. Tossing the fancy stuff back, I yank out a duffle bag I got as a freebie and fill it with a few T-shirts and some sweats. It looks like something Lilly would bring, and this makes me smile.

Reality . . . here I come.

emerge from my room to find Lilly and Poppy wringing their hands over me. Not physically, but they stop talking when I enter and grin at me in a placating way. As if I'm in the "special" classroom.

"I'm fine," I announce. "Are you fine, Lilly?"

"Why wouldn't I be?"

"I haven't been the best friend to you lately."

Lilly shrugs. "Whatever. Max and I took a cab, no big deal. You have bigger fish to fry. The fact that we haven't seen you in two months was more nerve-racking."

"Be sure and smile for the cameras, girls. And Lilly, you should make sure they spell your name right in case there are any fashionistas wanting to buy your stuff."

"What should I do?" Poppy, our gauze-wearing chiropractic friend asks.

"Tell them you're the 'Before,'" Lilly jokes. "Or the *Glamour* 'Don't,' and we're on our way to make you over."

"You know," Poppy says angrily, "people just really don't think that much about what you wear, Lilly. You have an over-inflated ego or a deep-rooted insecurity that should be addressed."

Lilly gasps. "Heresy! You're speaking to a designer. In my

world, people care what you wear. If they didn't, I'd still be poring over spreadsheets in finance."

"I'm just saying, I show up like this everywhere," Poppy lifts her gauzy, Nightmare-on-Polk-Street skirt. "People don't really care."

"That's because you look like Nicole Kidman, Poppy." Lilly shakes her head. "People don't care because you're gorgeous. Don't kid yourself—you make it acceptable. Try being homely and dressing like that and see how far you get. Quasimodo in gauze does not have the same reactions. Case in point? If I went on *Oprah* and jumped on her couch to tell her I was in love? They'd come out with a straightjacket. Tom Cruise gets away with it because he's gorgeous."

"You both worry too much what people think," Poppy accuses. Then she gets her natural-healing expression on and takes her Zen tone. Here it comes. "Self-esteem comes from the Lord, not other people. Why should we care what others think?"

"Well, my church congregation seemed to care," I say, recalling with too much emotion my Sunday experience. "When I walked into church, there were whispers, and they didn't even try to mask their disdain that I should enter a holy place. They'd convicted me, painted me the scandalous woman, and I never even had the chance to defend myself."

Lilly nods. "Yeah, your church always stunk, though. You just never saw it. I knew when we showed up that night to your singles group that that gang didn't feel the love."

Lilly is right. She usually is. True, she's often right without much thought given to tact, but still.

"It would be really nice to believe people didn't care." I sling my bag over my shoulder. "That they gave you the benefit of the doubt. But people love to witness failure."

"You didn't fail," Poppy says. "You made a mistake. Anger doesn't do any good."

I feel said anger well up within me like a marshmallow boiling over an open flame. "You know, if it was Johnny Depp I was accused of adultery with, well, so be it, gossip away. But a guy without a job, who was living off his wife in Daly City while I thought he was off in Nashville making his way as a Christian artist? Now that's just humiliating. Scandal with Brad Pitt is one thing, but it takes on a whole different feeling with Andy Mattingly, bigamist and small-time con artist."

My friends just let me rant. They know scandal with Brad Pitt really holds no better appeal. *Scandal* is an ugly word for a reason, and the scarlet letter is alive and well in today's free society. Even in liberal San Francisco.

Poppy grabs my duffle from me and nearly knocks herself over. "What do you have in here? Are you toting pickles now, too?"

She opens my bag, and I look away.

"Need a little self-help fix, Morgan?" Poppy pulls out the first book: *The Purpose-Driven Life*. The second: *Dr. Phil's Life Strategies*. The third: *Making Peace with Your Parents*. And the fourth: Max Lucado's *It's Not about You*. Both of them are staring at me as though I'm a complete stranger now, as I'm not exactly the inner-search type. I'm all about the outer search and heading to Nordstrom when the pressure mounts.

"Have you been watching *Oprah* again?" Lilly asks.

"I'm remaking my life." I shrug. "Those are books I've collected over the years." *But never actually read*, I add silently. Confession: I usually go to a boutique until the feelings of "Daddy angst" dissipate, as his Visa payment expands. Mission accomplished.

Poppy shrugs. "You got a Bible in here?"

"Oh! I'll be right back!" I run and grab the Bible that Lilly covered for my wedding that never happened. She made it out of the shantung silk I bought for the gown, and it's one of my very favorite things. First, because she made it, and next because I think of Marcus when I see it.

Thinking of my almost-first marriage helps take some of the sting out of my recent sort-of-second marriage. Marcus and I may not have been getting married for love, but we did love each other in a very special way. His death from liver disease really put me into a place of mass confusion.

"So we're ready?" Poppy asks when I run back out.

"We are."

The scent of my father's expensive cologne lingers in the room like an invisible cloud of his very being. I can almost make out his shape. "Did my father leave?" They nod and I feel relief that I can just disappear under the radar.

Mrs. Henry is nowhere to be seen, and that's just as well too. We have never actually liked each other, but from what my father tells me, she was good to my mother. I vaguely remember that, but Mrs. Henry's rudeness to our surviving family has far outweighed anything good I remember. I was too young, and my father was too desperate at the time. All I know is the woman hovers like a ghost and is just as creepy.

"Let's go," Lilly says, and she wears her anxiety by shaking her hands nervously. Lilly has a difficult time sitting still. I'm still not sure why she comes with us to the spa; she practically has to force herself to sit through a treatment—like she's getting tortured. She has the personality of a hamster on a running wheel, as if slowing down will leave her hovering between up and down, so she can't stop.

"Okay, one more thing before we go," I add as we head towards the elevator. I take a deep breath and say out loud what I've been thinking since they hauled Andy off to the pokey. "I've decided that part of the reason I fell for Andy again was that I'd created a false image in my mind."

"Sure," Poppy says.

"You're just figuring this out?" Lilly adds.

"So, in order to prevent that in the future, I've decided I need to learn what it's like to live in the real world. So I was thinking maybe we should take Lilly's car."

Now granted, calling Lilly's car *a car* is a stretch. It's definitely what you might call authentic living, in that it was purchased from a neighbor when she crashed it, and proudly it displays all the reminders of that day. Once upon a time, it came into this world as a Saab. Now she calls it the Slob, and it's my Cinderella carriage into my new life.

"You're kidding, right?" Lilly asks. "I'm not sure my car will actually make it to the spa, Morgan. It's a five-hour drive. Isn't there some other way to start? Like maybe getting drugstore lipstick versus Bloomie's or something?"

"Come on, it will be fun!" I enthuse, anxious to get on with Life in the Real World. "I need to have a dose of authenticity. To experience what the rest of you have struggled for. Otherwise, I don't know if I can give this all up, and I have to give it all up or I'll never be able to tell the Andys from the Princes."

"So you want to slum it, is that right?" Lilly asks.

"*Slum* is a harsh word. I want to know what it feels like to drive in a normal car where you're not garnering attention for your ride."

"Oh, we'll garner attention, all right." Lilly shrugs. "But sure, whatever."

We take the elevator down to the parking garage where Lilly's car has been hidden by the doorman to keep its "realness" away from my fellow penthouse dwellers. The bellman brings the car around, and I get another glimpse of the Slob. Oh dear, I don't remember it being quite that bad. I start to nibble on my lower lip, knowing full well my snootiness is going to get me nowhere in the real world. I sing that song in my head about stepping out of my comfort zone, into the realm of the unknown, and the doorman opens the Slob door.

"So let's go!" I pile into the back and see the earthy leather seats, ripped by its former owner's dog. I also smell cleaning supplies. Lilly has a little issue with Lysol—an addiction, you might say. The air is stifling, hanging heavy with the deep, antiseptic aroma I've grown to associate with her (and the hospital during my mother's illness).

"Feeling real yet?" Lilly laughs.

"It's fine," I lie, holding my breath while I pump the button to open the window.

"Oh, that window doesn't work. The wreck, you know," Lilly informs me. I gasp for air since I've been holding my breath too long.

"It is not fine," Poppy says as she slides in. "When are you going to get married, Lilly, and have Max buy you a decent car? This thing was a piece a decade ago."

"I can't believe you said that, Poppy! Since when do I need a man to take care of me?"

We both look around the car, but neither one of us says what we're thinking to Lilly. She's a sadist, but at least she has good taste in men.

"Sorry, you're absolutely right." Poppy slinks down in her seat. "It just seems like an obvious decision. You two adore each other. You drive a complete piece of trash and live in a dump. He's wealthy, gorgeous, lives in the Marina, puts up with your nana, and is dying to get married. You do the math."

"Getting married would only add more stress. This business is going to be my success. No one is going to say I married into it."

I understand Lilly's feelings. She loves Max Schwartz, heir to a San Francisco hotel dynasty, and she won't have anyone belittling their love by saying she wants his money. But it does make me wonder. Then I see the faintest sign of a tear in her eye. Lilly is not the tear-shedding type. "It will work out."

As someone who has been slowly seduced by and is now officially owned by my father's money, I can't say I fault her. But I don't know that I'd take such drastic steps to prove it. Driving in the Slob for one day is a big enough step for me.

"Morgan was born into prosperity, Lilly. No one minds that she drives a BMW. It's expected of her."

Yeah, so my father buys me a new BMW nearly every year. Not so much for me, but so his reputation for being the finest father in all of San Francisco isn't harmed. I look up to tell them this, but they're talking amongst themselves, not interested in my input, so I go back to looking out the window, staring at Bob the bellman, who's patiently waiting for us to haul this thing out of here.

"Since when have I ever done what was expected of me?" Lilly points out. "And besides, now Morgan wants out of her prosperity, and we're in the Slob. So it can't be all that great."

They both turn around and look at me.

"Can we go now?" I ask. "You two bicker like an old couple. We're supposed to be relaxing this weekend, getting me away from all the turmoil, remember? Poppy, you know better. Spray some essential oils or something. Chill." I cross my arms and sit back against the open wound of the seat.

Lilly starts up the car, and I bet they heard it on the top floor. This thing sounds like a turbo-diesel jet!

We drive out onto the busy street, where reporters are waiting by leaning against their cars, ankles crossed, cigarettes poised. But they take one look at the car, decipher that one of the maids is leaving the building, and go back to smoking. We are home free!

Until Lilly sticks her head out the window and blows a

raspberry at them. With a rush of double-takes, they all chuck their cigarette butts and dash to their cars. But they're parked the wrong way on the street, and Lilly and Poppy laugh all the way down the hill.

"Very funny," I say. Poppy and Lilly are still laughing, until the Slob starts to sputter and coast unnaturally roughly down the hill. Lilly rolls to the edge of the street and double parks.

"What are you doing?"

"I'm pulling over, Morgan. The car stopped working. This is what us real folk call 'car trouble.' Adam Ant wrote a song about it in the eighties. You might want to download it on your iPod." Then she giggles. "Oh wait, real people can't afford those."

"Start it up again!" I demand. When I hear myself, it sounds amazingly like Veruca Salt. *Daddy, I want it now!*

"Listen, at least the Slob didn't do this to us on 101 in the middle of nowhere," Poppy says brightly.

"No kidding," Lilly agrees. Then she turns around, after pulling on the emergency brake, and faces me. "Need I remind you whose brilliant idea this was? Two blocks, that's how far we got. You drive a 645i convertible, Morgan. And in the real world, that's better than a piece of junk. First word of advice: real people are practical. They take the good car."

We clamber out of the car and gather around it like a casket at a funeral. People are honking as though we actually have any control over the situation. I get out my cell phone and press a button.

"What are you doing?" Lilly asks, snapping my phone shut.

"I'm calling the bellman and getting a tow truck. I'll have my car brought around and we'll be on our way. Our first treatment is early tomorrow. We need to get on the road."

"Oh no, you don't," Lilly says. "You want to see how the

real world works? The real world waits here for a tow truck driver while every San Franciscan yells obscenities for being in middle of the road. That's what the rest of us do, Morgan. You have to learn to enjoy it. Sometimes I like to wave when people yell at me. Welcome to reality, baby. I don't want to take anything away from your experience."

Reality bites.

At this point, the photographers catch up with us and start clicking away and screaming in my face:

"Miss Malliard, did you marry Andy Mattingly?"

"Did you know he was married?"

"Will you be getting an annulment?"

"Does Andy wear boxers or briefs?"

"Okay, that's disgusting!" I point and yell at the journalist, but Poppy comes up in my face and whispers a reminder. "Morgan, don't say a thing."

I know better. My father has told me this my entire life:

"Be above reproach."

"Don't sink to their level."

"They're nothing but parasites."

But right now, the rules hardly matter. As they huddle together in their mass of flailing limbs, flashing bulbs, and taunting questions, the memory of my mother's funeral invades my head. They all look just as they did then, still hoping to capture a small piece of my mother. And I imagine that's exactly what I am to them. I start to wilt.

"That's enough. Normal people don't endure this. Call your bellman, Morgan."

Poppy pulls me into the foyer of another elite apartment complex on the street. Their bellman helps me to a sofa and offers me a glass of cool water. I accept it gratefully and cross my legs, admiring my new shoes. Real people definitely can't afford these shoes.

The bellman is kind and grandfatherly, and I wonder what my life would have been like if my father had been like him.

"Do you have a daughter?" I ask him.

"Three," he says back. Then he taps my shoulder. "And I know you didn't do anything those papers said you did. I can see it in your eyes. I always know when a woman's lying." He taps his temple. "That's what comes with living with four of them."

He smiles genuinely, and I feel my whole body relax. Just one person believing in you has that effect.

He goes off to the door to shoo away the leeches and make sure they don't enter the building.

"Lilly, you were right. I think my foray into the real world should probably be a smaller step than the Slob. As you always say, 'Rome wasn't built in a day.'"

"Good call," Lilly agrees.

"So, shall we go?"

I figure the real world has got to be better than this.

"You know," I muse to my friends. "Christopher Columbus had a tough time finding the new world, too. It was fraught with setbacks. Why should my journey be any different?" I lift up a fist. "Let's burn the ships!"

Poppy rolls her eyes, "That was Cortez who burned the ships, not Columbus. Your history knowledge rivals Lilly's geography skills."

"Whatever." Like I'm taking a GMAT here. I know one thing: the real world can wait until I'm exfoliated.

chapter 3

've been called a dumb blonde in my day, and I think that's unfair. First, because I'm not really blonde. And second, because I made it through college without the help of tutors, overly friendly professors, or my father's money.

Now, I'll grant you that falling for a fake Christian rock star wasn't the high point on my learning curve. Definitely not the move of the sharpest crayon in the box. But, in my defense, Andy Mattingly did write poetry that rivaled Yeats. Sure, it might have actually been Yeats, but at the time, I thought I was his beautiful muse who inspired him to greatness. I made myself believe that loving him enough would propel him to musical prominence.

We'll get to my narcissistic fantasies later, but for once in my life, I felt loved for who I was, not who I was born and shaped to be by my father.

Wishful thinking is my Achilles heel.

I'm through with this kind of fairy-tale life. Always waiting for the glamorous rescue where the hero rides in on his white horse (or white Beamer—I'm not picky) and takes me to his castle (conveniently located near Nashville's Music Row). Yeah, I put way too much thought into it, I know. But after two failed attempts at engagement, I'm beginning to see the error of my ways.

With God's help, it's my turn to be the knight. I'm going to get myself a real job, find myself a church where my tithe isn't public knowledge, and I'm going to prove to everyone who called me an adulteress that I am an innocent woman. Perhaps this is all over-reaching, but I have to start somewhere.

Right after this pedicure.

The automatic chair's thumper rises roughly up and down my spine, rolling me to a state somewhere between relaxation and downright annoyance in one fell swoop.

"So Morgan," Lilly says, lifting her foot out of her vibrating bath. "What do you hope to accomplish with all those books when we get to the spa?"

I should mention that our Spa Del Mar only has facials and massages, so we always stop on the way to get pedicures together. Sort of an aperitif.

"I'm going to get a job," I say proudly. Though in my head, I'm thinking, *What on earth would I do? What time will I have to get up for a real job?* I haven't a clue. My dad opens his store at ten a.m., but most of his clients prearrange to be there, so he goes in when the customers want him and when the Japanese tour buses roll into town. Other than that, he hires a well-dressed employee to stand there.

Maybe I should start small and be one of those perfume sprayers I try to avoid at Bloomingdale's. I could so outrun those old ladies with my sprayer at the ready.

Both my friends are avoiding eye contact, but I can see them grinning at the idea of me scanning the classifieds.

"A real job," I add. "I'm going to be thinking about what I'd like to do with my Stanford business education and my experience in the diamond industry." I take a sip from my iced tea while they mull this over.

"Break out the Lysol!" Lilly says through her giggle.

"What's so funny?" I ask, slamming my glass back on the table.

"Your experience in the diamond industry?" Lilly throws her head back, only to get punched by the manic chair. "No offense here, Morgan, but walking around fancy parties wearing your dad's jewelry isn't exactly working in the diamond industry."

I'm ready for her. "Maybe not, but I've learned a thing or two about real estate in the process. Which is where my dad actually makes his money." I lean back in the chair, trying to give the impression of serenity. "I've helped him acquire and renovate a few buildings. Hah!" I point at them. "Wiped those smirks off your faces, didn't I? You think I'm dumb, too, don't you?"

Poppy sways her head back and forth. "Heck, no, we don't think you're dumb. We wouldn't hang out with you if we thought so. We have our reputations to protect."

At this, we all laugh.

"We do think you're a bit naïve," Poppy says gently. "You've lived a pretty sheltered life."

Her comment stops me for a moment. Naïve? They've got me there. I did climb into a limousine thinking Andy Mattingly was suddenly wealthy and famous. That was definitely naïve.

"I've been naïve," I admit. "But I haven't been sheltered. I've tasted death with Marcus succumbing to liver disease before our wedding. I've tasted loss with Andy not being who I thought he was. And I've lived utter humiliation with the whole of San Francisco knowing my mistakes. Lilly, when you got dumped by Robert, was it front-page news? If anything, I'm thrown to the dogs, not sheltered."

"Must we bring Robert up?" Lilly rolls her eyes. The very mention of Robert is enough to break out the Lysol in bulk for her. "And Robert was just slowing me down so the right man could find me."

Poppy turns off her overzealous chair, and we quickly follow suit. Much better.

"Tomorrow, someone else's business will be plastered in the news. They'll forget about you, Morgan. It's not like you're Michael Jackson," Poppy offers.

"Did they forget about Hugh Grant in the backseat of a car? Tom Cruise jumping around like an idiot on Oprah's couch? Pee Wee Herman? Did we forget any of that?"

"Well, no, but this is San Francisco, not Hollywood. Only the people who've watched you grow up under your father's care. If your father hadn't been so outspoken on traditional values in the liberal capital of the country, no one would pay this any mind. People like to see the mighty fall," Lilly says. "And your father did sort of set you up. The press was just waiting."

"It probably wouldn't have been so bad if I wasn't twenty-nine and still living with my daddy, Lilly. See, you knew that it was fundamentally time to get away from your nana. Those things didn't register with me. You lived in squalor to make your own way."

Lilly wrinkles her nose. "Squalor? I mean, I know it was bad, but it wasn't that bad. You make it sound like there were rats eating off my floor or something. Besides, squalor to you is probably anything under two million dollars."

"Wait a minute," Poppy says. "We understand life isn't going your way, Morgan, but you can't expect to invoke sympathy from the living-with-your-daddy part. You have to add that you live on Russian Hill—which I thought was Nob Hill until you told me, but whatever. You have to add that you're living in an eight-million-dollar penthouse, with an area big enough that you might never see your father, and you employ a full-time maid who actually makes your bed and picks up your dry-cleaning. Because that sort of negates people's general sympathy. It's sort of like 'Let them eat cake' and 'woe is me,' you know?"

I haven't told my Spa Girls the worst of this yet. I feel like if I don't say it out loud, it won't be true, and no one will ever know how bad it is—how inane I've been. Lilly and Poppy won't hate me; we have too much history. But I've taken the dumb-blonde bit to new heights. (And once again, I'll have to apologize to real blondes because to be really worthy of the title, it should be "dumb, mousy-brown-haired girl," but that sort of loses its ring.)

By the end of our pedicures, Poppy has painted her toenails a wheat color, Lilly a bright pink, and I've gone for scarlet. I think it's the only appropriate choice given the circumstances.

After we pay, Poppy stops us outside the salon. "Morgan, this is your weekend, and I don't want to take anything away from that, but I have a slight confession to make."

Perfect timing!

"You have a confession?" Lilly asks. "It's all right, Poppy, we love you even though taupe isn't a nail color."

Poppy doesn't give a hint of a smile whatsoever. From her somber expression, I have a feeling it's going to rival my own news. In a way, I hope it does. I wait with bated breath.

chapter 4

As we gather in the convertible, it's obvious that Poppy isn't sure she is ready for her deep admission of guilt. But unless we were Catholic, she's not going to get a better confessional than my Beamer. And with my own circumstances being so dire, I'm ready to absolve her of anything. Go in peace, my child.

"You didn't murder anyone, right?" I ask, feeling pretty confident in her answer.

"Of course not!" Poppy yells.

"Run over a kitten?" Lilly asks.

"No!" Poppy shouts.

"I know what it is," Lilly says confidently. "She ate fast food, and her temple is very, very angry. All that hydrogenated oil is in her system now, like the small amount of yeast in the dough. Sin has infiltrated."

"Enough!" Poppy removes her flip-flops and puts her freshly painted feet on the dashboard. "I've . . ." She lets out a deep breath and fills her lungs fully before starting again. "I . . . kind of talked to the newspaper about you, Morgan."

"Me? What? No, no, no. This is your confession! You didn't talk about me. You wouldn't!" Poppy hides her face and Lilly glares at me. I rein myself in a bit. "This is me, Poppy.

You know better than to discuss me with the press, right?"

She doesn't answer, and I keep prodding, "Right?"

Again there is silence. Poppy's not looking at me. I try to remain calm.

"Okay, so you talked about me, but I know you wouldn't say anything bad. You must have a good reason, so let's hear what happened. I'm ready for the truth."

Deep breath from Poppy.

"Okay." I scratch my temple. "It's all right; this is some easily answerable offense, so go ahead, tell me."

Another drastic exhale. "Actually . . ."

My heart starts to pound, and I feel it in my throat as if I'm Jim Carrey in *The Mask*. I brace myself for the words, because I'm thinking if the queen of Zen thinks it's bad, it's certainly not good.

I close my eyes, "Go ahead, hit me with it." I tighten my fists and ready myself for the barrage I know I don't want to hear.

"I sort of told them how you met Andy and how you fell in love."

I open my eyes and look at Poppy twisting her red hair like a three-year-old. You know, thinking back on my history, I believe dumb blonde might be too kind. I have been dumb as a plank.

"It was before I knew Andy lied. The journalist was so nice, Morgan. I thought it was so cute how you met, and I thought he was excited for you like I was, and he tricked me."

Gee, imagine that. "You didn't tell him we met on the Internet?" I cringe. My father will die at this information. He parades twenty eligible, wealthy bachelors a month in front of me, and I resort to the Internet. (Now this speaks to the quality of men he selects, but he'll never see it that way. He'll see it as the equivalent of me wearing a "For Sale by Owner" sign.)

Poppy bites her lip and vacillates between shaking her head and nodding.

"You did tell him. Well, I can deal with that, Poppy. Lots of couples meet on the Internet; there's no shame in that. I mean, even in the Bible, Rebekah met Isaac in sort of an early blind date, right?"

Both my friends nod with too much enthusiasm.

"You didn't tell them we met in a Christian chat room, did you?"

She starts with the Lady MacBeth hand-wringing thing again.

"Poppy!"

"Look at it this way, Morgan," Lilly pipes up. "It's all out in the open now."

"Not quite," I say, pursing my lips like the Church Lady. "But enough is out for my comfort level." I've decided confiding my own news is not exactly the top of my priority list today. Confiding in people is what got me into this mess.

Well, that and falling victim to a fake rock star, but whatever.

After a long, silent drive to the spa, we wheel up to the familiar entrance of Spa Del Mar. Del Mar implies by the sea, and this is true—if you take about a ten-mile drive on a winding road. But Spa Del Mar is nestled in the eucalyptus, oaks, and rolling hills that signify California, and it makes you feel as though you've stepped back in time to when men like Zorro roamed the landscape.

Men like Zorro. Now why can't they make guys like that nowadays? A wealthy, Antonio Banderas-look-alike don who fights against the injustice of the elite. That's what I should have been looking for—someone to come in and fight against my father's rent gouging in Union Square. But no, I had to go and find myself a Robin Hood to steal from me and give to his wife. I bet if my father had read to me more as a child, none of this would have happened.

We check into the spa and clamber up the stairs with our goods. Lilly's toting biscotti and Diet Pepsi, which, trust me, beats her weird fetish with the pickles. Poppy has all her voodoo drinks for us to detoxify. And me? I've brought a normal obsession: chocolate, of course. Big DeBrands truffles with coffee beans on top for that final, happy caffeine buzz after the chocolate paradise. Lilly and I generally gag down Poppy's detoxification drinks, and when she heads off for her facial, we guzzle mocha truffles and Diet Pepsi by the gallon. Ah, detox—it's so cleansing.

Once in the room, we spread out and drop our stuff, exhausted from our long trip. After the pedicures in the agitated massage chairs and the car trouble, it's just been one thing after another.

"I think you should take the first facial tomorrow, Poppy," I say in my best yoga voice. Lilly looks at me, and we share a knowing glance. That's right, chocolate and Diet Pepsi for breakfast!

Poppy comes beside me and sits on the bed. "That is so sweet. I am really looking forward to this trip. You girls are going to feel so much better after these elixirs I brought. One has rhodiola for stress and to enhance immunity, vitamin A for beautiful skin, and a combination lactobacillus-evening primrose oil and garlic to help Lilly get her yeast balance right. She just really needs to give up the pickles and the sugar. Terrible for yeast."

"Yummy," Lilly smiles. "I can hardly wait."

"So how's your dating world going, Poppy?" I ask, anxious to hear about someone's social life other than mine. Of course, I know my friends really want to know more about Andy, but

I'm just not ready to give that up. I was pathetic. Is knowing the depths of my patheticness really necessary? The best defense is really to attack first. I can't imagine Poppy wants to discuss her love life any more than I do mine. But once again, she surprises me.

"Well, we have a new guy who has been coming to the singles group. He's very businesslike, not my type at all, but there's something about him. He has really good energy, and he seemed very interested in talking after Bible study about my love of natural health care."

Lilly and I look at each other again, sharing a knowing uh-oh look. I'm sure I've mentioned the fact that Poppy looks like Nicole Kidman. Granted, Nicole Kidman dressed like Whoopi Goldberg, but knockout gorgeous regardless. Often, men are very interested in the natural-healing sermon because they're interested in the hot redhead who's discussing it.

And they call me naïve.

"What does he do, Poppy?"

"He's a venture capitalist."

Also known as vulture capitalists in the Bay Area. Not a great sign for gentle-natured Poppy. "You say you met him in church?" I clarify.

"He made his money on some widget in Silicon Valley, and now he wants to help other engineers make their fortune. That's his passion. Because, he says, first and foremost he's an inventor."

"What's his spiritual gift?" Lilly asks.

Now Poppy looks to the spiritual gifts of the Bible like an astrologist would look to the stars. She loves to know what makes a man tick and what God created him to do. Most important, she wants to see if he's following that will and listening to the voice of God. How the Lord will ever find a man to fit into Poppy's marital shortlist is the world's eighth wonder, but I suppose He's in the business of miracles.

"His name is Brad, like Brad Pitt. But he doesn't look like Brad Pitt."

"Are you disappointed in that?" Lilly asks.

"Not really," Poppy shrugs. "Brad Pitt doesn't really float my boat."

"Well, now, you've got to tell us, Poppy, because I can't imagine: who does float your boat? Give us the Hollywood equivalent, please. Tom Cruise?"

Poppy is not the type to have a Hollywood hero. In fact, I've never heard her discuss men in general. Unless she's telling us about their poor kidney function or bent spinal cord.

"Too boyish."

"Hugh Jackman?" I offer.

"Too tall." She puts her fingers over her mouth and goes into deep thought. "I think, maybe Harrison Ford as Han Solo."

Still waters run deep. "The lovable scoundrel. I wouldn't have guessed it. I mean, I knew you liked Johnny Depp, but who doesn't? But the pirate mercenary of Han Solo, now, that is a surprise. Proof that there's a lot going on under all that cotton, isn't it, Lilly?"

"So does this Brad look like Han Solo?"

Poppy laughs. "No, he sort of looks like Vin Diesel without the muscles. Yeah." She thinks about it a bit. "A skinny Vin Diesel."

"You got a bald guy?" Lilly kicks off her shoes so they hit the wall. "Life is so unfair." Lilly thinks the root (no pun intended) of her issues is her bad hair, but considering she's snagged herself one of San Francisco's hottest bachelors, I think her issues lay closer to commitment phobia. I'll have to look that up in one of my self-help books this weekend.

"Are you dating Brad Diesel?" I ask.

"Well, he hasn't asked me out. We just talk after church is all." Poppy goes about opening the French doors on the balcony to let in the scent of sulfur from the hot tub below. She's avoiding questions, and if I didn't know better, I'd say Poppy is interested in this Brad.

"Administration." She turns around from the curtains, wearing a dreamy smile. "His gift is administration."

Seeing her smitten expression and acknowledging my own lack of opportunity—not to mention luck—I fall back on the bed. "I'm going to die a spinster. If I can't get a job and afford my stylist, I'm going to die a mousy-brown-haired spinster with bad, store-bought highlights. Oh." I put the back of my hand on my forehead. "The agony of it all."

"You need to think about this getting a job business, Morgan. You don't know how to be poor. You should leave it to the professionals," Lilly says.

She should talk. She's poor with style. She knows how to sew and how to create fabulous looks from nothing. I look Lilly straight in the eye. "I can be poor, Lilly. It's not like it's a skill to have no money. I won't have to learn how to dress for the right occasion. Poor people don't have occasions to go to, so what is there to know?"

Lilly laughs so hard, she snorts like a pig.

That's attractive.

"You have to know how to look professional for work and how to buy enough Payless shoes to go with all your outfits. You can't veer from a standard color palette, or it involves extra accessories at Claire's and Payless, and that's more than you can afford. So you stick with something you have shoes for."

"No biggie. I have shoes for everything."

"Okay, so let's say you get a job at Starbucks, and you have to wear a pair of black pants. You're going to hobble in to work for an eight-hour shift on Jimmy Choos? Is that what you're saying?"

"Well, no, I have some Taryn Roses that I could wear."

"And when someone spills espresso on your three-hundred-dollar mules, you do what?"

I hadn't thought of that. "Surely even poor people know better than to be dribbling on three-hundred-dollar shoes."

Lilly throws herself on the bed. "You are hopeless. Normal people can't imagine spending that kind of money on a pair of shoes. That is a major purchase in their home. An appliance! This is what I'm trying to tell you—not because I think you're stupid, Morgan, but because I want you to be successful in your life changes, so I think you need to take it slowly."

"If I take it slowly, I'll never go anywhere." I grab the Diet Pepsi out of Lilly's bag, and even though Poppy is watching horrified, I twist it open and take a swig. "It's now or never."

"All right, Morgan. I'll bet you can't live on my salary, without a car in San Francisco, for one month," Lilly says.

"No car is better than that Slob you drive now."

"Oh, you think so," Lilly is still on the bed, doubled over in laughter. "That handbag you have there, what is it?"

"It's a Hogan. You know that, Lilly. Like there's a designer you're not familiar with."

"That bag right there is your rent for the month. Welcome to the world of pleather, honey." Lilly pulls out her organizer, jots down a number, and shows it to me. "If you take me up on my dare, this is the amount you have to live on. You can live with me and pay me half the rent for the month, but the rest is up to you. Food, clothing, entertainment—this is it. I'm there for you every step of the way, but if you're really up to this, prove it. Or go running back to Daddy again."

"You really think I can't do this?" I look at the number, and my stomach churns. I think I spend more a month on coffee. "How do you buy lattes with this?"

"Have you seen those ads for frothy cappuccinos on television?"

"A mix?" I ask, aghast.

Poppy is pouring one of her elixirs at the desk, and she's shaking so bad from laughter, she's spilling it.

"You don't think I'm capable, either, Poppy?"

"I just don't think you have ever thought about money. It's not important to you because you have an abundance. But I don't think being poor is your thing, Morgan. We should go with our gifts. Yours is giving. God made you rich because you'd give up anything. You'd never keep anything to yourself when you could share. If you were selfish, I'd say this might be worth a try."

"So I'm not selfish, but I'm clueless?"

They're both looking at me, their mouths open like the Caldecott Tunnel, clearly unable to think of a response that wouldn't be a fib. They do think I'm clueless.

I think about what I would look like if I were a classified:

Wanted: Single Eligible Bachelor
Must be rich for my giving personality.
Must be willing to overlook a little boyfriend baggage.
Must find the clueless sort charming.

And this is from my best friends. Imagine what people who don't love me think.

"Lilly, I'll take you up on that bet, and I'll prove to both of you that I may have been living in my father's world, but I'm coming out, and I'm doing it on a shoestring. A very cheap, non-designer shoestring."

"The Red & White Ball opening is next month," Lilly warns me.

"I have a friend who sews and I understand Wal-Mart sells fabric," I counter.

Poppy spills her elixir all over the desk. "Can you see Morgan in the *Star Wars* bed sheet gown? She'll be all the rage."

"I'm going to read my self-help books now." I head to the balcony and the plastic chair. "You two certainly aren't helping."

As I sit on the plastic chair, though, I'll admit, I have a huge tinge of fear pricking the back of my neck. Well, okay, I look up to see it's really the plant on the balcony, but my point is the same: I'm not worried about living without money. I'm worried that I am not a person anyone would care about without money. And that when my Spa Girls figure out what I really did, I may find myself living without these wonderful, carefree retreats.

chapter 5

I am a selfish creature. It's not just the designer clothes, the penthouse, or my 645i that make me so. Those are just symptoms of the deeper disease. The truth is I can't remember the last time I did something out of the goodness of my heart. Oh, I've brought Lilly little makeup samplers and paid for the spa trips. But it cost me nothing. Not really. I don't pay the Visa bill, so my generosity has been a sham. It's a hard realization for me—feeling that when the Bible says our works are filthy rags, mine are steeped in gasoline with a match at the ready.

So much for detoxification.

When Lilly put aside time to design a wedding gown for me, she gave of herself—her time and her talent—when it wasn't convenient to do so. When Poppy sat with me all day while I sobbed over losing Marcus, she gave her sympathy to me, and brought me out of that dark place. She gave of herself.

But me? Really, I have given nothing that I couldn't afford to give easily. How odd my friends should find me the generous and giving one. When in fact I clutch everything tightly out of fear that if I don't buy them, I'll be in want for friends and people around me. What a wake-up call that my faith is little more than me holding God in my special box. I don't trust in the Lord, even though I claim to, week after week. What I really trust in, apparently, is that trampoline of safety called cold, hard cash. And if it were gone, could I jump freely knowing His hand was there to catch me?

After my hot rock massage outside under the magnificent oak in the garden, I'm excited about living with Lilly in her loft. I know she challenged me on a dare, but the truth of the matter is she's offering me her place while I get my act together. Another case of her giving to the least of these.

But I'm looking forward to the change. And a change it will be. I've always had everything I needed. As a child. As a teenager. Everything I needed by my father's standards, that is. Which I'm not certain was the best measuring stick. Even my college dorm room was equipped with the best of everything, and I lived by myself instead of with a roommate. My father worked overtime to prove to me I was above the norm and entitled to better. It's a wonder I ever had friends. I was bred to be better than them.

Not anymore. I'm going to start small in my gifts, like cleaning Lilly's apartment, or cooking her dinner, but I'm going to learn how to do things for other people. I am going to learn to clean a bathroom.

The masseuse puts a spa robe over me, and I wiggle into it and decide to walk the gardens before going back in the room. The truth is I ate one too many truffles this morning, and I feel like I'm going to explode after the massage. Gluttony is never pretty.

I sit on a bench under a jacaranda tree and close my eyes to the peace of the moment.

"You look relaxed," a male voice says.

I look up to see an unfamiliar face, a man wearing a suit

shirt opened three buttons to reveal a small, pleasantly spaced tuft of hair. His smile is genuine. Not that I'm the greatest judge of character. But I like the look of him. He's elegant and educated in his demeanor, but not too smooth or slick. Still, when I think about my heart stirring in any sort of male direction, I have to stop and take stock. I am the girl written up in the papers for running off with a con artist.

"Do you mind?" He puts his hand out towards the bench.

"Feel free," I scoot over and go back to closing my eyes, sniffing the deep, earthy scent of eucalyptus. I feel him beside me—not his actual touch, just his presence. I sneak a look at him and find him staring at me. I immediately sit up and pull my robe tighter around me.

He clears his throat. "Sorry. You're very beautiful in person. I wasn't expecting that."

"Excuse me," I say as I get up. See what a doormat I am? Creepy man in a suit at the spa, and I'm apologizing before removing myself from his presence.

"Please don't leave," he calls out, and for some reason I feel myself turning towards him.

"What are you doing here at a spa? And why are you using a bad bar line?"

He laughs out loud. "That was a bad line, but I can assure you, I meant it with the utmost sincerity. If it gives you any solace, I haven't been in a bar in years."

"And I can see why. You're not exactly smooth."

He laughs again. "No, I'm not."

I scan him again, with my arms crossed in front of me. "So what are you doing here? In a suit?"

"I followed you here."

"Why?" I deadpan. I feel completely safe. I'm in the Spa Del Mar, my home away from home. He doesn't feel frightening. (Which is probably reason enough for me to hike this robe above my knees and make a mad dash while I still have time to avoid a new scandal.) But there's something about him that makes me very curious. Just like a cat on its ninth life.

He clears his throat but doesn't answer.

"Why did you follow me?" I ask, suddenly feeling my absence of makeup as nudity, plain and simple. The robe does nothing to assist that emotion. "Can you do me a favor and answer what's so exciting about me that people want to read?"

"Do you want the truth or a story?"

"Which won't hurt my feelings?"

"You're a girl with everything. There's nothing we like better in America than watching someone with everything lose it all. You're the American gladiator. It's not personal."

"Trust me. It is personal. So what do you want from me, Mr. Suit? A good juicy piece of gossip on who I'm dating right now?"

He shrugs. "That's not really the angle of my story or why I'm here. *Time* magazine said it best when—"

"*Time* magazine?" I gulp as I feel my lids slide shut. Oh, please tell me my pathetic life is not going to be a feature story. "Why would you possibly be interested in me?"

"I'm here to ask you about Andy Mattingly, the man you married."

I can't breathe. I yank the robe around my neck tighter, but it's already practically choking me. "How did you know I married him?"

"I found the marriage certificate on record in South Lake Tahoe. Everyone assumed you went to Vegas, but I traced your phone records."

I stand up and point at my newfound "friend." "Aren't you thorough?" I walk over towards him and, in a fit of daring, bend down to look at his feet. "I knew your socks would be perfectly coordinated. You cross your T's."

He smiles.

"It wasn't a compliment."

He moves farther over on the bench and slides his long legs out, leaving two lines in the dirt with his high-end loafers. "Sit down. I'm not here to bother you. With the advent of the Internet and cross-country dating, I'm here to find out why women . . . " He looks over my figure. " . . . who could clearly find themselves dates fall for these men. I'm sure your father is interested in the same answers."

"Did you expect to find I had a third ear in person?"

"Truthfully, I expected you to be stupider."

"Well, now, don't sugarcoat it for my sake. How do you know I'm not stupid? I was married for three hours to a man who tried to take my father for my trust fund. Does that strike you as exceptionally brilliant? I haven't worked a real job outside my father's store so I'm not the career woman you might imagine. How exactly do you see me as intelligent? This, I have to hear."

"You went to Stanford; you can't be too low on IQ if you went to Tiger Woods' alma mater. There has to be a wrinkle or two on that brain of yours."

"You think?"

"I came to help you, Morgan."

"Help me? Oh, mister, I've heard that before, but here's a newsflash for you: stalking me is not helping me. It's just creeping me out, even if you did dress nicely for the occasion. You're still no better than your standard street-beat man who sucks on his cigarette waiting for me to leave a party."

He touches his chest. "Ouch. Now that hurt. My suit is Italian silk. Couldn't you at least have noticed?"

"A well-dressed stalker—that's just what I was hoping for. Now, leave me alone, or I'll call the police." I walk towards the hotel section of the spa, but he doesn't get up and follow me.

As I turn around to stare at him, he laces his hands behind his head, all confidence and bravado. He looks satisfied, as though he got what he came for, and this thought unnerves me. Because I can't for the life of me think of what I might have given him, and the fact that he looks so satisfied makes me want to take a fist to his jaw.

"Good riddance," I call as I open the spa door.

He buckles in the middle and jumps out of the bench, rushing behind me. But when I turn to look at him, he stops as though he hasn't a care in the world and starts to kick the dirt as if it doesn't matter if I stay or go.

And I know it does.

"I knew you were bluffing! See, I am not ignorant!"

"Is this your Andy Mattingly?" He pulls a wallet-sized photo out of his breast pocket, and my heart jumps at the sight of Andy.

"That's him," I say as I drop my hand to my side, not feeling nearly as confident as I did a minute ago.

"Did you know his name is really Arnold Kellog?"

"I married a guy named Arnold?" Thoughts of *Green Acres* reruns and the pig invade my mind.

"You weren't really married. You never consummated the marriage."

My jaw drops. Now I am most definitely creeped out. "How did you know that? Did you have a camera in our room or something?"

"Phone records. Your father hired a private investigator. He was working with Andy's current wife—well, his third one, actually. She called Arnold on his cell phone soon after the marriage took place, and you answered his phone."

I look to the dirt. "He was in the shower."

"Arnold did—"

"Please call him Andy, for my sake."

"He did one thing differently with you, Miss Malliard. Andy, I believe, really did love you. He was trying to earn enough where if you looked in his checking account, you wouldn't think he was marrying you for your money."

This forces an unnatural laughter from my belly. "Somehow that doesn't bring me any comfort. Do you plan to tell me who you are? Besides the wearer of fine Italian suits?"

"George Gentry."

"Now that sounds like a fake name."

"Tell my mother, then. It's the truth."

"You'll forgive me for scoffing. I've had my fair share of surprises with men and their fake names. George Gentry, I wish you the best of luck in your endeavors. I'm here at the spa to forget about all this, though, and I'd appreciate it if you'd just leave me out of your investigation, or whatever it is you're up to."

"Poppy said–"

I twirl around. "You're the one who talked to Poppy," I accuse.

He nods and looks to the ground, "That's me."

"You've got what you came here for: the dumb blonde in need of your deft journalistic prowess to make me real to the reader for my incredulous naiveté."

Rather than take the hint, George Gentry bends over the water pitcher filled with ice and lemon slices that sits beside the door and pours me a tall glass. "We aren't bitter, are we?"

Okay, so who am I to pass up cool, lemony water offered by an espresso-eyed hottie, even if he is a jerk who knows far too much about my personal life. All I can say is that it's a good thing I didn't sleep with Andy. I'm not sure I'd want to hear that report.

I take the glass. "You haven't broken the story yet on my being married to . . . " I pause for a minute before getting up the nerve to say his name. " . . . Andy. Why not?"

He pours himself a glass of water, and takes a swig, the drops from which bead at the top of his straight mouth. "I'm not a reporter, Morgan. I'm a lawyer." He focuses on my hand. "That's some ring you've got there." His eyes narrow at my striking blue diamond. I close my left hand around it. "Did Andy give you that?"

"Mr. Gentry, Andy couldn't pay to have this ring sized. Even if my father gave him a discount."

He laughs. An endearing and warm laugh that rings with truth. And I find myself gazing into his eyes wondering what's wrong with me. Why don't I meet men who are who they say they are, who don't follow me into spas, and who don't dress up for the stalking occasion. Is that too much to ask?

"Like I said, I wish you luck with whatever it is you're up to." I place my hand on my collarbone, and I blink several times, unable to keep myself from trying to figure out what he could want from me. I don't want to ask.

"Morgan? We were worried." Lilly suddenly appears under the screened porch and eyes my acquaintance with the tenacity of a shark. "Who's your friend?"

"George Gentry, meet Lilly Jacobs, my best friend and fellow Spa Girl. You'll want to get that into whatever it is you're up to. I think it adds to the airhead element. I get pedicures and facials often, and I've been known to get pretty beat up by massage chairs. They have a thing for me." Sort of like handsome, egotistical men without real jobs.

Stalking up to him, Lilly reaches up and grabs George by the collar. "Listen, if you mess with Morgan—"

"Lilly!" I shout through unexpected laughter. For a sprightly little thing, you wouldn't want to mess with her.

George gives a small grin at my beloved pit bull of a Spa Girl. "Arnold—I mean Andy—is scheduled for arraignment next week. Will you be there, Miss Malliard?"

I melt a little more. "Call me Morgan. You're intimate with my phone history; it's only right."

"Lilly, a pleasure to meet you," George sets the water glass down on the table and chances one last glance at me. As he walks away, he tosses over his shoulder, "I can explain everything if you give me a chance. Please trust me, Morgan. I can help you."

That's what they all say.

chapter 6

"H ow do I look?" I ask Lilly. We're back in her apartment, and while I had a great, relaxing spa weekend, we're about to destroy it by attending Lilly's church's Sunday Night Singles. She's determined that I get "back in the game," and she says my church is a bunch of peacocks trying to impress one another, so it's time I saw what a normal church function is like.

Can you tell me why a church must always name their singles' nights? Is it to make you feel like a complete moron? I mean, I remember in high school we had Broom Ball Night and I'm not seeing much of a difference. I'm sure the name is meant to imply fun, excitement, where-the-action-is, etc., but somehow it's more like there's a beacon of light over my head reminding the world I can't get a man over the threshold. (Except one who's bringing another wife to the party.)

Maybe we need to change the connotation of *single*. Maybe call it "Night of the Independents." No, that sounds too political. I know: "Land of the Free."

I know marriage shouldn't be my end goal, but when you throw us all into the same room with the heavy fog of desperation that comes with the title "Sunday Night Singles," it motivates us toward wanting to graduate. I mean, the animals on the ark went two by two; they didn't group together and rush towards the hottie giraffe when she came late, did they?

"You look great." Lilly interrupts my thoughts. "No one will ever know it's you. Not a label on you but mine."

Lilly has outfitted me in something she calls "retro chic" and it's reminiscent of a time in fashion history you'd just as soon forget. I have a badly dyed shirt with sleeves flowering at my hands like a wild Easter lily and the ugliest cowboy boots (with rhinestones, I might add) you ever saw. Cowboy boots in San Francisco! Isn't there some kind of law? My saving grace is the pair of Lilly Jacobs designer jeans. Now this girl can make a pair of jeans. They hug you in all the right places and create a long, lean line that tells the world, "My legs do go on forever; so what of it?"

Lilly's quest in my fashion nightmare is to show me that I rely too much on money/clothes to make a statement for myself, and if I'm going to make a statement, I should find out what mine is. Heavens, all I can say is I hope this ain't it!

"So what kind of statement am I making?" I ask her. "Besides that I lack self-respect, and an iron."

"That you're above having clothes speak for you. You're an enigma wrapped in a mystery. What man wouldn't want to find out more?"

"One that had good taste?" I offer. "And with this wrinkled shirt, you have completely eliminated all obsessive-compulsive men from my future."

"You need no more men with psychological diagnoses in your future, true?"

I wilt a little. "Yes, I guess you're right. But what about a man who realizes I don't match and don't have a real handbag?"

"Then he's probably gay and not looking at you anyway," Lilly says easily. "When's the last time you met a man who noticed your handbag?"

"You've been in the fashion industry too long."

"Isn't it the truth? Sometimes Max will do things like put a suit on, and I actually get nervous that he knows how to coordinate. I am definitely paranoid."

"You need to get out more."

"You need to be out less," she counters.

"Well, this is the outfit to do that in," I admit, scanning the boots one more time and feeling like I'm going to a great Halloween party. It is October.

"You look gorgeous. There's no way I can fix that." Lilly nibbles her bottom lip. "But maybe if you don't wear any makeup . . ."

"Can we go now?" I am not giving up makeup. A girl has to have a little self-respect. I mean, Queen Esther got a year of beauty treatments before meeting the king to talk. I can't see how dressing like this is biblical, and we are going to church.

"You know—" Lilly holds her fingers and thumbs like L's, framing me. "Your statement now is that you're friendly, not too concerned with fashion, and approachable. Before, you always looked so put together and elegant, only the car salesmen were going to introduce themselves."

"I beg your pardon?"

"Salesmen have the courage to come up to you. They face rejection all day long; they're prepared for you to say no. But a quality man? He might be too fearful to approach you."

"Not today."

"Exactly!"

"Maybe I like salesmen." I'm a wee bit offended. Why shouldn't I want a man willing to come up to me? I mean, if he's too much of a doofus to approach me, is he worth knowing? My father has sold diamonds his whole life, and he'd make a good husband. Sort of . . . kind of . . . okay, not really.

"It's not about them, Morgan. You're too beautiful. You just attract the wrong sorts. Look at all the supermodels and their loser husbands—is that what you want from life? Your name tattooed across someone's bum?"

Well, she's got me there. I can handle being compared to a supermodel, but the reality of their boyfriend choices and my own are far too similar for comfort.

"I'm not really interested in dating, Lilly. I just want to practice having a normal conversation. Maybe talk about how the 49ers look this year, or something."

"Which is why we're going to my church group. You won't be tempted."

"That's not a great thing to say about your church group."

"But it's the truth. Their idea of a hot date is for you to come watch them play videogames and tell them how manly they are. Tempted yet?"

"Grown men play video games?" I ask.

"Man, you are so naïve."

"Not really. It's the same in my world. There are men who ride the ponies, and they want you to come down to the Circus Club and watch them compete while they trot around on a horse. Same thing as the video games, just add money."

Lilly looks at me, disgusted. "Please don't talk anymore. Are you ready to go?"

"What does Max think of you going back to the singles group?" I ask, reminding her of her boyfriend.

"Let's put it this way: Max has been to my singles group. He's got the midseason starting anyway." Lilly shrugs. "He's so busy working, I barely see him, but he has no worries. He is definitely the man for me."

Max, Lilly's boyfriend, is a television critic for a local paper. Really, he's a hotel heir in San Francisco, but he refutes that part of his history. He got tired of living his parents' dream a long time ago, and I have to say I admire him for it.

But I'm just not sure I can pull the same thing off. These cowboy boots alone are enough to send me running and screaming back to my father and his credit cards. I'm a people pleaser by nature, and I worry people will not be pleased with tonight's image. I'm not pleased; why would anyone else be?

Since we've been home, my father has called my cell phone incessantly. His messages are basically, "Why would you want to live in squalor when you have a perfectly good penthouse?"

Now I know where I got that idea to call Lilly's home "squalor" in front of her. I'd obviously heard the term a few times. (The fact that Lilly's still my friend speaks volumes.)

Actually, the loft is not bad in terms of city dwellings. She keeps it clean, albeit smelling too much like Lysol. Her refrigerator is empty. She claims it's because she's been gone this weekend, but it's not like I haven't been here before. Lilly weighs about one hundred pounds, and she forgets to eat. Now if you put food in front of her, she'll wolf it like a vacuum cleaner, but she won't go out of her way to eat. She's one of those people who are naturally thin, with waiflike qualities, while she consumes cheap chocolate in unlawful quantities.

Her former roommate, Kim, lives upstairs with a man Lilly once kissed: Nate. Kim and Nate have been cohabitating for two months now and they enter Lilly's apartment at all hours of the day. No one in the building apparently owns a piece of electronic equipment that is not community property. The Tivo is up and down stairs, the television, the sewing machine . . . You name it, they just walk in and out of each other's places to use it like they're living in a Hare Krishna cult. I've seen it before when I've been here, but even in the last two hours, I've seen how constantly and eerily codependent they are. Kim has already been down for a single egg and a can opener. While she was down here, she dropped off the coffee bean grinder for Lilly. Which is odd since there is no coffeemaker in the loft. I imagine that's coming at some later rendezvous.

My first thought is to flee. To run back to my dad's and ask Mrs. Henry to make me something to eat. But one look at Lilly and I think about all she's accomplished with so little, and I just can't let her down. She has hired homeless women, taught them to sew, and rented out an empty warehouse in the fashion district and become a part of that neighborhood with her business. All in two months time and with very little start-up money. I, on the other hand, bought three new pairs of shoes last week that would pay the women's salaries for a month. I'm not proud of it, but there it is in all its ugly glory.

This—living with Lilly—is like moving to Kenya for me. A completely different culture, and just as foreign.

"Let's go," I say.

"Let's." Lilly grabs a can of Lysol and stuffs it in my over-sized canvas—yes, canvas—bag. Gone is my pebbled leather and carefully-stitched Hogan in favor of a black canvas bag that reads, "Got Milk?"

"What are you doing?" I pull out the can of antiseptic.

"The bus driver won't let me bring Lysol on the bus. He knows me."

"There's a reason for that. Do you think I'm going to smuggle contraband on the bus? It's my first ride. Like I need any more humiliation. Getting kicked off Muni would be the final straw, don't you think?"

Lilly purses her lips and grabs it out of my hands. "Don't say I didn't warn you."

I'll admit it: ten minutes later I figure out that we should have taken the Lysol. What can I say? Did I know that part of humanity doesn't believe in antiperspirant? There seems to be a rather large contingency of them who ride the bus.

Wait, maybe that could be my ministry and life's purpose! Buying Right Guard for the underworld! Lilly tells me sometimes it's cultural, but I have yet to meet the culture who wants to stink. Although, maybe they have a point—they got the seat to themselves on the bus. Lilly and I are crammed onto one seat, hugging my "Got Milk?" bag and dreaming of Lysol. Lilly's fetish is starting to make sense to me, and that's just frightening. I can see myself getting older, crocheting rhinestone Lysol cozies and inviting people into my home with the plastic-wrapped sofas and fruit-shaped refrigerator magnets.

The bus spits us up outside the church like Jonah landing on Nineveh's shores, its doors closing before I'm officially out, giving new meaning to the phrase, "Don't let the door hit you on the way out." Once inside, I see that Lilly's singles group consists mostly of men over forty losing their hair and their waistlines. I wouldn't have noticed, except they look exactly like the men my father has been trying to set me up with for years. The only difference is that my father's men can afford better hair plugs and they've all been married two or three times.

Lilly loves bald men, and it's like a convention in here. I can't believe she didn't find the man for her in this bunch. I have a theory that the men of San Francisco work so hard they lose their hair early, and clearly there are a few workaholics here. Of course, Lilly herself was a workaholic and often didn't make time for her singles group. Which may be how she missed all these candidates and ended up with Max.

(I have to wonder, though, why hair is such a big deal to guys. They obsess over it like we obsess over our bust size. And really, women don't care about a guy's hair. I look at the eyes. I look at the hands. But the head? Not so much.)

"Hi, Lilly. Who's your friend?" A young man with a full crop of hair approaches us and takes my hand gently. It's very chivalrous.

"This is my friend Morgan. Morgan, this is Steve Bandy. He's a dentist."

I pull my hand away. "Nice to meet you." I smile pretty and show him the investment my father has made in my mouth, but I'm sidetracked by all the new surroundings. The walls are hospital green, and there are music and movie posters taped to the wall. "Is this the teen room, Lilly?" It looks exactly like where I once played broom ball.

She just shakes her head; apparently, it's my clue to shut up. As I walk around the room, everyone smiles at me, and I gleam back, wanting to explain the cowboy boots, but knowing it's part of the deal. *I'm finding myself!* I want to shout. *I'm somewhere under these ghastly clothes.*

In the corner, there's a man playing the guitar, and he just arrests my attention. My mind immediately shifts to Andy and all I've done wrong and just how many conscience warnings in my head I ignored. The guilt is overwhelming. The room starts to feel claustrophobic and stifling. I'm reaching for the wall to steady myself when the guitar player looks up and there's something in his eyes that pulls me towards him. I'm almost there when I feel something stop me.

"Where are you going, Morgan?" It's Lilly. She is pulling on my shirt.

"I was just listening to the music."

"He's tuning his guitar." She looks at me strangely.

"Is he really?" I ask the question, and truthfully, I don't know the answer because I'm mesmerized by this man. He just seems to look right through me. "Who is that?" I ask. "Playing the guitar, who is that?"

"His name is Kyle Keller. I don't really know him too well,

but he's the part-time music pastor." Lilly pulls me aside and introduces me to someone else, but I don't hear what she's saying. There's something about that man playing the guitar. I just feel like he's sitting there, waiting for me to come over, and I can't get to him. It's not really an attraction thing, just intrigue, like he has something to say to me and I must hear it.

The singles pastor, a man of about forty, sits beside someone I can only assume is his wife, as she struggles to keep two toddler boys looking like good little church children rather than the obvious terrors they hope to be. My money is on the boys. The mother, a young woman with a pretty face and thin, muscular arms wrestles the boys in place without missing a beat, and the pastor begins speaking. Everyone files into place, and the pastor opens up with a "pre-message" that, I have to admit, I don't hear a word of. The pastor introduces worship and we listen to Kyle play solo while the words pop up on a blue screen behind him.

After worship, we break into small prayer groups and "share." This has been bred out of me, so I don't say a thing, but I listen and nod with my most compassionate smile as everyone talks about the horrors of work and increasing rent. My eyes follow the guitar player as he gets up and leaves.

No one knows who I am here. That is both freeing and utterly frightening, because no one really cares either.

"So, Morgan, if you don't have a job, maybe we could pray for your job search," Steve Bandy, the dentist dandy, says.

"Yes!" I point at him. "That would be a good idea. Pray I'll get a job."

And a life.

And an image.

Please!

chapter 7

After a solid night's sleep, I wake up to the roar of traffic on Highway 101 and my mother's picture on the front page of the *Chronicle*. Lilly must have left it for me. My heart plunges when I see the familiar glamour shot and my mother's poised elegance. How on earth she managed to have just the right pose every time there was a camera near remains a mystery. She was like a bat, hearing the high-pitched sonar squeal of the photographer and turning with extreme precision towards it with a gracious smile.

I open the paper to the article in which she's mentioned, and there again is the picture of me in Andy's arms. The headline reads, "Like Mother, Like Daughter." I crumple the paper and don't bother to read whatever tripe they've dredged up today. I ran off with a loser, big deal. As if I'm the first. Where is Britney Spears when I need her?

But my mother's photo does give me pause. When my mother, Traci Malliard, is spoken of in public, both my father and I don a sorrowful, reverent look that would make even the most callous of journalists cower in sympathy for our shared pain over her untimely loss. There are, of course, the persistent rumors, but we never speak of them. We stand shoulder to shoulder and protect her memory as if she was Mother Mary herself. When in fact she had far more in common with Joan Crawford—more than the fact they were both actresses and liked fire-engine red lipstick.

Life with my mother, when she was alive, was a persistent nightmare. My father escaped to his work, acquiring more and more real estate deeds and business deals to make himself feel like a man and escape her wrath. But whatever he owned, she wasn't impressed with, and so at night he would come home to hear her estimation of his worthlessness.

In contrast, or perhaps because of her snappishness, I thought my daddy hung the moon. I would hear my mother shriek at him behind slammed doors, and his eerie silence, ignoring her as though she was a mere gnat in his great forest. My mother was the great enigma to me. The woman behind the closed doors. She was truly a beauty—her nose is still a favorite of the plastic surgery set—but as far as warmth? She made Mrs. Henry seem like a cozy log cabin. At least from what I remember. I remember being frightened of her and avoiding her at all costs.

Still, my father cared for her physically until the bitter end, keeping Mrs. Henry around to nurse her through her horrible fight with ovarian cancer. My mother's once-glowing skin became ashen gray and her voluptuous figure withered away to a mere skeletal remnant. I don't know what her faith was when she passed, but I am ever-hopeful. Yet sadly realistic.

Speaking of realistic. I look around to the concrete walls in Lilly's apartment—the dusty windows twenty feet off the ground, the lack of art—and I laugh nervously. The dysfunction here is no different than in my own beautiful surroundings at home. We are broken people, regardless of station or environment, and my need for Christ becomes ever more apparent, like the one ray of light shining from the west bank of windows.

As I sit here on Lilly's futon and open my Bible, I am ready to delve into my history and leave it behind.

Doorbell.

Right after I get the door.

I get up and open it to see my father in his double-breasted suit, his countenance missing its usual bluster, and it's like a sign from above. As I let him in, I kick the balled-up newspaper under the futon.

"I'll get my things," I tell him.

He shakes his head. "I'm not here to get you."

But he looks parched, his color wan. I can't see him like this without remembering how my mother treated him, and I worry that I am exactly like her. He doesn't have the paper in his hand, and I wonder if he's seen today's dirt. (And where are the journalists when there's a real story? Like that I wore rhinestone cowboy boots to a social function? Now that is scandalous.)

"You're not here to get me?"

"Do you want me to be?"

I think about this for a minute. "No, actually, I'm job hunting today."

I wonder for a moment if he notices my clothes, how they lack the proper fit and the labels he's grown to recognize as my favorites, but he seems to be involved in his own thoughts and pays my appearance little mind.

"Good for you, sweetheart. I hope you find a good one. Don't let them pay you anything less than what you're worth."

Which, as an unemployed, unskilled laborer, I have to wonder is what, exactly?

"If you're not here to take me home, why are you here?"

"I've met a woman."

Lord have mercy.

"You've met a woman?" I'm fearful. Granted, I only know

my father's love life to exist in my mother, but let's just say his track record rivals my own. Maybe it's a curse. I take some comfort in the idea that maybe my future is mapped out and I'm merely a victim of my genes.

He looks me straight in the eye. "I didn't think I'd ever consider marriage again, Morgan. But I am. I think I can trust her."

"Trust her as in you could buy a car from her? Or as in she wouldn't steal from the store if left there alone."

"Trust her as in I could avoid a prenup."

"But you won't, of course."

"True. One can never be too careful."

"Where did you meet her?"

"At the club."

The thought of what he has in store for me as a stepmother sort of frightens me. Will she be twenty-four? Married fourteen times? Have a little trouble with the bottle? What could it be? The fact that I haven't met her is hardly a mystery. Daddy usually doesn't take women seriously enough to share them with the world. His idea of good publicity is to have a new woman on his arm at each event and keep the media guessing.

My question is aimed at her. How in the world does she need him enough that he feels it's necessary to tie the knot? And where exactly does this leave me, his codependent partner in life?

"Daddy, why would you want to get married? I thought you and I had discovered we're free spirits." Translation: warped human beings who cannot function in the world of relationship.

"Morgan, I've finally realized that you're becoming your own woman. It's time for me to start having my life now. I've raised you and you're ready to fly."

I know this moment generally comes a bit before a kid

turns twenty-nine, but I'm a slow learner.

"Daddy, what about Andy?" I ask, wondering if he'll see I'm not as ready for flight as he might imagine.

"I never expected you to do things perfectly. Granted, I didn't expect you to do things with quite so much lack of perfection." He rolls his eyes at this. "You've had your Andy; you didn't marry him at least." He pauses and claps his hands. "I did marry your mother."

Daddy, I blew it too. "So when will I meet her?"

"That's why I'm here." My father checks his watch. "I need you to meet us for dinner on Saturday night at the club. I'm going to be making my announcement public and I want you there to celebrate. Maybe the leeches can print something good for a change, no?"

"Can't I meet her beforehand?" I want to be prepared if she has a bad facelift or a puffy pink nose from an enlarged liver and too much alcohol.

"Morgan, your grammar, and you must stop questioning my decisions." He looks at his expensive shoes, and his expression shifts. "You're just like your mother sometimes. I don't need you second-guessing my decisions. Do you understand?"

"It's good to be accountable once in a while, Dad. I just want to meet her before I have to plaster on a fake smile in front of people. Is that too much trouble?"

"Your mother taught you how to handle social situations; you'll be fine. You could have met her at home, but you're the one who left. Made me trudge across town to visit this box you're living in." He checks his watch yet again. "Where are the windows in this place, Morgan?"

"At twenty-nine, I left home. I'm twenty-nine, Daddy, and I've been gone all of two days. I would think with a new woman in your life, you'd be happy for my independence."

He gazes around the loft, and that marked disapproval

I've tried my entire life to avoid comes to his face. "And this is what you have to show for it?"

"I've been a little busy, Daddy. Working in your shop, attending functions with the jewels. I didn't have time to build the life I might have. I'm just now discovering what that might be. Give me more than two days to build it, all right?"

"Shouldn't you know by now? This whole searching for self business is just a way people avoid work. You have a fine job wearing the jewels and honing my sales pitch. I don't know why you need more. It buys you all the things you love, doesn't it? You prefer this?" He raises his hands to the industrial ceiling.

"Yes, I do."

He brushes his tongue over his teeth. "You're an ingrate, you know."

"Just like my mother," I finish for him.

"Don't blame others for your problems, Morgan. That's how your mother got to be so selfish. Everything was someone else's fault. She would have blamed me for the cancer if she could have."

This inflames me. Suddenly—perhaps because for the first time in my life I'm standing up to him—I'm seeing my dad in a different light. Rather than just distant, he seems cruel. I'm apparently seeing the brusque, sharp personality my mother saw on a daily basis, and all at once I think maybe their lack of love wasn't completely her fault. Maybe she yelled because he never heard her otherwise. I know shouting seems to be the only thing that penetrates that thick skull of my father's. Even Mrs. Henry has been known to shout when she needs something taken care of. No wonder my father thinks all women do is yell.

These thoughts are so disturbing. I wish I had more time to contemplate them. I gaze at my father as though I've never known him and wonder where the truth of my childhood lies.

"I don't really want to go to the club. You can introduce her without me." Besides, if I go the emphasis will be on me, anyway. "I can't come on Saturday night." I search for a reason, but what does it matter? He'd belittle anything as an excuse, anyway.

"You can come, and you will. I won't have the city taking away the moment from Gwen to notice you're not there. Saturday night is her night, and you will not upstage her with your absence. It's time you grew up, Morgan."

It is time I grew up, and I'm going to start by finding myself something to do on Saturday night. "I think you should leave, Daddy."

"You want to live like this forever, Morgan? Where you're struggling for food and a decent living arrangement? You think this is romantic? Your mother lived like this until I rescued her, and let me tell you, she was living no picnic."

My father's face is red with rage, and I know he sees my mother in me right now, but for once in my life, I don't think that's such a bad thing. I'm proud to have her spunk and her fire while he tears down the world I've created. Well, the world Lilly has created.

"I'm not pretending to be poor, Dad. I'm discovering who I am and what I like to do. Newsflash: I don't like to wear diamonds and attend parties with people twice my age every night. There has to be something more than dripping in jewels and getting my picture taken."

"Which is why you ran off with that Andy character, and look where that got you. Maybe there isn't anything more, did you ever think of that? Maybe you're searching for something that doesn't exist and wasting my time and money in the process."

"Maybe I am, but it's a free country. I can search."

"Not without a credit card. It may be a free country, but life costs money." Again he glances at his watch to let me know how much valuable time he's wasting with this conversation.

"I should think you'd be happy I ran off with Andy. It was good publicity for the store."

"It was terrible publicity," he spits. "Men refused to buy their girlfriends trinkets for fear of being seen at the store."

His comment makes me sick to my stomach. He really does care more about the sale than the dozens of marriages he's helped crumble. In truth, he was thrilled for the publicity, and it's only now, when my comment doesn't serve his purpose, that he chooses to rewrite history. "There's more to life than money. You've got enough now to retire a million times over; why can't you go enjoy yourself? Maybe take your new wife to Fiji or something?"

"I enjoy working. It's the only thing that life rewards you for." My father reaches for the doorknob and takes another glance around the room. "What is that smell?"

"It's Lysol. Lilly likes things to smell clean."

"Saturday night at the club." He yanks open the door. "I'll see you then and introduce you to Gwen. She's a good, solid person and she doesn't yell."

Well, now there's a profession of love. "I can't be there." I say it as much for myself as him.

"You will be there. You've done enough to damage my reputation in the last six months; you're going to help me rebuild now or you really are going to find yourself in the school of hard knocks."

"I'm not." I cross my arms, and I feel them trembling. I have never stood up to my father this way, and I can hear my blood vessels pounding in my temples.

"You are, Morgan."

"I'm not," I say, like a testy teenager.

"This is for your own good—you come or I'm cutting you off."

"Meaning?"

"No exclusive gym, no country club, no shopping in your little shops with my credit cards."

My mouth gapes open, but I quickly shut it for fear I'll inhale too much Lysol. I have lived my entire life trying to please this man, but there is no appeasement. There is only my total and complete annihilation of self.

"You're threatening me?" I ask.

His tone softens to the soft sell. "You leave me no choice, Morgan. It's not like that, and you know it." He gives me his best "close the deal" smile. "When people live a privileged life there are things that go along with that responsibility. You have been given so much, and I don't ask for a lot in return."

"And my responsibility is doing what you tell me to do." I raise an eyebrow at him.

"Morgan, you are not prepared for the world that your friends live in. Do you realize that you've lived a very sheltered life, and when you're in contact with the real world, things like Andy happen?"

"A parent's job is to prepare children for the world." My words are like an icy sheath cutting through him. He cannot stand criticism of any sort, and I have just told him that if I am remarkably lame, it is his fault. I see him clench his teeth, and his jaw twitches with unreleased fury.

Through his tightly bound porcelain veneers, he growls, "You are well prepared for the life I raised you to live."

"But I think I want something different."

He looks around the room again. "This is fun for a while, isn't it? Living the life of a struggling single woman in San Francisco? So romantic. But you'll see how fun it is when you can't run home and be protected by my credit limit. You'll see how fun it is when you can't fill yourself with those expensive lattes and don those fancy shoes."

Like a weight, I suddenly hear my mother's words. Her vicious accusations against the man I thought loved her intimately even in the face of her steely bristling. But with unusual clarity, I see that my father's love is conditional. It always has been, but I can honestly say until this moment I never saw it. I only tried harder to please him and live up to his expectations because my mother was so appallingly bad at it.

Now I think maybe that was her choice—to jump off the boat and swim for her life.

"So you'll be there Saturday night." He reaches for the doorknob. "If you aren't, I'll have no choice, Morgan. You've got a responsibility to the Malliard name: you either keep your commitments, or you give up the privileges that are afforded with it."

He starts to walk out the door, his line in the sand drawn.

"You never told me her name?"

"Whose?"

"This precious wife you're taking. You never told me her name, other than Gwen."

"Gwen Caruthers. She's in real estate and sold me my last property."

Apparently that's not all she sold him.

With that, he shuts the door, determined that I will be there on Saturday. I slump down on Lilly's futon, and I feel like all along I've thought my dad was a respected member of the military, only to find out the SS on his uniform stood for Nazi.

I have to know more about my mother. Something tells me I don't remember everything as it was. Not only do I have no image in this life, but apparently, I don't have a credit limit either. This reeks. Poor, I think I can handle, but I should at least stand for something. Every Christian should.

chapter 8

My cell phone trills, and it's a number I don't recognize. "Hello," I say warily.

"Morgan?" Andy's voice emanates from the telephone, and I'm lost between wanting to ask him so many questions and realizing he is at the root of my newspaper popularity. A million thoughts run through my mind, but like a cat, I feel my back arch.

"What do you want?" I ask, thinking, *Why on earth didn't I grab a restraining order to keep him from my vicinity?* I mean, the papers would have eaten that up, and I missed a golden opportunity.

"I need to see you, Morgan. I'm out of jail, and I have to explain. The newspapers have it all wrong."

Oh my goodness—five minutes with him and I'd probably be married again. I have this weakness for the sales pitch, and I still remember how I felt when he catapulted me off the ground in that fashion show. Now that was an emotional high. . . .

Reality check: bigamist here.

"You know, I don't think so. But thanks for calling. Best of luck to you now."

"Morgan, please."

"Please what, Andy? Or should I say *Arnold*?"

I keep my hand on the button, but I don't hang up. I want to hear an excuse. I want to know he loved me, and even though I hate myself for waiting on such a myth, I stand here, hope filled.

"I just wanted to be who you wanted me to be."

"I wanted you to not be married, for starters."

"My marriage was not really a marriage."

Oh brother. *Click.* I do it. I hang up, and I feel empowered. Perhaps it wouldn't take so much for the average woman to get fed up, but I am not your average woman. I am your typical love-starved socialite without a solid dating history. I've only known dates as an act for the media. I don't remember my heart ever being involved like this. It makes me feel so incredibly stupid.

After my talk with Andy/Arnold I feel dirty. I need a bath. But there's no bathtub in the loft, just a small stall shower. That's the one thing that tempts me to go home. I miss my double-head, full-sized shower with the removable spray handle. Lilly's shower has this trickle that is so paltry, I'm almost embarrassed for it. It's like this little stream of "I think I can, I think I can." But it can't.

"Hello?" While I'm standing there musing about plumbing Lilly's upstairs neighbor, Nate, appears at the front door, which is propped open with a shoe. "Lilly said you had half-and-half here," he says.

"In the fridge." I motion towards the pink, outdated appliance and Nate helps himself. "Lilly's having coffee and then she said to tell you she'd be down. She wanted to let you sleep."

I nod, feeling a bit guilty for tossing Lilly out of her own place.

"Tell her she doesn't need to do that."

"I couldn't help but overhear your conversation."

I brush my fingers through my wild morning tangles. "And?"

"I think you're being too hard on yourself. Kim fell for a con artist, too. Remember when she took Lilly's check for the business?"

"This is not making me feel better, actually."

"I'm just saying, it happens to the best of people."

And Kim, too, I think. "Tell Lilly she's free to come down-stairs. I'm awake."

"Will do," he says, lifting the half-and-half in a sort of pathetic toast to my ignorance.

I don't trust Nate. Not as far as I could throw him. He's too smooth, always in the right place to dole out wisdom and play the understanding male. When in fact he's probably no differ-ent from Andy: a dog in sheep's clothing.

My cell phone rings again and I can only assume it's Andy with more excuses and more tools to tear down my armor.

"Aren't you going to get that?" Nate asks.

"No," I say without further explanation.

"Do you want to come up for coffee?" Nate is handsome in a scholarly way. I sort of imagine him as the hot professor you had a crush on in college. But his friendship with Lilly is a mystery to me. He and Kim live together but don't feel truly satisfied with one another, as if they're always looking around for someone better. I would prefer Lilly find another place to hang out, but she's an adult, and they seem to share her love for reality television.

I feel my eyes thin as I stare at him trying to figure out his motive. I think about his question: do I want to come up and see the other half of the appliance brigade? You bet. I want to know what's up with the constant sharing and why he can't seem to have a life with his girlfriend alone. "Thanks, Nate, that would be nice."

I slip on a pair of flip-flops Lilly left by the door and follow Nate up a dingy set of stairs to a hallway that is almost elegant by comparison. There's even a painted cement walkway that's straight out of *Architectural Digest*. But when we reach his apartment, I go into shock. The cabinets are a light maple with stainless-steel appliances, and Nate's furniture consists of black particle-board shelving for his equipment and industrial-type chairs. It's minimalist at best, with a shock of red here and there. And something else—a smell that about bowls me over.

I see Lilly sitting prettily on the scarlet vinyl sofa that's straight out of a 1950s doctor's office. As I look at her, her coffee cup in hand, I bring my fingers to my nose as casually as possible. *How are you in here?* I want to ask her, but she's sipping her coffee and everything seems fine. An older cocker spaniel ambles across the floor, and I suddenly find the source of the scent.

"His ear leaks," Nate explains. "That's the smell. Were you wondering?"

"Want some Vicks VapoRub?" Lilly asks me cheerfully.

Nate hands me a cup of java, and I feel the distinct need to wretch, not play house and drink coffee. I thrust the cup back towards him. "I need to make an urgent phone call. I forgot something."

I rush down the stairwell, exhaling and gasping for air as though I've been on the moon for a time. And they say Starbucks is expensive? Man, the price of Nate's coffee is intolerable.

There's a man outside Lilly's door when I come to the ripped, tenement-by-comparison hallway. It's Max Schwartz, Lilly's boyfriend—and would-be fiancé if she had an ounce of common sense, but at the moment there is only her business and her goal of proving to everyone she doesn't need him.

Including Max. The entire situation is ridiculous and unnerving, and as someone who has absolutely no prospects for a job or a legitimate boyfriend, it's painful to watch.

With Lilly's sharp sense of smell, you'd think she'd have better instincts. Max is of average height, has a strong, sexy nose and chiseled facial features, and a receding hairline a la Matt Lauer. Max comes from big money, but he doesn't live like it. And yet where is Lilly? She's up with two people who are shacking up. One stole twenty thousand dollars from her (she got it back) and the other kissed her and then moved in with the roommate who stole the money. And they call me naïve.

As far as choices go, Lilly's in desperate need of counsel. And yet she thinks I'm here to help me.

My cell phone is trilling again, and I press it off, making a mental note to get a new number. Here's the thing: when you marry a man who has already married a few other people, it's best that he doesn't have your phone number. You'd think when someone has been in jail for bigamy, he would sort of get a clue. But I guess if he'd sort of gotten the clue in the first place, he wouldn't be a bigamist.

Max Schwartz is still standing there, all gorgeous. I'm currently thinking Lilly is in desperate need of a lobotomy. At least a good spa weekend where we slap some sense into her.

He's staring at me, waiting for me to speak.

"Max, it's good to see you."

"You, too, Morgan. Is Lilly here?" He looks around the apartment as I open the door, and I watch as his expression falls.

"She's not." I point towards the ceiling, indicating Nate's. "She's just upstairs, Max."

Max nods solemnly and walks towards the stairwell leading downstairs. "Thanks, Morgan. Tell Lilly I stopped by, will you?" He's still limping from a badly broken leg and the surgery that followed. Before he starts down the stairs, he looks back at me. "You're not hanging out there, too, now? What does that guy have up there, pixie dust?"

"Coffee. Aren't you going up to see her?"

He walks back toward me and shakes his head. "I don't think so."

"Max, you're not giving up on her?"

The corner of his lip turns up. "Never. We share a love for being on the scene."

"On the scene? Lilly? If there's a person with a more mundane life than Lilly, I really need to hear this. The girl thinks picking up the newest Lysol scent is living large."

He laughs. "It was a joke."

It's the first time I can remember Max being humorous about anything. He was raised by a stoic father like my own, and if we're taught anything, it's to keep our emotions to ourselves. San Francisco society doesn't want to hear about your problems, unless they're huge and scandalous like my own and can provide gossip and sell papers. Otherwise, keep it to yourself.

"Come on in and wait for her, Max. I'll go up and get her." I start to shut him in the apartment, but he stops the door with his hand and shakes his head.

"I'll give her a call when she's home. She'll have to be getting to work, and I have to stop by the hotel to do something for my father."

I grab his arm, and he stares at me, his lids heavily laden with fatigue. My thoughts run amok. *What if I'd fallen in love with a man like Max? A healthy and generous sort who was willing to commit and—here's the kicker—willing to commit only once instead of getting a group rate on brides.* The idea is laughable, however, because Max Schwartz would have been completely respectable to my father, and if there's anything I've learned to avoid, it's a man my father approves of. My dad has given me a solid foundation for life, and I must say, one of the bricks in it is avoid men that look too good on the outside. I just have to find the right balance between fixer-upper and marked for demolition.

Max looks at me softly, and it feels like the first time he's noticed me, and not just in anticipation of Lilly. "Hey, I'm sorry about what the newspapers are doing to you, Morgan."

I shrug. "It comes with the trust fund, I suppose. Nothing more fun than watching a rich person go down."

He laughs. "I suppose it's true."

I slap his arm. "Except when you're in the paper, it's for your latest good deed. When I'm in the paper, it's to tell the world I've made yet another bad boyfriend choice."

"You'll get it right," Max says absently.

I hear Lilly coming down the stairs. How do I know it's Lilly? She's preceding her steps with the swooshing sound of Lysol spray. Apparently, the stairs are ready for their close-up, or the mixture of dog and espresso has finally invaded her nostrils. Max turns quickly towards the stairwell, and his expression changes instantly to anticipation. He is gone. Thoroughly enamored with Lilly Jacobs and unable to wrench himself free of her antiseptic scent. I can only hope she has the presence of mind to see what's in front of her.

"Lilly!" He walks towards her, and their eyes meet, and it's as though I have disappeared from the planet. I never once thought I could feel jealousy over one of my best friend's joy, but I feel anger welling up in my chest. Lilly has a man who loves her like this, and he's not married to someone else, and there is nothing stopping them from a future together. I honestly don't remember a man ever looking at me like that. At least not when it was real. Andy looked at me like that and made my stomach churn with excitement, but it was little more than modern-day mythology.

I watch Lilly's expression melt into Max's before she straightens her shoulders, smiles slightly at him, and then takes on an air of indifference.

"Max, what are you doing here?"

"I thought you were coming over to sketch last night. I waited up for you until it got to be ten, and I figured you wouldn't come that late. The night was clear and the Bay lights looked incredible. I thought you would have loved it, and I just couldn't believe you weren't there to enjoy it."

"I took Morgan to the singles group and then I was just tired, so I went up to Nate and Kim's to watch a movie and just crashed."

Max's face doesn't flinch, but I'm astonished. She was tired? When Max Schwartz was expecting her, she just decided not to go? I know we all cling to what's comfortable, but hanging out as a third wheel for Nate and his honey should not be comfortable for Lilly compared to a night with her boyfriend, all cozy and cuddly overlooking the San Francisco city lights. Lilly is hiding something, and I can't imagine what it is, but I hope she figures it out before Max Schwartz hightails it out of her offbeat life. And she's left with Nate, his girlfriend, and that wretched smelly ball of fur.

"You could have called." Max's jaw tics ever so slightly, but Lilly hasn't noticed; she's folding fabric on her futon.

"I didn't know I needed to check in." She turns around, clearly challenging him and hoping for a reaction. I am so going to hurt her.

"I didn't ask you to check in, just to have common decency. You are my—"

"Well," Lilly cuts him off with a sinister stare. "I'm common. Did you expect anything less? Sometimes I miss out on the decency part."

"I would think anyone raised by your nana would have the manners to make a phone call."

"Well, maybe you should go home and tattle and let her know how she failed, too."

Max's eyes flash, and he turns on his heel faster than I thought possible for someone who just had surgery. He looks weary and unwilling to put up with whatever obstacle Lilly has prepared for him next.

"Have a good day, Morgan." He brushes past me briskly. "You're going to have to face this, Lilly." His voice drips with ice. "This is not a temporary situation. There are conse-quences." He exits and slams the door behind me.

Lilly doesn't look at me. She just keeps folding fabric, fingering the delicate red silk. When enough time has passed that she's certain I'm not going to question her, she looks up.

"What movie did you watch?" I ask, more curious than ever about her behavior, but unwilling to turn her away by asking.

"*Sense and Sensibility.*"

"And which is it you have?" I ask her, referring to the storyline of a sister who loves with all her emotions and a sister who clings to her reason, pushing away love.

"Both, I should think. I printed out some jobs off Monster.com for you. Some of them sound really good, and I think you should get a résumé off as soon as possible."

"My father is getting married," I blurt. I hadn't realized the news was there lurking beneath my cool facade like a cougar who lies in wait for its prey, but there it is.

"He's pushing me. Too much, too fast," Lilly says with a shake of fabric.

"My father?"

"Max. He wants me to meet his mother and be the kind of

wife that's expected of him. But I'm no socialite. Why can't he just understand that I love him? I'm not called to be a woman like . . . well, a woman like you, Morgan. I'm just not ever going to be that person."

"Fair enough, but just be warned there are more than a few women willing to be that space in between."

"I know that. Do you think I don't know that? My nana has always said it's just as easy to fall in love with a rich man, but it's much, much harder."

"I'm sure I'll cry you a river tonight. Would you even care? Let's say I swoop in and take Max off your hands. Our wedding is announced in next month's society page. Are you bothered by that? Just remotely?"

"You wouldn't do that."

"I was engaged to a man dying of liver disease and married one who was a bigamist. How can you be so sure of what I might do next?" I cross my arms and slip off the flip-flops. "Max is a solid man, and he'd be a great husband. I'm not immune to that reality, and in case you haven't noticed, I'm more than willing to build myself a family."

"You're my Spa Girl," Lilly giggles. "As if you'd break the golden friendship rule. Even bad friends don't steal boyfriends."

"I might." I shrug. "I have a thing for suffering men, and you are certainly making Max suffer. That's how it starts, you know. I let him cry on my shoulder . . . Yada, yada, yada."

I haven't convinced her. Lilly just laughs this off. Now I have to say, Max is definitely tempting, but only because I've seen the way he looks at Lilly, and the reality is he won't ever look at me like that. To him, I might just as well be a wooden plank on the Embarcadero as a San Francisco socialite with the right connections. Max made up his mind who he wanted a long time ago, and it's my mission to make sure he gets her. Because Lilly Jacobs was made for him, and if she's not bright enough to see it, I will definitely help clear the windshield of her mind.

If I've learned anything in my recent history, it's how fragile real love is. Sometimes we need to be hit with the two-by-four that is reality.

chapter 9

This Monday morning has taught me one thing. There are more annoyances in life than salons being closed. Really. Looking for work is a completely humiliating experience, and it's not nearly as easy to make money as I thought even two days ago. People are not actually clambering to give me a job, and they don't consider my fine wardrobe a benefit to their office. Though they should.

Even though I'm not wearing my nice clothes (Lilly is still working on that image thing; let's hope she's over that soon!), I look like I'd have a nice wardrobe. People should know— the blue diamond I wear on my right hand is only a small taste of the excellence I've created in my image. Yet I've walked into countless offices and allowed receptionists in ill-fitting clothes to look me over like a piece of meat, grab my résumé as though it's riddled with snot, nod without comment, and send me on my way. Without a job, no less!

A few days ago, I would have walked in confidently, my legs striding long with Jimmy Choos to lead the way, and snapped my fingers to get what I wanted. But today? Today I have a pair of cheap "pleather" mules, and besides looking like Nurse Rachet, I feel like the ugly stepsister crammed into Cinderella's itty, bitty slippers.

There's one last lead on my job sheet and though my feet feel like hamburger, I'm determined to finish the day. The job is not in a great neighborhood, and I'm leery of going, but considering the luck I've had, I schlep on over, imagining myself in Christian Louboutin, and hold my head high as I enter the last office. I shut the door behind me, and the receptionist looks up and then back down at her paperwork.

Honestly, my first thought is, *Could I really live with this carpet while I worked?* It's busy, and I'm sure filthy, and it matches the ghastly chairs and the bad artwork. But I think about being in my father's perfect shop, with all the blue halogen lighting beating down on the flawless diamonds, and I remember I have nothing to show for it. So maybe the carpet isn't that bad.

The receptionist is that type of redhead that's straight out of the bottle—the mahogany sort that resembles the hue of a fine antique English desk. Good for furniture, not really so great for hair.

"May I help you?" she asks in that annoyed, get-out-of-here tone.

"I'm Morgan Malliard. I was hoping to drop off a résumé." And if you're willing, I'd love to offer hue advice.

"We're not hiring." She looks down, blending in with the faux cherry desk.

Be nice. Be nice. Be nice.

"But if you were," I give her my best San Francisco's Jeweler smile, "I'd be perfect for this job you have listed here on the Internet." I hold up the paper Lilly printed for me. "Maybe you could pass my résumé on for me." I look up at the marquee to see just what it is they do in this office. "Advertising," I say aloud. To which the redhead mouths "Duh" as though she's not directly in front of me. One thing about growing up in the city, I've learned that people see no reason to withhold their opinions.

I'm not deterred. No one with hair color like that is going to intimidate me. "I've done a great deal of marketing for the Union Square merchants and know many of them. Perhaps you could just give this to your boss and have him give me a call."

"Look, princess—" The redhead has clearly forgotten her hormones today. But like a beacon in the night sky, a man appears. Except when I see how he eyes me, like a lion at the zoo before they throw the meat out, my comfort dissipates. The redhead sees him, too, but it does nothing to redirect her attitude. "We're not hiring, but when the glass slipper appears, we'll call you."

I turn, nodding slowly to let her know I do understand. I mean, would I want to work here anyway? But something leaves my feet planted on the ground, as though I have something to prove here.

The woman refuses to look at me, though I'm still hovering over her. In my head, I keep hearing that little boy: "I see dead people." It's the bad shoes. I am completely invisible in bad shoes.

"So did you fill the position you advertised on Friday?" I blurt.

The guy flourishes a big grin. "We didn't. Are you looking for work, darling?"

Slimy.

Slick, like dirty oil.

Scary.

"Never mind," I say as I start to back out of the office.

"No, really, what type of work are you looking for?"

Not your kind.

The redhead continues to glare, taking an unnatural pleasure in our wooden conversation. Perhaps in answer to my obvious discomfort she finally offers, "Princess, I'll give your résumé to the boss."

"Do you type?" the smarmy guy asks.

"Of course I type." This is 2005. Who doesn't type? "As you'll see by my résumé, I have a Stanford degree in business and work in . . . I worked in advertising for years helping build one of the biggest San Francisco jewelry businesses in the city."

"Let's see that résumé." He grabs the sheet from the redhead, who has rolled her eyes into the back of her head like some creepy puppet.

"I'm looking for a job . . . in advertising," I add as an after-thought.

"Isn't everyone? I can't imagine why; it's a thankless job."

I figure, what do I have to lose now? I handled this guy's type every night of my life wearing my dad's jewels.

"What kind of work are you looking for?"

I surreptitiously pull a business card from the last office I entered out from my pocket and read the title. "Account executive," I say. "I'm an account executive. Excellent with the accounts."

He laughs. Apparently, I'm not as good as my father at the whole lack-of-knowledge thing and continuing to talk my way out of a mess. You would have thought I might have picked up more of his talent. "Well, if I hear of anything, I'll let you know." He allows his eyes to scan me and wets his chops. "I'll let you know very soon, Morgan," he says after another look at my résumé.

I need a shower.

Mr. Smarmy disappears from view after the necessary wink. I refrain from comment even though I consider it my duty to pass on to men that winking is not sexy. It just makes them look creepy—although this guy didn't even need the wink for that. That was an added bonus. And it takes everything within me to not stick my tongue out at the redhead. But painful shoes have certainly cleaned up my attitude.

As I exit the office, I slam into someone in the hallway and I drop the folder that contains all the job leads. I'm bending down to pick them up when I notice that the man bending to help me is someone I recognize. It's George Gentry.

George and I both gaze at one another, and he thrusts the loose papers at me and stands abruptly. But he doesn't take his eyes off me, and I can't tear mine from his.

"Who are you?" I ask. I look at the nearest door, which advertises a law firm, then I look at his suit. "And don't tell me you're from *Time*. Who are you really?"

"I already told you who I am, Morgan. You just didn't believe me. I'm a lawyer. A lawyer late for a meeting." He turns to leave, but I grab him at the wrist and force him to look me in the eye. They're deep russet brown, the color of a California redwood, and they have an honesty to them. But I know he's lied to me so my dreamy fantasies about his character are just that: fantasies.

"You also told me *Time*," I say facetiously.

He hands me a card. "I never said I worked for them. You inferred that. I was about to give you a great quote I'd read there. Look, I can't explain to you right now, but someday, Morgan Malliard, when a man isn't waiting for me to ensure he doesn't go to prison, I'll tell you everything." He places his hand on my arm. "It won't be long now. What are you doing here?" he asks as he drops his hand.

"Looking for work."

He eyes the door I just exited. "Find anything?"

"Human vermin," I joke. "But no, not really a job."

"I can't talk here. I'll be in touch." He jogs down the hallway, and as I watch him disappear into the elevator he gives me a smile. I honestly hope he'll wink at me, and I realize it's not really the wink, it's the bearer of the wink. But he doesn't wink.

I scan the card. "George Gentry, Attorney at Law." I look at the door he just came from. It says "Lemur and Lemur, LLC."

My dad hired him. The question is why. Is it serious?

Truthfully, I don't even care. As much as he's annoying me, George has a trustworthy face (not to mention smart-sexy in the handsome news-anchor mold). And I imagine that if Lilly hadn't shown up the other day at the spa, I probably would have ended up spilling anything he wanted to hear. I'm a sucker for a pretty face.

Sigh. I wouldn't know the truth if it were cast before me in stone. Naïve might be too gentle a word to describe me. Dumb-as-a-box currently seems more apt.

chapter 10

It's been one full twenty-four-hour period without my designer clothes or the heels to go with them. I personally think I've learned a lot about character and human potential by the experiment, and I've discovered my image is just . . . well, it's just better off in quality clothing. Study over. Call the fashion journals. I know I sound spoiled, but I long for my comfort zone. Some people find it in sweats; I'm partial to Marc Jacobs. "Where are my shoes?" I ask Lilly when I get back into the loft and toss the Got Milk? bag to the floor. "I'm never going to get a job dressed like this. The receptionists are dressed better than me."

"I took them back to your father's house this morning after you left. We don't have room here, and I thought you'd agreed to the conditions." She's bent over her sketch pad. "Trust me, people get jobs without couture, or imagine the unemployment rate."

Now I could get huffy. I could explain that my father threatened to leave me destitute or that soon my clothes will be last season's, or even that she had no right to touch my stuff. Or I could just go buy some Dr. Scholl's corn pads and deal. From the look of Lilly's lack of sympathy, I imagine that's what I'll do.

Switching gears, I pull George's card from my pocket and I study it, rubbing my hands over the raised letters and thinking of him. His eyes seemed so sincere today. There was an intensity, a scent of importance to him I couldn't quite understand. But then I remember that day at the spa, and his arrogance, and I feel a sense of anger rising.

"Why on earth would he lie to me? A complete stranger?"

"What?"

"Nothing. I'm just thinking out loud. Do you remember that guy from the spa, George Gentry?"

"Sure. Is he still following you?"

"I think I might have followed him. I met him at a law office today."

"What did you want to do for dinner?" This is a question that's really wasted on Lilly. She doesn't care what she eats, or even if she eats. She somehow manages to get enough calories into her slender hips to keep moving and buzzing around life like an ADD bee flowering the whole of San Francisco with her pollen.

She turns her sketch pad, studying the angles. "I've got some Cup O' Noodles in the cabinet. Shrimp or chicken?"

"That is not dinner, Lilly. That is a camping snack. 'Just add water' is a direction for a facial substance, not a meal. Do I need to go to the grocery store?"

"I guess you do if my Cup O' Stuff isn't good enough for you. Or maybe you could phone Mrs. Henry and have her come by on her way home and create a seven-course meal for you. Cleanse your palette before the pâté and all that. Tell her to bring the good china; mine's at the shop."

I drop my hands to my sides and feel my smile disappear. And suddenly everything—the agonizing shoes, the stupid Got Milk? bag, the humiliation of hawking myself to ungrateful companies, not to mention the fact my whole life has suddenly become a whole lot harder than it was even a week ago—comes crashing down on me. I've had it with Lilly's comments. I'm ticked. I'm fumbling with my future while Lilly's grasping hers by the horns, sketching her spring line with confidence. I'm envious that she just naturally knows what to do in her life and that she has so much initiative that she can push away a perfectly good man like Max and not be the worse for it. I haven't even had enough initiative to get rid of the cell phone number my ex-boyfriend (I can't bring myself to say *husband*, and since the annulment is complete, helped along by the fact that we were never legally married, I'm going to stick with *ex-boyfriend*. It makes me sound like less of a loser. Sort of.) keeps managing to call me on.

I cross my arms and glare at my friend. "Lilly, maybe I don't know all that you know as a street-smart San Francisco girl, but I'll tell you what—not once did I ever make you feel like less. Not once. When you didn't have money and couldn't afford fabric? When your roommate stole your check? Did I ridicule you? No, I gave you my credit card and what you needed." I feel the knot in my throat rising painfully under the words. I hate conflict (and truthfully, doing everything my father has told me to do, I've never really faced much conflict).

I slip on the excruciating shoes and I exit Lilly's apartment, slamming the door behind me. It's only when I'm in the dimly lit hallway that I realize how limited my options are. If I go back home to my daddy's, everything they say about me will be true, and I will be forced to admit I am inept, naïve, and most likely my mother's daughter. Of course, part of me wants to whine that it's not my fault. I know I've been given everything in life, and perhaps I shouldn't have taken it all, but I didn't know anything different and I never prepared for the alternative. One doesn't spend her entire life rich and yet contemplate poverty. Maybe as a Christian, I should have done this all along.

The realization stuns me that I truly am twenty-nine with nothing to show for my life except a trail of paunchy old men my dad hoped I'd marry. (And something tells me I can't exactly print that in the Stanford alumni newsletter.) I do what my father always told me—stand up straight and try to focus on the positive:

I have my degree.

I have my health.

I had good shoes. (It is better to have loved and lost than never to have loved at all.)

However, none of these things adds up to a life purpose, and I don't have the first idea what I could do for a job. My father always just told me where to be, and like a good little lemming, I went. And now, as I stand here waiting for my next cue, there is no director.

But I can't spend my entire life looking for someone to direct me—I have to make a choice. It's just at the moment I have no idea what.

As I reach the stairwell, I stop to ponder where exactly I'm going and I hear someone breathing. A dark shadow envelops the wall and crawls up it like an ever-expanding black widow and I jump back, pasting myself against the wall in stark terror as the labored breathing gets louder and closer. The shadow grows, darkening the wall, and leaves me nowhere to run. But just as I'm about to turn back towards Lilly's apartment, Max Schwartz skips up the last step, letting out a deep exhale. I whimper as he gives me a tender smile.

"Morgan, what are you doing out here?"

Just then, Lilly opens her door and calls out my name. I turn back to look at her, and then to Max again, but I can't speak. I'm still catching my breath. I grab his hand to let him know I'm acknowledging his presence, and then I rush down the stairs, unsure of my destination, but feeling the desperate need to run. What I wouldn't give for an Internet-ready tread-mill at my gym.

When I get downstairs, there is no car waiting for me. There is no doorman to bring my convertible around. There is only the orange-streetlight glow and the steady rush of traf-fic noise and rhythm of honking horns.

"Morgan?"

"Ah!" I grab my heart as it pumps furiously.

"It's me—Nate. Do you need something? A cab, maybe?"

I feel my head bob up and down as an aura of peace floods my senses. Someone to take charge.

Nate pulls out a cell phone and dials for a car. Then he sits down on the stoop with his bag of groceries and telltale San Francisco sourdough baguette protruding from the contents. I sit down beside him, thankful for his small show of chivalry even if I can't quite place his motive for playing Superman.

"You don't have your purse. Do you need some money?" he asks and I relish the thought that someone notices me. Anything about me, even if it's a complete lack of organiza-tional skills. At least it's not the scarlet letter.

I find my voice. "No, I'm going home. The doorman will pay the driver, and then Daddy can pay it back."

"You're going home already?"

"I didn't have much luck finding a job today."

"It's been one day."

"One day too many for me, I'm afraid."

Nate puts the grocery bag aside and settles back into the stair, his elbows resting on the landing. You would think it's a bright, sunny afternoon on the San Francisco doorstep, not a chilly, foggy night, as easy as he makes this motion. "You know what I love about you, Morgan?"

This I gotta hear.

"You just have elegance, like Grace Kelly. You make your environment look better." He shrugs in his carefree manner. "There's a poised way about you, like a human gazelle, and people are just attracted to your presence, just to possibly have a smidgen of your glamour. You're just like your mother that way."

"Thanks," I say, rolling my eyes. Maybe I can take my glamour to the unemployment office.

"You're not understanding what I'm saying. It's an extreme compliment, and I don't give them out easily or undeservedly."

Nate is quite savvy, and I imagine he does have some good advice for me, but with the harem that generally surrounds him, I'm more than a little leery. Especially with my own history of a supporting role in a modern-day harem.

"You're right. I'm not understanding, Nate. Do you want to elaborate?"

"Well, for instance, you could tell someone their entire stock portfolio was worth nothing, nada, zilch, and they'd be happy to hear it from you. Or that their dog needed to be put to sleep, and would they like a shot or a pill for that?"

I laugh out loud. "This is a gift?"

He laughs, too, and his eyes crinkle at the edges in their very charming manner. Nate has this gift of making you feel as if you're the only person in the world when he's speaking to you; he's never sidetracked or in a hurry and the reason Lilly and Kim both flock to his side is obvious. My fears of being on the street have all but dissipated, and I lean towards him to hear what helpful advice he has, even if it is against my instincts.

"San Francisco is a happening place, am I right?"

"You are." I agree.

"It's like New York—if you can make it here, you can make it anywhere."

"True, but obviously I can't make it here, so are you suggesting I move? Maybe look for something in Iowa?"

"You really don't know what you're good at." He says this with just the right amount of flirtation, and I feel myself becoming more uncomfortable.

"I'm good at buying shoes and spending my father's money. But it's a funny thing, I can't really do anything with that skill. And neither of those brings in a lot of cash."

Nate just shakes his head, clearly frustrated with me. "You know the in's and out's of the city, where the chic people go, where the 'yesterday' restaurants are, and where they wouldn't want to be seen. That's a gift."

"But not really a marketable one." I start to imagine what God would want from me, and how He loves an unselfish heart. "Do you think I'd make a good missionary?"

Nate is not a Christian, and yet this makes him laugh. "You'd make a fine missionary to wealthy people. I'm not so sure if you're ready for the streets of Calcutta just yet."

What I love and envy about Lilly (even when I'm annoyed with her) and her friends is that they tell you the truth. Their version of it, anyway. In fact, just try and hold her nana (who raised her) back from telling her the truth. My father, in contrast, has always blindly encouraged me, so it never dawned on me I wasn't actually perfect for each and every station of life. Until now.

"So I'm not cut out for the mission field." I cross my arms in front of me, pulling my sweater around my chest. "What is my graceful gift good for, exactly, Nate? Is there a place out there that cares if I type prettily?" Truthfully, I don't know why I'm listening, other than I want a friend to sit with me until the cab gets here. Nate couldn't dole out career advice any better than Martha Stewart.

"When you came into my apartment this morning, what's

the first thing you noticed?" he asks.

"You have a lot of computer equipment."

"Hah!" He points at me. "That's not what you noticed. You noticed the smell of my dog, just like everyone does. He stinks."

Which begs the question, *Why doesn't Nate have a Lysol fetish?*

I nod subtly. It is what I noticed. It's horrible.

"His ear drains. He wouldn't survive the operation, or I'd fix it." Nate explains. "You never said a thing when you walked in. You just coyly handed me back the coffee cup before excusing yourself."

Yeah, and running for my life. "Your point? I didn't want to be rude."

"Did Lilly ever think about being rude? About wiping VapoRub under her nose before entering? Or passing it around like a party favor?"

I laugh, picturing Lilly and her freakish scent issue, sticking out her jar of Vicks like it's a fine champagne at a wedding.

My cab pulls up in front of the building and Nate stands, leaving his groceries on the stoop. As he's walking to the cab and opening the door for me, he says one last thing. "My point is you could be a stylist and tell people what to wear, a hotel concierge to tell people where to be, or an event planner to showcase what you wealthy people buy. There are any number of options. You just need to think outside the box and stop looking for things beneath who you are. Embrace who you are. You're the daughter of San Francisco's Jeweler; your mother is the infamous Traci Malliard. One does not come by successful genes like that for nothing."

As I slide into the cab's seat, Nate shuts the door and taps on the window, which I roll down. "Thanks, Nate."

"People aren't reading about you in the papers because

you screwed up, Morgan. They're reading about you because you're a fascinating human being, and if I may say so, you're hot like your mother. Being fascinating and hot is marketable all by itself. Your father knew it, and now it's your turn. And if you tell Kim I said any of this, I'll deny every word."

As the cab starts to roll away, I look back at Nate picking up his groceries, and I smile to myself. You know, when the fog of life is closing in, strangling you with its soupy presence, a word of encouragement is like a ray of California sunshine. Even from a charming engineer who is full of garbage. There are people in life who do nothing more than show up. Nate is one of those people, I think. He enters stage left, plays the nice guy role, and then quietly slithers away.

But he thinks I'm hot. That is most certainly encouraging.

chapter 11

My pulse races as I come to my street and the Russian Hill neighborhood I call home. Or did before this weekend, anyway. Like the red dirt of Tara, the stained cement of Hyde with its cable-car tracks in the street sustains me. I am beckoned home by its power, the grunting chains in action beneath the asphalt, the clanging bells like a symphony to my ears. Polk's gleaming shops and bistros are begging for my return. I am home. Where good food is plentiful, and my view of the Bay awaits me. There is no guilt, no pain of failure; there is only the sparkling promise of life within my co-op.

I roll into my comfort zone, and the cabby stops the car. A doorman I don't recognize opens the cab door.

"Who are you?" I ask.

"Dylan."

"I'm Morgan Malliard, and I'll need my cab fare covered until my father can repay you." I step out of the cab and notice the doorman pause. Snap, snap. Let's go.

He looks at me awkwardly. Most likely he has no tips lining his pockets because he is not good at what he does. "Miss?" He touches the tip of his cap.

"Cab fare," I state plainly. "I don't have any money on me.

There should be some in the till in the lower drawer of your office. If you'll pay the man, my father will see to it there is twice the money in your paycheck." This is how the system works. Hello? "How long have you been here?"

"No one said anything about money. I'm here as a job, to earn money, not to put it out."

Looking at this poor man's expression, I wonder how many men just like him I walked over without thought to their humanness. Here in the garage of my building along with the cab driver and the doorman, it dawns on me for the very first time that these people are working jobs. Someone is paying them for their services.

Which is more than I can find someone to do for me. "I'll be back," I say to the cabbie. I start for the elevator.

Dylan holds his palm up. "Just a minute. I'll handle this." And he gets on his closet phone, trying to appear official. When in actuality he's probably scared to death he's going to make a mistake. Nobody stays here long without learning that people who live in this co-op are short on "nice" when it comes to cold, hard cash.

I wait beside the cab as the driver taps the steering wheel to the hip-hop beat of Jay Z. The doorman comes back out, shaking his head back and forth.

"You'll have to hold on," I say into the cab, and I go to the doorman's phone and buzz my father.

"Yes?" Mrs. Henry answers, her telltale aloofness putting the fear of the devil into children everywhere. I hear that witch music from *The Wizard of Oz* as I picture Mrs. Henry riding a bike. *I'll get you, my pretty.*

"Mrs. Henry, it's Morgan. I'm downstairs and there's a new doorman." I turn away rather than let him hear my conversation about his ineptness. "I need cab fare, and I don't have any cash."

"Your father has guests."

"And I have no money. Put my father on, please."

"He's asked not to be disturbed."

"So they'll disturb him later when I make my one phone call from the pokey. Is that a better option? I'm sure he won't appreciate the headline in the morning's paper."

Click.

Now the cab driver is getting annoyed, and he's turned the radio up so it sounds like a downtown barrio in the parking lot, which infuriates the doorman, who has completely lost control of his building. And I'm just standing here in painful, ugly shoes wondering what to do next. This whole scene would be tolerable if my feet were happy.

"I'll be right back." I head to the elevator and put my card in for the penthouse. Upstairs, the doors open with a ding, and I see my father sitting at the oval dining room table with two men I've never seen before and a woman. Not a normal Richard-Malliard-San-Francisco's-Jeweler type woman, either. There are blueprints rolled out in front of them.

"Daddy? I need cab fare."

He stands up and reaches into his pocket, pulling out twenties, but my appearance seems to garner no emotion whatsoever. Is it any wonder I take the money and run in this life? I grab three of them and slide back into the elevator. By now I'm sort of wishing I'd just stayed at Lilly's and had some Cup O' Noodles. It would have been far less disconcerting. Who on earth are those people? And what is my dad tearing apart now?

Before I can escape, Daddy pulls me out of the elevator. "No, no. You stay here." He hands the money to Mrs. Henry, who is hovering nearby. "Go take this downstairs for Morgan." He pulls me towards the table, and the men stand.

The woman remains seated, checking me out like I'm a

piece of meat in her local butcher shop. Let's just say it looks like she's never met a pork chop she didn't like. She has an angry line in the center of her forehead that points to a bulbous nose that is red from too much drink, but she has freshly sanded skin from professional dermabrasion (I'd know the look anywhere) and a waddling neck that is completely out-of-sync with the plastic complexion. *She should have had the neck done, too,* I think. She looks as though someone stuck Barbie's head on Mr. Potatohead.

"Morgan, this is Gwen."

To my horror, he reaches out to Mrs. Potatohead. Oh no, no, no, Daddy. She doesn't even know to stand up when introduced. This cannot be my forthcoming stepmother. She is missing grace, decorum, and she's wearing cheap shoes! And she has hired two straight men to decorate. (How do I know they're straight? Well, first off, I do live in San Francisco. Second, one is wearing a wrinkled shirt and the other has sandals on with socks. There's not a gay man in the city who would be caught dressing like a tourist or in wrinkles, unless they were currently fashionable.) This does not bode well.

I don my favorite plastered smile, "Gwen, what a pleasure to welcome you into Daddy's and my home."

"It's going to be our home soon enough. I want to introduce you to Sven and Jackson. They'll be redesigning the penthouse to be more conducive to married life."

"Conducive?" I ask with sickly sweetness.

"We will be newlyweds, darling. We'd like to see the master suite expanded, since—" She raises her eyebrows at my father. "—well, since we'll be newlyweds."

Eww.

I give a hollow laugh. "Right. Well, what will you be doing exactly?" I realize I'm about to get a detailed bedroom explanation. "With the house designs, I mean." Here Sven and

Wren, or whatever their names are, swing into action and unravel the blueprints.

"We'll be leaving your room, honey," my father assures me.

"As a guest room, and you're welcome anytime," Gwen chimes in.

"Actually, I live here, Gwen. Hasn't my father told you that?"

"Well, of course you do, honey, but in every chick's flight, there's a time to leave the nest."

And sometimes, there's a time to pad it with another layer of living. Bring on the down feathers.

"Daddy and I thought fifty might be a good age." I giggle again, falsely, but I'll tell you if Daddy had a plan to keep me in my bedroom until I died of old age, here she is. I grind my heels into the hardwood floor. Currently, I have absolutely no intention of going anywhere. Not for my agreement with Lilly, not even for a date with Johnny Depp himself.

"We'll be moving the bedroom into this hallway and giving them the panoramic view of the Bay. Your room will be moved over here where this—" Sven pauses. "Where this coat closet currently stands."

Oh Gwen, this is the best you've got? Honey, you don't know my father from Adam. "Daddy, won't that drastically reduce resale value? To have such a large master suite without a living area with the view?"

Gwen swoops up the plans. "We were just discussing how we might rework the spaces."

"Well, I hope you rework it to take advantage of the views, because that's what adds the zeroes to the property value. Sven and Jackson, do you have architects working with you?"

"We prefer to work alone," Jackson says with a fake British accent. Dude, this is San Francisco—like we don't know a fake accent when we live in one of the world's most international cities.

"You may prefer it, but this building has very strict codes, and all changes must be approved by the co-op board. I can tell you, you'd never get these plans past the co-op board." And if we have any luck at all, Daddy will never get his new fiancée past the board. But alas, they have no jurisdiction there.

I don't know why I don't like her. Daddy's had girlfriends before, but they always made sense to me. They were either scandalously young and beautiful or some social mogul's widow who could provide entry into a new circle he hadn't yet broken. There's always a reason my father does anything, and this particular girlfriend doesn't give me that reason. She's not wealthy, or I would have heard of her, and the fact that she has a real job makes this whole scenario completely intimidating. I don't think my father is actually capable of true love, so it can't be that.

"Morgan," my dad says gently. "You probably want to freshen up for dinner, and then we'll discuss this further. Go ahead."

I look at Gwen, and then Tweedledee and Tweedledum, and make my way into the bedroom. Oh my goodness, I feel absolute euphoria seeing my room, its view, and the six hundred-knots-per-inch rug my father bought me. *May I never take it for granted again,* I think as I bend down and kiss it. Then I rush to my bed, tear off the covers, and touch my sheets. Oh, it's heaven to feel a real thread count. Oh Auntie Em, I had a terrible dream.

The lights below are just starting to flicker on one by one, twinkling against the deep violet sky. That's another thing I've taken for granted. In Lilly's neighborhood, the sun disappears so quickly, but on Russian Hill it slowly descends behind the mountain, putting on a light show for all who care to watch.

Being at the edge of the ocean, we are some of the last to bask in the daily sunshine.

In my bathroom, I see my sunken tub with its city-lights views calling out to me, and I run the tap to fill. Normally, I'm a shower girl, but something about this day calls for decadence and the luxury of a bubble bath. I find some bath gel that's been imported from Italy to sit on display and pour it lavishly into the streaming water. The scent of lavender and honey fill my senses, and I feel as though I'm dreaming. Have I always lived like this? Because today it feels like I never actually noticed.

There's a knock at my door. With the way I'm feeling, I'm just certain it could be Johnny Depp. But I open the door to Mrs. Henry, her face pinched, clearly upset that she had to schlep downstairs and pay the indigent cabby. She sees such jobs as beneath her. I suppose I did, too.

"Yes?" I ask kindly. The fact is Mrs. Henry has the answers I need about my mother, so this is my first attempt at making nice. I think about the threat my father made about Saturday night and sniff the bubbles, knowing all I'll have to give up if I don't answer to him. And Gwen.

"Dinner is nearly ready. I wanted to give you fair warning," Mrs. Henry says.

"What about your room? Where will it be? In the elevator shaft?"

"Miss Morgan, I can't really say." She pauses, composing herself from her true emotions. "It's your father's home and if he and the future Mrs. Malliard choose to remodel, that's their private business."

I laugh. "If you think I'm going to sit back and let this woman take over our home, you haven't learned a thing about me in all these years, Mrs. Henry."

"I know you have enough of your mother in you to fight."

She gives the slightest smile. "This is a phase. An infatuation. Your father has had them before."

I look out the door and watch Gwen rub her hand along my father's arm. "What can he possibly see in her?"

Mrs. Henry crosses her arms. "She's bossy. He likes them bossy. Always has. The more they kick him to the curb, the more attractive they are to him. I think he likes to see himself as a professional bull rider who can last longer than the eight seconds."

I laugh out loud. "I'm sure there's a Freud story in there somewhere. But in the meantime, I think I'm going to need your help, Mrs. Henry."

What Mrs. Henry lacks in warmth, she more than makes up for in work ethic. I don't ever remember her missing a day of work or being sick. The *Mrs.* part of her name is a little misleading. She divorced early on, but she kept the missus-nomer because she thought it gave her more credibility.

Occasionally, I see what my mother must have seen in Mrs. Henry. I see a friend and a confidante, and an ally who will not let my father go down without a fight.

Mrs. Henry leaves me to my bath and I sit and ponder the situation. The one thing that really doesn't add up is Gwen's lack of beauty. My father deals in beautiful, sparkling goods, and he once held my shimmering mother in his case for all to envy. Gwen Caruthers has something I'm missing, and I'm bound and determined to find out her appeal. It's not that I care that she's homely—hey, if that's what he wants, I'm all for it. It's just so completely outside Daddy's nature.

I may be working on separation anxiety for myself, but that does not mean I'm leaving my father with a faulty piece of Velcro, either.

turn the bathwater off and scoop up a handful of bubbles to sniff them as I gaze out into the twinkling lights across the Bay. "Life is good." Well, *this* life is good, anyway.

Just as I'm about to slip off my robe, the bedroom phone rings. I think twice about answering it, but what can I say? I'm a slave to the phone. Isn't it every girl's hope that Prince Charming is on the other end? Remember, I just want that one good fish.

"Hello."

"Just what do you think you're doing?" It's Lilly. "One offer of Cup O' Noodles, and you slip off into the night? Morgan, weren't you even a Girl Scout?"

"No, that green is horrible on me. Besides, the other mothers didn't want their daughters around my mother. They said she wore too much cleavage and set a bad example for their girls."

"Enough of the woe-is-me pity party. I don't think the girls would have even known what cleavage is. You're making this up. Are you coming back here? Nate said he put you in a cab, and Max was worried because he said you were white as a sheet."

I look at the bath and take a whiff of the swirling, aromatic scents. "I don't think I'm coming back, no." Because life here is really good.

Lilly is quiet for a moment.

"So, we'll do a spa trip soon?" I ask cheerily.

"No, we won't do a spa trip soon," Lilly barks. "You are nearing thirty. You cannot live with Daddy forever, Morgan. Maybe it's none of our business. Maybe you'd prefer if Poppy and I just stayed out of your life. But you said you wanted our help. You said you wanted to be responsible for yourself and learn about reality. Well, Cup O' Noodles is reality, honey. You can buy them for a paltry fee at Costco and live large for a month."

"Dried vegetables gross me out, Lilly. Besides, it was really more your comment that ticked me off." Currently, I can smell fresh artichokes cooking, and I know Mrs. Henry will have a delicious cream sauce on the side for dipping. Maybe real butter and lemon juice—oh, I so love that. Maybe she'll have the beef with tarragon she makes. I feel my mouth watering at the thought. "Yeah, I'm not coming back."

"Fine, Morgan, this is your life, I'm not going to meddle. If you want to be the princess of San Francisco, you go right ahead. It's good work if you can get it."

I should have known Lilly wasn't going to offer up any apologies. "It really is my life."

"I know now when you say you want help, you just really want to be told your life means something. I can understand that. Your life means something—you're Richard Malliard's daughter. Woo-hoo!"

"What are you mad at me for?" I ask, suddenly incensed.

"I'm mad at you because you say you want to get out of this vicious cycle you're in. You say you wish your church did more to help the poor. You say you wish your father would have faith in something other than diamonds. You say all these things, but they mean nothing to you, Morgan. Not really. If they did, you'd do something to change your life, not fall back into your precious down comforter and city views. Get yourself a life!"

I look out the window and feel a pang of guilt. It does rock up here.

"Someone has to witness to the wealthy," I say confidently.

"Last night at singles, did you meet anyone who cared who you were?"

"Not a one. It's like those people never pick up a paper. Which is good and bad, I suppose. They don't know about my history, but they probably don't know if we're out of the Cold War either."

Lilly exhales. "You are living in a fishbowl, and there is an entire world out here waiting for you. People who gaze up at the bowl, but who actually get to be part of the audience and participate. Climb down out of your tower, Morgan, or don't say we didn't warn you."

"What do you think is going to happen?" She acts like I'm in a Lifetime movie or something. "I'll be suffocated in a bad facial accident?"

Again she's silent for far longer than is comfortable. "I think your faith is part of the show, Morgan." She clears her throat. "Personally, I think right now if Jesus Himself walked up to your doorway and asked you to come with Him, you'd look back." She pauses to let this soak in, and I have to say, it's like a fist across my jaw. "Just like Lot's wife, just like the rich, young ruler. You're about the stuff."

My first instinct is to deny every word and turn right back on Lilly and her self-righteous preaching. "Letting your boyfriend sulk and wait around for you to come around to marriage? Where is that on your faith scale? It is by faith we are saved, not by works so that no man can boast."

"Faith in what, Morgan? Your daddy's credit card? How is living one day in my apartment and not finding a job having any faith?"

Her words pierce me. I've never had my faith questioned by anyone, and how dare she? She doesn't know my heart, nor my motives. How can I possibly leave my dad in the clutches of that woman who will systematically destroy all he's built, starting with this penthouse?

"Lilly, it's not that I don't appreciate what you've tried to do, but my father is going to marry someone who I think is out for his money. I have to stay here or I'll find my trust fund dwindled to nothing, not to mention the crime she wants to perpetrate against this penthouse. Would you let your nana suffer when you could stop it? My dad has worked hard for all he has; he'd be crushed if it were gone." I don't relay the fact that I miss my great bathtub, or that I was completely the third wheel at the loft, and that I just feel lonely and so falling in my soft, downy nest is just what I need to do right now.

"It's his money, Morgan. If he chooses to give it to his new bride, that's precisely the reason you need something to fall back on. What if they marry and your dad keels over without ever changing his will?"

"You didn't answer me about Max. Are you going to marry him?" I tap my foot against the travertine.

She ignores the question again. "We're not talking about me. Let the money go. If you get a job, you won't need your dad's money. You can live in my place for as long as you want, and Poppy would love to have you if you want to get away for the weekend. She's bored senseless down there in Silicon Valley."

"Newsflash: I'm not qualified for anything, Lilly. My résumé is a mishmash of celebrity parties and grunt retail in my dad's store. I can barely remember what I majored in, much less any of the information I learned. Basically, I have a Stanford degree in Johnny Depp movies, because that's about all I remember, and that's not exactly marketable."

"You're not trying. Nate talked to Max, and he's going to get you a job as a concierge in his father's hotel until you can find something better."

I swallow hard and look at my bath drawn to perfection and steaming up the beveled window's view, creating a frosted, hazy, Monet-like scene. "I don't know anything about being a concierge."

"Max is here. I don't want to dress up, but I want good food for dinner, and within walking distance of Nob Hill. Where should we go?"

"The Nob Hill Café on Taylor."

"No, wait a minute," Lilly backtracks. "I think I'm in the mood for Italian."

"Venticello, but you should probably dress a little. Not too much—dressy-casual. Doesn't Max know where he wants to take you?" And how on earth did we get from me renouncing my Christianity to restaurants?

"Well, we'd like to see a play afterward, and I heard *Cats* was good."

I start to laugh out loud. "Lilly, I don't think *Cats* has played here for a decade or so. Gogol's *Overcoat* is playing at A.C.T.; see if you can get into that. I think you'd love it!"

"You're hired!" A male voice comes on the line.

"Excuse me?"

"It's Max," the deep voice says. "My father is looking for a new concierge, and you're our woman. We can't pay what the Mark Hopkins or the Fairmont pays, but then again, you don't know French or Japanese," he stops for a moment. "Do you?"

"Max, I appreciate what you're trying to do, but—"

"But what, Morgan? You forget I've lived your life. Do you

really want out? Or do you just want to fall back into Daddy's arms and have the rest of us leave you alone? It's your choice, but there's no going back once they've taken full possession."

Max Schwartz was offered a significant share in his father's hotel chain, but he turned it down for his love of words and television. Perhaps it isn't the most lofty of positions, but he did escape with enough money to live in the Marina and be on speaking terms with his parents.

I peek out and see Gwen bent over my father, her rustic cleavage enticing him to avoid the facts laid out before him in blueprints: tanking real estate.

I quietly shut the door again. "Of course I want out, but one has to make plans. You don't just move out when you have no job and no income. Besides, my father needs me right now."

"Your father will always need you. It's his *modus operandi*. Trust me. I'm offering you a job, Lilly. You can have it for as long as you need it."

"I don't want to be a concierge, Max. I appreciate you trying to get me a job, but I don't want to answer tourist questions all day. I think my skills entitle me to more than that. Tourists annoy me."

"That's fine," he says shortly.

"Tell Lilly I appreciate what she's trying to do, but I don't want her help right now. I need to be here for my father."

"I'll pass that along."

I place the phone back in its cradle, and I notice my bath doesn't look nearly so inviting. She's ruined it for me, Lilly and her incessant nagging. People are so anxious to get you work, when all they do is complain about it. I fail to understand their actions.

The phone rings again, and I shout into the phone, "What?"

"Morgan?" It's a male voice I don't recognize.

"Who's calling, please?" I ask, anxious to find out if my private line got out to the press.

"It's George Gentry. I met you today again in a hallway in the financial district." His voice is buttery smooth, just like I prefer them. I wonder how many wives in the closet this one has.

"I know who you are, George Gentry. You're the man who let me believe you were a journalist. Today, surprise, surprise, you're a lawyer. What's next—tomorrow will I get your FBI card? And are you planning to continue popping up every-where like a terrifying jack-in-the-box? If so, please bring chocolate so that I might appreciate your presence."

He clears his throat. "Right. Well, I need to speak with you, Morgan, on a legal matter."

"Mr. Gentry, I have no interest in meeting with you or hearing what you have to say. For all I know, your business card is still warm from the Kinko's printing press. You do forget, sir, that I've been the target of many a con man and fallen for each and every one. I'm now what you might call savvy."

Don't I sound the epitome of confident? But I am curious about what he has to say, what he's up to, and what any of this has to do with me. And his sable eyes have nothing to do with it.

"You have every right to be leery, Miss Malliard, but I think you're going to want to hear why I've been following you. We can meet in a very public place. You name where you'd feel comfortable. A coffee shop? A hotel lobby, maybe?"

"Now it's 'Miss Malliard' you're calling me? Such formality for someone who informed me I didn't consummate my marriage and seems to know my every move. I would think we're on more intimate terms, Georgie."

I don't like the way I feel after these words. I don't like

what I've become after Andy. Fearful of everyone and suspicious. It's not becoming.

"Morgan, aren't you even curious why I might want to talk to you? How I know so much about you?"

What really makes me curious, I suddenly think, is why I want so desperately to talk to him.

"Not in the least bit," I lie easily. "I keep hearing that Police song 'Every Breath You Take' and thinking 'stalker.'" Even if he does look like heaven on a stick. The fact is Andy looked that way, too. I'm so inclined to trust the wrong people. I can't take a chance.

"I understand your objections, but you should know that you'll be served papers soon. Along with your father. I don't usually send warnings, but you've been through so much, and I didn't want to catch you by surprise. Your father knows all about this. I thought you deserved equal treatment."

He hangs up on me, and I feel my heart race. Suddenly I wish it was safe to run in the night streets of San Francisco. I feel this intense need to expel energy, and nowhere to go with it. I reach in and let the water drain from my bathtub and slip into a cashmere sweater and my Lilly jeans. I unlock my desk and pull out two hundred dollars in cash, stuffing it into the pocket of my jeans. Opening my bedroom door, I see that the destruction of my father's penthouse is still on the table.

I rush through the apartment and catch my father's gaze for a moment. He's no match for the evil threesome of dire decorating, but I'll worry about that when I get home.

"I'm sorry, Daddy, I have to run out."

"Will you be home tonight?"

Whatever Mrs. Henry is cooking, it smells delectable, and I wish I had time to eat, but I want to escape and if there was a safe landing, out my bedroom window would have been preferable.

Lilly's loft simply wasn't far enough. I never truly left my comfort zone, I never got the peace I needed to figure it all out. I think best in my car. Hopefully, I'll get in and know exactly where I'm running to.

"No, Daddy," I shake my head. "I won't be home tonight. I have some things to figure out." As Gwen is deeply entrenched in conversation, I stare deeply into his intense black eyes. "Have you ever heard of a George Gentry?"

My father grabs my elbow and pushes me backwards into my bedroom. "Where did you hear that name?"

"You know him?"

"Has he contacted you?"

"Sweetie!" Gwen's whiny voice screeches from the dining room, echoing off the travertine floors. "We need you to tell us how high the bookcases should be."

"I'll be right there," Daddy growls. "Has he contacted you, Morgan?"

"Who is he, Daddy?"

"Just another leech, Morgan. No one you need to concern yourself with. Make sure you stay away from him until I tell you differently."

I think about relaying the information about papers and being served, but something holds me back. "Right, Daddy."

Mrs. Potatohead hollers again.

"Daddy, you should really tell her we don't yell in the house. An inside voice, I think they tell the preschoolers at church."

"You're going to love her, Morgan. I know you will. It will just take some time alone for you two to get to know each other. She's brilliant."

His comment is really more command than gentle prophecy. Somehow, I don't see myself feeling the love.

For lack of a better place to escape, I drive straight to my health club. After placing my car in the skillful hands of Johnny, the best valet on earth (my father simply must put him in his will), I enter the hallowed halls of Square One. Kingston Crane is working behind the long, rock-faced counter, the song of dripping water in the wall-length fountain behind him giving the eerie echo of a natural fountain in a well-equipped cave. I want to feel relaxed walking into the carefully architected building, but Kingston's presence unravels any sense of well-being with his creepy gaze and moist, glossy, maraschino lips.

Kingston is the living, breathing clarification of why I will never be a concierge. With a shrewlike face and black, darting eyes, Kingston is the boy who ate paste in school. The boy whose mother glued his hair down in a shellacked side part. He moves frantically and erratically, like a rodent caught in the bottom of the garbage bin looking for his way out. I can only imagine how he got this job, since I'm pretty sure he strikes the entire club the same way. He's the face you will eventually see on an episode of *48 Hours* with someone commenting, "There was always something not right about him."

"Miss Malliard," Kingston mews.

"Kingston."

"May I help you, Miss Malliard? Did you have a question for me?" He leans over the counter and licks his lips freshly.

"Is there someone for a pedicure at this time of night? Perhaps Julia's still here?" I look at the clock above Kingston's small head, and it ticks loudly at three minutes before eight.

"Of course there is. Why don't you relax in the sauna, and I'll get the room set up. We haven't seen you in a while, though you have been keeping yourself busy, I suppose. You look as though you've gained a little weight, so it's good to see you back. Maybe you'd like some personal training?" He grabs a calendar from behind the counter.

"I'll be in the whirlpool or sauna when Julia is ready for me."

It takes every Christian principle I've been taught not to comment on his lack of masculinity as I head down the glass-mosaic hallway into the changing room, mumbling the entire way, and unlock my locker. My swimsuit hangs neatly alongside my goggles, and I reach for the suit and a fresh club robe. The towel girls, as Lilly calls them, have all gone home for the day, so I pick up a fresh towel, ponder the nearby whirlpool for a moment and then decide the sauna is more of a departure from my regular reality.

A charge of cold air hits me as I exit to the hallway. But it's nothing next to the icy chill of reality that next bolts through my system. Outside the door, leaning against the wall, is something I never thought I'd see. I feel my soul flutter within at the sight of Andy Mattingly. (Or Arnold, depending on who you believe.)

"Andy, what are you doing here?"

"You won't answer my calls. My brother's a private investigator, and I had you followed."

Right. And Agent 007 is on the case. This guy wouldn't

know the truth if it sprouted eight legs and crawled up his back. "How did you get in here?"

"Turns out Kingston was a little short today."

"He's a little short every day."

"On cash. He was a little short on cash."

Andy or Arnold, whatever his name is, strikes such an image. His well-groomed, sandy-brown hair is so upstanding and proper. His amazingly sincere hazel eyes are dazzling and captivating. And every last inch of him is a mirage. A hauntingly gorgeous oasis I want so badly to be true, but that has evaporated, along with all my dreams that anyone will ever live up to what I hope for.

Kingston must be his spy, his undercover agent in the pathetic surveillance he's set up. "I don't imagine Kingston will be much richer when management learns he let a felon into the club."

I'm walking briskly toward the exit to the foyer when Andy steps forward and stops me with his eyes. Those gentle eyes that belie everything he personifies.

"I'm sorry, Morgan," he says with a convincing tear. Straight out of the soap-opera playbook. He'll be taking off his shirt for his close-up any minute now. How did I miss this the first time?

I just stare at him, blinking away my own sudden tears. Partly because I loved this man, but mostly over my own stupidity at having loved a fantasy. I can hear his words, and I know now there is not an authentic one in the whole verbal string. But here's a question or two I'll have when I meet my Maker: *Why give this guy those eyes? And the ability to talk like that?* I know I won't be the only one with those questions. Heck, I know already I was one of two.

"You should use your powers for good, Andy Mattingly, or whatever you're calling yourself today. How could you marry two women? How could you possibly think you'd get away with it?"

"I wanted to start fresh. I didn't target you, Morgan. You weren't a financial mark like they keep saying. I truly fell for you when I saw you in church that day. I was going to leave the life of crime behind me and—"

"Sing? Which is why you went to Nashville, right? Oh wait, you didn't actually go to Nashville; you went home to your wife."

"You said you loved music, and I wanted you to love me, Morgan. I would have learned to play the guitar."

"Oh brother. Really, you can do better than this."

"I would have been good for you, Morgan. I would have treated you like the queen you deserved to be."

"You are positively pathological." I'm trying to step around him, but he keeps forcing his way into my path.

"I'm starting fresh. Karen has applied for a divorce." Andy/Arnold bends down and flashes me a small gold ring. "Marry me, Morgan. You married me once; marry me again."

Out of curiosity I pick up the ring and notice the inscription within: "Karen, my love always, Arnold."

For some reason, this strikes me as hysterically funny, and I start to laugh uproariously.

"Karen wanted you to have it to show you we have her blessing."

Oh heavens, was I ever this stupid? "God rescued me that day, Arnold. There is nothing so beautiful as the crisp white linen of a Reno annulment, and I own one and my consummate freedom." I let out a ragged breath. "I hear divorces are a little trickier, a little harder to come by. Good luck with that."

I start to walk away, and then turn back. "Although, you may not want to lose Karen so quickly; she must be a saint." I drop the ring on the floor and it clinks down the glass tile, bouncing several times before stopping in the corner. Arnold dives for the wall, and it occurs to me: Karen has no idea where he is tonight or where her ring is. My heart breaks for her. What did he tell her to get the wedding ring wrenched from her finger?

I turn completely around and face him, unbothered by his presence or his good looks. "Did you tell her you were going to buy her a bigger ring tonight?"

He physically gulps, and I guess we have our answer.

And then, as Andy bends to pick up the ring, reality twists again and I see another man walking down the hallway. He's wearing a suit. A familiar suit. Once again, I'm face to face with George Gentry and his forest-brown, compellingly beautiful eyes. If the Lord wanted to send me a temptation, George is wrapped and ready to go. Just like a puppy in the pet store at Christmas.

My first thought is shame. Shame that he should see me with Andy as if solid proof that the tabloids have their stories right.

I pull myself together. "Is this suddenly a public health club? Because if it is, I've got to tell my father he's paying way too much in dues. Clearly, they'll let anyone in here."

George gives that smirk of a smile and walks towards me. "If you won't come to me, I'll come to you. I followed you here."

"Did you give me a chance to come to you?" I look over towards Andy/Arnold. "I can't even give you points for originality. It seems to be the method of the day, Mr. Gentry. If you were searching for originality, you missed your cue."

"So I see."

Andy and George make eye contact, and a flash of recognition flickers in their private, silent communication. I can only imagine what they each see, but my own imagination turns several corners. George says he's my father's lawyer, but the fact is he could be Andy's criminal defense attorney, and I may have walked right into both of their plans.

In any case, Andy rushes out the door.

"Do you always have that effect on people, George?"

"The same way you attract them, Morgan, I repel them. It's a gift."

"What are you doing here? I refuse to believe that it's an accident everyone has found me here tonight when I haven't been here for two months!"

"Not that you could tell." He lifts an eyebrow, and I turn away quickly for fear I'll fall into another smooth talker's trap. "I followed you from home. I'd gone to meet with your father and saw you pulling out. My car just unwittingly went after you. I just thought tonight was the time. We need to talk."

"Talk about your private investigator skills? You seem to excel at following me."

"It was made easy for me, Morgan. I'm not as talented as you might think."

"You were meeting with my father?" I ask. "About what?"

"That's why I wanted to talk to you. Is this a good time?"

"Not really, no. I came here to relax." I open the sauna door, and he follows me in, briefcase and all. "What do you think you're doing?" I ask.

"Taking a sauna. This is what rich people do at their health clubs. You came to relax. I came to talk to you. This way, we can both accomplish our goals and everybody's happy."

He searches the room and then takes a bucket of water and douses the hot rocks, sending a plume of steam billowing towards the cedar ceiling. "No wonder you work out." He looks back at me. "This is not bad. If you're going to be in the gym, this is definitely the way to go." He shakes his head. "It's not for me though. I don't like to work out with people. It's not really a group sport for me. I like to do it in front of the news. Sit-ups calm me down, work off the day's stress. Good for the blood pressure."

"You're going to ruin your suit in here." I'm just shaking my head, unable to believe he's sitting on a damp cedar bench in a European suit. He must be crazy, which would explain his following me.

"The suit needs to be pressed anyway. I'm saving on dry cleaning."

"Are you going to leave, or do I have to call security?"

"By security do you mean Kingston, the little man out front that I paid twenty dollars to get in here? Morgan, you could take him."

"You only paid twenty dollars? That's all the security in this place is worth? You could be a serial killer for all Kingston knows!"

"Actually, if you're going to pick from a line-up of serial killers, I'd think Kingston was more the type."

"If it will get rid of you, I'm listening. Who are you and what do you want? There are no more sordid details to tell and really, if you're in the bribing phase, you would have been better off to pay Andy for information."

"I have all the information I need, Morgan. This meeting is for your benefit."

"You've all managed to pick up on every last one of my weaknesses. I think I've sold all the papers I'm going to sell. I've run my course."

"I really am a lawyer. Not a writer. You said I was with *Time* magazine and I just kept quiet. We lawyers learn how to do that in law school. It's a skill. There's even a biblical proverb: 'Better to be thought a fool than to open your mouth and prove it.'"

I feel the sweat beading on my forehead and George

removes the jacket of his suit, hanging it on the hook for the water bucket. I notice he does not refresh the steam rocks.

"What kind of name is George Gentry anyway? You're sort of young to be a George, aren't you?"

"I'm the fourth George Gentry."

"I'm the first Morgan Malliard, and I'm thinking that's going to be it. Retire the name. I've broken the mold."

"Meaning you don't want to keep your name when you marry or you don't want to have children?"

"Both, I think. I've already been married, and I'd be a terrible mother. My mother was a terrible mother. I think it's genetic."

With a gasp, I cover my mouth with my fingers, realizing for the first time I have let my mother's secret out to the world.

George doesn't seem to notice. "And marriage?"

I shrug. "Well, that sort of speaks for itself, doesn't it? I can't seem to make it down the aisle with an official eligible husband."

"Can you hand me that towel there?" George asks and I hand him a hand towel, which he wipes across his brow. "It's a pity about your wedding. I saw your picture in the paper and you made a beautiful bride. Very Grace Kelly-like."

"That's what Lilly was going for," I say before realizing who I am speaking to. "But the world has seen me as a bride. What's the point now?"

"To marriage?" he asks. "I've heard making your friends wear bad dresses to the wedding is pretty cool. That's what my sister said, anyway. You get to know which of your friends prefer chicken or beef, who the annoying ones are, who want vegan. And you can seat your in-laws next to relatives you hate."

He laughs to himself, and it's utterly charming. I feel

myself smile, despite the harsh subject. I tell you, if I ever think marriage again, I'm going to think about a man who can make me laugh. Enough with the over-wrought romance.

I'm in full sweat mode when the door opens and slams us with chilled Arctic air. It's Kingston, sticking his little shrew nose in before the beady eyes focus into the darkness and lock on me. "Julia is here, Miss Malliard."

"Thanks," I say, wanting to reward him with a big piece of cheese.

George is sweating through his white business shirt, and it sticks to his outlined six-pack abs. I tear my eyes away as though I'm looking at the sun, but they dart right back. Lord forgive me. I'll say he does sit-ups.

"I've got a pedicure. If you'll excuse me." I stand up but George yanks the door shut and pulls me back down to the wooden bench.

"I came here for a purpose, Morgan, and I can't leave until I tell you what it is. I'm your father's lawyer."

I let out a laugh. "No, my father has been very clear about what he thinks of you, Mr. Gentry, and lawyers in general. I hardly think he's hired one."

He grabs my hand and stands in front of me. Although he looks like something out of a Calvin Klein ad, his eyebrows are lowered in severity and his abs are right in front of me, so I turn away. I know better than to put myself in this situation. When I look at George Gentry, I feel my defenses starting to wear thin. I want with everything in me to trust him, but I can't trust myself. I've never been right, and his mystic chocolate eyes hold too much ambiguity to make anyone comfortable. All these men following me? It's just not right. It's too convenient, and clearly he knew Andy. They're probably in this together, vying for the stupid San Francisco socialite who is easily amused.

"What do you want?" I snap, pulling my hand away.

"As you know, I followed you and your friends that day to the spa. I had to know if you were as . . . naïve as they said in the papers."

"And you found out I was."

He puts his forefinger to my lips, and I feel the heat from his body. It has nothing to do with the rising temperatures in the sauna, and I just can't stand myself right now. My desire to believe every man is Prince Charming is beyond infuriating.

"There's no easy way to say this, Morgan, so I'm just going to blurt it out. Your father is being investigated for tax evasion. I have a feeling we'll be hearing the indictments within the week."

For a moment I don't even think I've heard him correctly, and I shake the moisture from my ear. "What did you say?"

"Your father. An indictment."

"You're not a lawyer. There's client privilege. You wouldn't tell me that if you were my father's lawyer." I grin, satisfied that I'm not as naïve as he thinks I am.

"I'm your lawyer, too, Morgan. Your father has you as a business partner. A legal partnership. The insurance and most business accounts are in your name. You're younger. You get lower base prices on the insurance rates and other benefits. Is any of this ringing a bell?"

I'm shocked into silence again. I breathe slowly, deliberately, and think back to all the paperwork I've signed over the years. Hundreds of documents, maybe even thousands. I have lived my entire life trusting people to take care of me. Every day there was something new to sign, and I never read a word of it. I just trusted my father, like I trusted every other con man in my life. Suddenly marrying Andy doesn't feel quite so stupid as I try to deal with the notion that perhaps my father used me.

"Are you saying that I personally am being investigated for tax evasion?"

"And fraud, yes, Morgan."

I bury my forehead in my hands, burrowing into oblivion, wishing I could disappear. Then I look up again. "You're my lawyer?" Leave it to my dad to find the one lawyer in town who looks like a Calvin Klein billboard.

"If you retain me, yes. Your father has already done so, but you're well within your rights to retain your own counsel if you wish. He preferred you weren't told, and there's no legal need until the indictments come down. But we've had warning, and I thought it only fair to you if I'm going to represent you. You should have the warning."

"Are you any good?" I look at him in his sopping-wet shirt. As a GQ model, I'd hire him in a second, but a lawyer is a completely different story. I may be naïve, but something tells me a lawyer might be in my best interest. I can't help but wonder if Daddy's new love interest has anything to do with the word *indictment*.

George looks at me directly, eyes showing no sign of retreat. "I'm good."

"Will I be poor?"

"Not if I can help it."

"Will I be like those horrible Enron men who stole from middle America?"

"I promise you won't. That's not what's at stake here."

"Will I go to jail?"

"I'll do everything in my power to make sure you don't."

"You're hired, Mr. Gentry."

He looks at me for a beat, then slowly nods as if to himself. Suddenly he's all business as he opens the sauna door again. "I'll be in touch," he says as he swings his jacket over his shoulder and carries his moist briefcase down the hallway.

I watch him walk away and think this is the first time I've had a legitimate worry in my lifetime. Maybe the desire to get in touch with reality was God-breathed. George suddenly turns back and faces me. He opens his mouth to speak, but shakes his head as though thinking better of it and turns again.

"George?"

He turns back towards me, and I watch as he drops his briefcase, and moves towards me slowly, but deliberately. I can think of nothing else as his muscular frame approaches, and I feel myself swallow the lump in my throat. He stands before me, and I watch as his chest rises and falls with each breath.

"Tomorrow, I'll be your lawyer," he says as his face comes towards mine . . . and I feel the warmth of his breath on my cheek as he stops the motion. I hear him exhale as he pulls away and I release my own puckered lips. He never touched me and I swallow my disappointment. "I'm sorry, Morgan. It won't happen again."

It didn't happen now! I think to myself. He walks away from me down the tile hallway, and I think about my luck. It's just my way to find a man with potential who legally can't get involved with me. Worse yet, I will be paying him for the privilege.

I feel completely betrayed as I watch George disappear from view. If what he says is possible, it means my father used me, and his buying me an expensive, albeit hot, lawyer is not going to work this time. Declaring my independence from the cell block will be too late.

Julia is there to meet me as I walk the hallway, and I notice she's handing a baby to Kingston and giving him directions.

Understanding what my unnatural desire for a pedicure at nine p.m. has wrought, I start to jog towards her. "Julia, did you come in just for me?"

"It's not a problem, Morgan. We need the money. Diapers don't grow on trees, you know. Robby is usually home by now, but he's working overtime tonight."

Julia's precious baby girl is wearing a pink velvet sleeper and has a matching pacifier clipped to the little suit. She sleeps pleasantly.

"May I hold her a moment? I've never held a baby that small." I realize that isn't exactly invoking confidence in the mother, but she nods and hands me her bundle of joy.

"This is Shelby. She's five weeks old." Shelby is basically bald, but has a tuft of soft downy hair at the crown of her head. Her lips are tiny, red, and heart-shaped, and she's making a sucking gesture though there's nothing in her mouth. It's the sweetest thing I've ever witnessed. As I hold her to my chest, I feel her warmth and my complete content-ment and I wonder if I ever felt such peace.

"Is she always this easy?"

Julia nods. "She goes everywhere."

Maybe it's the seriousness of what I just found out, but looking at the baby, something changes inside me. I've never thought I could be a mother, or that I possessed any semblance of yearnings to have a child, but right now, I know differently. My stinging tears are fulfilled as I watch Shelby suckle and make small kissing sounds. I can't help but wonder if my future has already been sealed—years in prison and no chance of motherhood. And a future of unrequited love with inappropriate men.

Reluctantly, I hand her back to her mother, whose arms are outstretched and yet ready to hand over this angel to a waiting Kingston.

"I didn't know you came in for me, Julia. I never would have called you away from your family." I reach into my robe pocket and pull out the soggy $200 in cash that I brought with me. "I hope you can buy a few diapers. Thank you for coming in."

"Morgan, I can't take all this." Julia tries to shove it back towards me. "What are you thinking?"

"Take it. Trust me, you're doing me a favor. I might lose it soon enough anyway. I'd rather someone who needs it have it."

"At least let me do the pedicure."

I shake my head solemnly. "I'm not in the mood anymore."

I lumber back to the changing room and use my cell to dial Lilly's loft, which now looks like my only option for housing.

"Lilly Jacobs Design." Her cheery voice makes me smile.

"I think I'm in some trouble, Lilly."

"Do you want my help this time? For real?"

"I do. I need it desperately. I'm at my gym. I think I'll leave my car here if you don't mind getting me."

"I'll be right there."

For now, I'm just glad I can trust anyone. My mind veers back to the vision of George Gentry and his soggy briefcase and his lips so close to mine. I wish I could trust him. I wish I could trust myself.

I remind myself how he pursued me to tell me the truth and I have to wonder, why didn't my father bother?

chapter 14

Lilly drives up in her beaten Saab, which Nate got running again, and we smile broadly at each other when our eyes catch. Good friends know when you've been an idiot, and good friends forgive anyway. I climb into her car and throw my overnight bag into the backseat.

"So, do you want to talk about it?" Lilly asks. "I take it things didn't go well at your dad's."

I shake my head. "It's worse than you might think. Apparently, I'm under investigation for tax evasion. Me, who doesn't even shop on tax-free sales days. It's ridiculous. How exactly could I evade something I have nothing to do with?"

"Do you even pay taxes?"

"Of course I pay taxes." I look down to my hands in my lap. "Well, Daddy pays them for me. He says it's cheaper to have them done together since we're a limited partnership." With each word, I want to hit my head against the dashboard. To call me naïve was kind.

"That's what I thought, Morgan." Lilly shakes her head, honking at the traffic even though we have yet to leave the curb. "Do you think your father might have done something illegal?"

"Do you?" I ask her.

"Well, now that you mention it. I'm not sure your dad is someone I would trust."

"He's just a businessman, Lilly. He's always looking for the next tax scheme."

"Do you believe that?"

The question haunts me because I'm not really sure I do believe it anymore. "I know my father is not the warmest person, but that's a far cry from tax evasion."

"I hope so, Morgan."

I look out the window at the traffic as we wait to enter the fray. "All I wanted was someone to love me so I could take care of them."

Memories of my mother, coughing in the back room as she gasped for air, flood my mind. My father's eternal absence and the only world I truly felt comfortable in—the one I created for myself in my imagination. With my dolls, I was the perfect mother. I would bathe them, diaper them, feed them, and talk lovingly towards them.

"I know that, Morgan, but your gauge is off, because your needle doesn't point north. Your dad was never due north; he's more of a magnet on top of the compass screwing with your mind. Your mother, well, who knows what she might have been if she hadn't been sick."

"If I can't trust my father, who can I trust? I know the obvious answer is God, but I'm looking for something a little less ethereal for the moment."

"Lots of people, actually, but just because he's your father doesn't make him trustworthy, Morgan. That's all I'm saying."

"You don't trust anyone, though. Look what you did to Max the other day."

"True, but what do I have to gain by saying maybe you should look a little deeper into your father's orders?"

"I'm sure he just made a mistake. He got caught up in his

gambling ways and made a financial error. He'll get me out of it; he always does," I say, with more faith than I feel.

Lilly doesn't answer, which is more of an answer than I really wanted.

"When you were hurting the other day, a normal reaction for a father is not to put a three-carat diamond on your hand. Do you understand that?"

I really don't. That is my truth. When life gets troublesome, you're on to the next thing. To stop and feel it is the worst kind of agony, so you move on. When the pink diamonds don't sell, you invest in the blue ones. You make it popular for women to change their wedding rings. That's the fashion. That's . . . that's the lie.

"Can we talk about something else?" I ask her.

"So what about the concierge job? Does it sound better?"

"That was sweet of Max, Lilly, but I don't have the patience to be a concierge. Tourists bother me and I'm afraid I'd offend someone and get him in trouble with his parents. I can be humble, but I don't think tourists are the right place to start. Someone will show up in leggings, and I know I'll feel the need to tell them it's not the right look for them. That they look like a potato who's sprouted legs."

"You would never say anything unkind, Morgan. You are too well trained for that."

"It just doesn't feel right. I should know better than to follow my instincts, but—"

"No, that's exactly what your father has told you, but that isn't true, Morgan. You're not stupid, and you're perfectly capable of making your own decisions. If your decision is that the concierge job stinks, well, so be it."

"But I am nervous. I mean, if a lawyer is following me to central California, showing up at my gym, and calling my private line? I would think the indictment is probably imminent." I nibble on my lip, hoping she'll put me at ease.

"Take the job, Morgan."

I nod and lean back against the seat. I want this all to go away. "Oh, I'm sure Daddy's squirreled enough away in a Swiss bank somewhere that I won't have to worry about it."

In the orange hue of the street lights I see Lilly's mouth open and snap shut again.

"Go ahead, say it."

"This time, I'm worried for you, Morgan. Think about it, your dad's getting married after all these years. Is she wealthy?"

I try to catch my breath at the thought. "I don't know. I never thought about that. She's got bad taste."

"Does she look like your mother did?"

"No." I shake my head with force. "The exact opposite. She's quite unattractive, and much bigger than anyone else my father ever dated. Not that there's anything wrong with that. It's just out of the ordinary."

"I want you to have a job and some money of your own."

"Don't get me all freaked out, Lilly. Just because you trust no one doesn't mean I want to end up that way. You're letting a perfectly good man dangle by a string because of your fears."

"We just don't want to see you end up like your mo—" Lilly stops herself.

"Like my mother? That makes two of us." My mother was an unloved woman, a beautiful spectacle who was hated by her husband. Like the queen who came before Queen Esther or the wives before Bathsheba. It's my greatest fear that I might drink from that well, that the bitter waters of my parents' marriage would haunt me into my future. I learned it wasn't outer beauty that made the difference, but the inner, and I've become a doormat in response. Albeit a well-bred doormat.

As traffic clears and we drive away from the ritzy health club, which is more about image than any venture towards well-being, I think about the life I'm probably leaving behind. Even if I'm completely innocent of all charges, I'm not exactly setting the social example for San Francisco with my recent headlines. This certainly isn't going to help. Society enjoys its gossip, but it's also quick to oust anyone they deem as entertainment value. The life I knew is officially over.

"I won't end up like my mother," I announce in confidence. "I think with my heart."

"But you spend with your very well-trained Visa wrist."

I sigh. "Isn't it the truth? You know, it never actually dawned on me that I don't deserve a pair of five hundred dollar shoes that I want. I know you find that abhorrent, but it's been my world."

"No, Morgan, you're wrong. I understand the desire for nice stuff. When I was a girl, I just loved the clean stitching on good work. I know that once you've worn a pair of five hundred dollar shoes, it's hard to go back. But Morgan, for your sake, you need to go back."

She's right. The price of a pair of Zanottis isn't what it reads on the bottom of the sole, it's what my father tattoos on my soul in return. "I've paid a price for that shoe collection."

"Poppy called," Lilly says cheerfully, hoping to change my mood. "She is coming up tomorrow to help you pound the pavement and get the right job."

"She is?" This makes me smile. Poppy is like Underdog. She's always there to save the day. She was there when I cried pathetically on her shoulder after Marcus (my first fiancé) died.

"Poppy's worried about you. I told her you didn't want the concierge job and so she's coming up to make sure you're employed before you move back in with your daddy."

"She knows me well. Did you tell her I went back home?"

"I called her immediately."

"I tell you, Lilly, if you hadn't called? If you'd allowed me to step in that bathtub tonight? With the view of the city lights and all that sensory calm? I'd have been toast. Just the interruption gave me cause to pause."

Lilly shakes her head while changing lanes. "Consider me thanked. When you feel the thrill of doing it by yourself, Morgan, you'll know what I mean. It's a complete rush."

"What did Poppy say about the concierge job? Did she think I was ungrateful, too?"

"No, she thought you'd make a terrible concierge because you have no idea what things cost. She thought if you were asked for a cheap restaurant, you wouldn't have the first idea what they were talking about. Have you even had a Big Mac? Do you know what "Super-size me" means?"

"So she has faith in me." I can't help but laugh. Only Poppy could kindly tell me I'm an idiot. "No, I haven't had a Big Mac. Sue me, okay?"

"You know what she thought you'd be good at, and I think I agree with her."

"What?"

"You'd be a good stylist, Morgan. People would totally pay for your expertise in taste. Then you could spend their money—and we all know you're good at spending other people's money. You have a PhD in that."

"That's what Nate said, too. It would be good work if I could get it. But just how does one get a job where you spend other people's money?"

At the moment Lilly doesn't have an answer and we both sit quietly for a moment as she drives me back toward Lysol Land. I'm a bit shellshocked at everything that's happened. Tonight I thought I could run home, just like I'd always done, but I'm quickly learning that isn't possible. The rules have changed. My father's fiancée is here to stay, as is her bad taste, but he's obviously getting something out of the remodel. Daddy can be such a little boy sometimes. He loves to relinquish responsibility, because then nothing is ever his fault. I'm certain that's why I personally am named in the lawsuit, and why he's willing to let someone else rip our townhouse to shreds. It won't be his fault. Mistakes and Malliards do not mix—unless they're attached to me and, now, the future Mrs. Malliard.

"My father's getting married."

"So you said."

"I met her tonight."

"Is that why you're back at my place tonight?"

I just grin, even though Lilly can't see me in the dark.

"Do you like her?"

"Not in the least. I know my father has bullied his way into the social scene, but if my fake wedding and Daddy's little tax evasion lawsuit don't do us in, Gwen Caruthers is waiting in the wings—waiting to take the Malliards back to a place of shunned silence among the socialites."

"It doesn't matter, Morgan. You need to get out of there anyway. Just because you've always lived like this, it's no excuse. You've been saying the mantra of 'I don't know any different' for too long."

"I just hope my new room isn't six by eight with a toilet in the center of it."

"Your father may play some tricks with his money, but not to the point where jail is a possibility."

I wish I was so confident. Can you say Martha Stewart? "My dad would sell his mother for the next deal, and he would have rotted in a Russian prison were it not for Marcus. It's an addiction, not something he can control. If there's a way to make more, he can't help himself; he has to throw the dice. He's compulsive and the payoff is worth the risk." I gaze out the window at the soft orange glow of the streetlights. "I wonder how I'll look in orange."

"I wonder if you can have a spray tan in jail," Lilly ponders.

"Not helping!"

"I'm just saying with orange, you need a tan. It's a given."

"You'll never guess who I saw tonight," I try to say as casually as possible, because really it means nothing. "George Gentry was at my health club." I wait for Lilly's reaction while I feel my own reaction in my tummy. If only I didn't have that visual of the abs. So wrong. Yet the image keeps on popping in my mind, like muffins in the oven. The more I try not to picture those muscles, the more vivid they become.

"The guy we saw at Spa Del Mar? Morgan, you need to stay away from him. He's obviously following you, and you are not going through another Andy again. We are not going through another Andy again. And what kind of guy hangs out at spas and health clubs? Are his fingers manicured, because that's a sure sign."

"A sure sign of what."

"You can't trust a guy who gets a manicure. They're either gay or way too concerned about their appearance. It's too weird."

"Are you done?"

"Yes."

"He's my tax-evasion attorney, apparently. He's been trying to speak to me before the indictments come."

"So this George guy is your lawyer?"

"Daddy hired him for me, but I think George needed to know if I was guilty or not. That's why he's been following me."

"You want to get married too badly, and if some guy rescues you from the pokey, you'll start having all these Prince Charming fantasies again. We can't have that. Morgan, you need to stay away from men who find you. Can you get an ugly lawyer?"

"It's nothing like that. I've learned my lesson about men. If they come looking for me, I go looking elsewhere. You should see this guy's abs, though, Lilly. I don't know where he finds the time to be a lawyer because he looks like a Bowflex commercial and like he never leaves the machine. I mean, hot. Steaming-fresh-from-the-wok hot."

"Down, girl."

"Listen," I tell her. "I left my dignity behind a long time ago, somewhere on that fashion runway you forced me onto, so you don't have to worry about me being carried away into a waiting, stolen limo. You just have to worry they'll cuff me and read me my rights, okay?"

"You're taking it well, that's all I can say. It sort of worries me." Lilly pulls over to the side of the road. "Do you want a coffee or something?"

I look down at my sweats. "I don't have any money."

"I'll buy you a coffee, Morgan. It's the least I can do."

I shake my head, and she starts the car again. "I remember when you had nothing, Lilly, and you did okay. You even got a great guy in the process. This is the first day in the rest of my life—which hopefully will not be spent in business suits for countless lawsuits. Isn't it just my luck that *Court TV* might follow me, and I have to wear business suits with cheap shoes."

"You don't have to wear the cheap shoes anymore. I realized that was true torture for you." Lilly is quiet for a moment, then she inhales a deep breath. "I'll make you a business suit that gets you noticed."

I grin from ear to ear. "See? A good friend knows your weaknesses."

"A good friend doesn't let a good friend go on national TV with average business suits. Do you think they'll really tape it?"

"I doubt it. What could possibly be of interest to people?'

"Well, there's your mother."

"Yeah, there's that. Better make the suit just in case."

"I have a great one I'm thinking of already." Then Lilly says, "Okay, back to me. Max wants me to meet his parents."

"The horror! And this bothers you why?"

"They're apparently not happy that I'm Christian."

"Max is Christian as well."

"They're not happy about that either," Lilly explains.

"So come meet Gwen first, and you'll count your lucky stars. Animal-print sofas, Lilly. I just know it."

"I'm all about avoiding the conflict, Morgan."

But really, she's not. Lilly was born conflicted, and there's a dash of pit bull in her somewhere. "*I'm* all about avoiding conflict, so please spare me the lecture. You're not avoiding conflict, you're only prolonging it. You either have it out with his mother, or he leaves. Those are your options. Do you have any ambition whatsoever when it comes to a man in your life?"

Lilly shakes her head, "Not really, no. But I'm afraid this time, I have no choice."

"The right guy will make you fight tooth and nail."

"See, Morgan, you watch too many Danielle Steele movies. Life doesn't work that way. You date, you find out he's a loser and why, and you break up."

"The Gospel according to Lilly. How exactly is Max a loser?" This I gotta hear.

"It's true, isn't it? Not that Max is a loser, but that finding out the truth is heartbreaking. It's true of you. Morgan, you're just going to freak when I tell you what I did. Let's just say I have no right to be lecturing."

"Well, welcome to my world. I'll have to make sure you get the password." I cross my arms and lean against the seat as we circle Lilly's block for parking. "You know, we haven't learned a thing since we left Stanford. We were dateless then, and we're dateless now. Ten years, and we're in the same place. Me, thinking Prince Charming will rescue me, and you thinking Prince Charming needs to be beaten to a pulp for what men did to your family. And then there's Poppy, oblivious to the fact that men actually roam the planet. Maybe it's us. Maybe we need a new set of friends. You know, upgrade."

"Who would put up with us?" Lilly asks.

"Good point."

"Max is a good man, there's no getting around it, and he's got me hook, line, and sinker. But I've heard about women who marry into families where they aren't wanted. What would I know about putting on a dinner party? Or hosting a hotel event? I was meant to be an electrician's wife or something."

"Or maybe a television writer's?"

"If that's all he did, sure. But it's that heir thing. Gets me every time. For once, I think I'm in deeper than I could have imagined."

I sigh. "I just don't get you, Lilly. You'd walk across hot coals for your work, but you're not willing to walk across the street for a good man like Max. What is wrong with you?"

"One of the mysteries of the universe, I suppose."

Lilly once told me she was the anti-Morgan, and I think that's true. I'd march right in there, put on my best smile, and charm Max's mom like a snake—maybe even bring a few baubles from my dad's store—but I wouldn't let a man like

Max get away. Not for the likes of what might be. I suppose that's because I'm well versed in what's out there on the rack. Max is definitely couture.

"Let's go to the spa this weekend, Lilly."

"We were just there."

"I know, but I have an idea. It's a curse of sorts on the three of us. We have to break it."

"Now that's scriptural."

"No, you're not getting what I mean. Please, Lilly."

"I thought you were broke."

"You'll spot me."

Lilly laughs as we get out and lock the Slob (as though it's in any danger). She grabs my bag and hoists it over her shoulder. "I wonder who will follow us this weekend."

"For being a complete loser, people sure are interested in me. You have to give me a little credit. I'm like Angelina Jolie without the kids or Brad Pitt."

We both giggle and climb the stairs to the loft. She, wondering how to avoid her love, and me wondering why the image of washboard abs keeps appearing when I really should be thinking about how to avoid jail time.

chapter 15

started playing poor to win this bet with my friends, and granted, it was only this weekend I made said bet, but I'm feeling over it already. I'm thinking independence is over-rated right now. Had I an inkling that I'd be in court, I would have never agreed to leave my clothing. I can just see myself in one of Lilly's Goodwill numbers, stating, "I'm innocent, your honor! But it's true. These are horrific clothes, and they should have never entered the light of day. I'm guilty of bad clothing!"

Perhaps that's a bit dramatic, but I just don't know what the playbook is here. Take Poppy. She's famous for having beautiful red hair. What if someone suddenly stripped it away. How would she cope? Is being wealthy any different? It's not just about being rich; it's about being who I am.

I thought I'd learn to live without Daddy, but I never actually envisioned I'd have to live without his money.

And I probably won't. Daddy may be a gambler, but he's greedy, too, and somewhere out there, he has briefcases of cash just like in the movies. I'm certain of it. Absolutely positive.

Sort of.

I remind myself he's about to remodel the loft, and that's a million-dollar project at the very least. Then I take in a deep, cleansing breath and force the horrible vision of Gwen's decorating from my mind.

Waking up without a view is daunting. I see . . . walls. The consistent, berating horns of the freeway offer no respite from the world. It's a wonder Lilly doesn't head to the spa every weekend! Oh wait, that's me who does that.

I'm trying to concentrate on my morning devotion; it's been a long time since I bothered to spend any time with God. I mean, I figured He knew where to find me, but I suppose without Him, Andy knew where to find me, too. My Bible verse for the day is about being content in all circumstances. And I'm sitting on this futon thinking okay, yes, I can do this. I can be content. It's not about the four C's of diamonds or perceived perfection; I know that now. I have complete clarity. Vision, even. I am one with my very loud universe.

"I'm content," I say aloud. "And I'm lying on a lumpy futon listening to traffic without any idea of where the Bay is from here. How cool is this?"

"You might want to add you're not the least bit prideful, either." I nearly jump out of my skin at Lilly's voice. I turn to see her putting on one of her hats that she uses to mat her hair down to her head. "Get over yourself. You're not homeless, are you? You're in a San Francisco loft that if remodeled would be worth a fortune. Maybe we could hire Gwen?"

"I thought you went in to work already."

"I was up at Nate's getting coffee."

"What's up with that, anyway? Why are you always hanging out with him and Kim like a third wheel? I can't even imagine you can handle the smell." I snap my Bible shut as the combination of nagging and looking over the words simply doesn't feel right. "Why don't you avoid those two and buy your own espresso machine? It would be far less costly than schlepping up there everyday."

She thinks on this for a minute, sipping her coffee slowly and loudly. "I have no clue."

"No, you don't."

"Habit, I guess. It's good coffee," she shrugs. "Really rich espresso even when he makes decaf for me."

"How come you never hang out with your church group?" I ask, knowing full well I don't actually hang out with mine, either. It's something about that title: "Single." For me, it just feels wrong. I didn't hang out with all my loser boyfriends hoping for better, for the title of "Single." I should at least get the title "Actively in Pursuit" or "Working at It."

"I always feel sort of left out there." Lilly sips her coffee again. "They're all brilliant and have enough money to go out to dinner all the time."

"You do now."

"I know, but like I said, habit. I'm in the habit of being poor, and you could learn a thing or two from me."

"I surely could."

"I don't go often enough, I guess. To the singles group," she clarifies for me. "It feels like I'm the new kid who just moved into town. I had enough of that as a child, having a nana instead of a mother."

I allow these words to wash over me. "You know, I wonder if everyone feels that way."

"I doubt it. I think we have issues, Morgan. I would have thought if I could have a package like yours, my troubles would be over, but it's not true. You're just as messed up as me."

"Well, that's the truth."

"I think it's because the church looks at marriage as the goal. That was never my goal."

"Clearly," I say to Lilly, wondering why on earth she can't get past her fear of commitment. I mean, I should have a fear of commitment. What does Lilly have on me? I think the difference is I hold out hope. I think God has placed a man on this earth who will love me for who I am. Lilly already has one and therefore takes him for granted.

Lilly sets her coffee down and dons a serious look that is most unlike her. "Max is the one. I just hope I can convince his mother of that," she whispers, looking up towards the windows. She's all drama. Getting up, I find a bottle of dish-washing soap and hand it to her.

"What's this for?"

"It's our Oscar for Best Performance in a Drama. Have you seen the way he looks at you?"

She directs her gaze straight at me. "No, really. He's the right man for me. Things are just complicated, Morgan. I don't know quite how to explain it to you."

"You're thirty. I believe that's past the standard age for your nana. I believe the word *spinster* had been muttered, in fact."

"What does my nana know? She was a widow at my age."

"She knows she lived her life without a husband and hopes for something different for you. She also knows Max pretty well, and loves the man. What more do you need? Besides, he's the one . . . just because you're afraid to meet his mother."

She shakes her head. "You don't know what you're argu-ing. Things are complicated. We need to work them out. Someday, I'll explain it."

"I have time," I say, stating the obvious. I know Lilly's had her fears; with a very particular nana, she was always afraid to make any type of mistake. That's why leaving finance for design was such a huge leap of faith. But if I had to leap, please, let there be a man like Max on the other side of the chasm. Because, baby, I'd so rather go over the ledge knowing I tried.

"My nana told me to marry a man who could take care of

me and who was smarter than me because it's nearly impossible to respect a man otherwise. And the Bible commands us to respect the man." Lilly's nodding her head, as if all this sounds completely brilliant.

"And you don't respect Max?"

She smiles to herself. "I do. More than I thought possible."

"Lilly? You're not making any sense. I think the Lysol has gotten the best of your brain cells. Maybe you should go back upstairs and get some caffeinated coffee."

"There's that whole heir thing. Don't let the name fool you—my nana raised me Italian. I don't know anything about being classy. But I can make a mean bowl of spaghetti."

I start to laugh. "You're kidding me, right? Sophia Loren is classy."

"Only because she's older. She was kinda trashy when she was younger. There was all that talk of affairs, lack of clothes in photo shoots. . . ."

"I am not going to argue Sophia Loren. If you want to be classless, you go right ahead, but you can't blame your heritage. Or Sophia Loren."

"I don't even know the right fork to use in a fancy restaurant, Morgan. I know how to make really good homemade ravioli, and I own a thirty-year-old piece of starter for sourdough. Otherwise, I've got nothing. Something tells me that Max's mother would want to throw anything old like that away. What if she wants to throw me away?"

"How does it make you incompatible? They live in Florida."

Lilly's expression falters. "She'll hate the way I dress her grandkids."

"So I'll dress them when she comes around or you have pictures taken."

"He's a good man," Lilly continues. "He's gorgeous, smart, secure, good to my nana—I'd do everything the same."

"And you love him, Lilly. Don't forget that part. You sound like you're talking about an interest-free loan, not the man you love. Not everything is practical."

"I'm comfortable here. At Max's, I look at his granite countertops and I think, *I can't possibly keep these clean*, but I know that's my future. He's not moving in here."

"So you'll hire a maid."

"I don't want to become everything I despised at Stanford. I didn't want to marry money, Morgan. Is that so hard to understand? There's something romantic about struggling together."

"You think so? You're not marrying money. You're marrying Max. Would you rather the money was all at risk for him? That his father had put him in some type of tax scheme?"

Her forehead wrinkles in confusion. "Maybe."

"You're warped."

In my mind, I replay the desperation on Max's face when he looked for Lilly that day. I wanted him to follow her, to play dead for her, but I realize now that was wrong. Lilly doesn't want to be chased or pursued by love like I do. She wants love to feel like a scruffy, time-honored, fuzzy slipper, not a glass one like I've searched for.

I look down at the stunning solitaire on my right hand. It's a rare blue diamond, a brilliant cut in an amazing hue of aquamarine. My father's hoping to start a new diamond trend in San Francisco. I'm sure he invested before the scandal, and as I gaze into its clear blue depths, I wonder if any man will ever care enough to give me a ring like this without wanting to profit from it. My own father is incapable of such a feat. I imagine my odds aren't good.

"I want to be loved," I say. "You want to be comfortable. So here we are, alone with a futon. Just two girls and our steamer trunks full of baggage."

Lilly sits down beside me and grabs my hand to look at the diamond. "That's an amazing stone."

"Wouldn't it be something if it's all I had left?"

"How do I make him believe me, Morgan? That I'm not the wife his mother expects, so he can warn her?"

How does she make me believe it? I mean, if I had a man look at me like that. If there was a man on earth capable of feeling about me like Max does, I'd give up anything. I can't identify with Lilly at all, because I've waited my whole life for unconditional love—at least the closest you can come to it here on earth. I searched for it in my mother, followed my father around for it, and mistakenly allowed a con artist to make me believe it was present.

I know my contentment should be in Jesus. I've read the Book. I know how it ends. But I also feel the chill of my discontent around me, and the longing for someone on earth to weather the storms of life with me. My goal is Jesus, but I still want someone to walk the pathway with me. Just one good fish, Lord! I've been alone my entire life—besides my father and Mrs. Henry. I want someone who notices I'm actually there. Is that too much to ask?

"I don't know what to tell you. I think you might have figured it out before now. Would you really be willing to walk away from Max?" I stand up and reach into the fridge for a Diet Pepsi, which I pop with vigor before Poppy gets here and ruins my fun.

"Never," she admits. And I have to say, it's the first time I can remember Lilly being truly honest about how she felt. She was so afraid to want something because her nana might tell her it wasn't the right thing, but I think Lilly has finally come into her own.

I watch Lilly pick up a picture of Max, and the look in her eye is evident. She loves him with all her heart, but Lilly lost her father, and her mother abandoned her. People she loves are known for leaving, and someone needs to convince her Max is different.

"Max might leave, Lilly—people are flawed. But I don't think he ever would. I think he would cherish you and support you, and most important, I think he'd tell you when you were full of garbage. Like today, for example. But if you're looking for perfect, you've got to look up."

Her eyes fill with tears, "I couldn't stand it, Morgan. If he left, I mean."

"But you can stand looking him in the eye and telling him you won't meet his mother?"

She wipes the tear away with the back of her hand. "His mother will hate me."

"Max is not a mama's boy, or he wouldn't live across the country from his parents. Lilly, if I made a play for Max—not that he'd notice me any more than the doorknob—but if I came on to him, what would happen?"

She starts to laugh through her tears, "Max is really not all that great on the flirting business; he probably wouldn't notice. No offense to you, Morgan."

"I'll wait for Poppy downstairs." I don't know why, but I just can't take Lilly this morning. I suppose it's because she has what I want in the palm of her hand, and she won't even wrap her fingers around it and embrace it.

In contrast to Lilly's pursuit of all things vocational, I am a serial monogamous dater. I have always had a boyfriend to parlay me to the next social event, a man about whom the paper conveniently estimates his net worth in terms of how likely I am to marry him. Without a boyfriend, I feel empty, incomplete, and just plain lonely. I suppose it comes from being virtually ignored by my parents.

But isn't that so hip? To blame my parents for all my

problems and not take responsibility for the fact that I don't know how to be alone.

Clearly, I have a long way to go on this contentment factor.

"Before you go, I made you something." Lilly jumps up from the futon and goes to her coat closet, which is a mish-mash of so much stuff, you almost expect the bowling ball to come rolling off the top shelf like on the Flintstones. "It's for your job interviews. Remember? I told you I had something for you for court."

"Lilly, what on earth?" It's a gorgeous black pant set, with long sleeves and starched white cuffs and a collar. It's very nautical. Very chic and extremely gorgeous. "It's incredible, Lilly. You never cease to amaze me with what you can do with that sketch book of yours."

"It's from my collection this fall. This one is your size, so I brought it home last night. I thought it would help in the job search, and it's completely in your budget: free. I'll make something new if there happens to be a court date."

I dash behind the Chinese screen and climb into the new outfit, starved for the feel of fresh clothing on my limbs. In this, I know I will be able to get a job. I feel like a million! And it didn't cost me a thing. Now I know how Daddy feels when he collects the rent. Advance to go, collect two hundred dollars.

"So you'll meet Max's parents and you won't freak out on commitment while I'm gone?" I say while I admire my image in the mirror.

Lilly nods. "You'll stay away from my Max?"

I laugh. "Lilly, he's all yours, but I've got news for you. Max sees no one but you in the room, and if I were you, I wouldn't give him the chance to question his affections. Or next thing you know, you'll be on the front page of the news-paper in the arms of a bigamist."

I slip into a pair of comfortable Cole Haans, which I snuck over, and head out the door feeling like the San Francisco executive I'm about to become. My reality just got kicked up a notch. Financial District, here I come. And this time, I'm dressed for the occasion.

chapter 16

feel like a new woman in front of Lilly's building. I don't even have matching accessories, and I still walk like I'm on the runway. That's how one knows good clothing. Lilly's designs are enough without baubles and trinkets, though I'd never let my father hear me say that. That's blasphemy to a Malliard. Good clothes always call for fine jewelry, my dear. But seriously, Lilly really is a talent, gifted with fabric, like I'm gifted at sniffing out the best spa products. Too bad she's socially inept. Well, I guess it's not actually too bad, because if she and Poppy weren't socially inept, we never would have met and bonded. If there's one thing that's good in my life, it's that I have friends as strange as me. Just in their own particular way.

Poppy honks the horn of her Subaru Outback. You can tell it's Poppy's because it's the only Subaru in town without the mandatory bumper sticker of the following persuasion:

Free Tibet

Love Animals—Don't Eat Them

KQED (public television)

Pro-child, Pro-choice.

No, Poppy has none of those bumper stickers, but rather a big silver Jesus fish on the back of her Subaru. The car, which is a cranberry red and as sporty as you can go with a Subaru, is perfect for getting her to her little mountain hikes.

While we're on the subject, what is the actual point of hiking, can you tell me? Does the view not look just as good from a well-appointed balcony? Having a goal is really not necessary to enjoy the outdoors. I want to tell Poppy this, but she doesn't get it. Any more than I get her desire to view the Valley from nearby peaks. Sweating for fun is completely outside my realm of understanding, unless a sauna is involved.

I head towards the wannabe SUV. She honks the horn again to let me hear its cute little whimper, and I climb into the passenger seat.

"Hey, thanks for picking me up. I needed the moral support, because working world, here I come!"

"Great outfit. Is that one of Lilly's?"

I nod. "Isn't it fabulous? I printed some leads off the computer last night, and instead of business, I'm going to concentrate on the fashion sector. I thought we'd start at some of the boutiques I used to frequent."

"Good idea. And I have a lead for you I think you're going to like. It's right up your alley." Poppy turns off the radio, which is playing some new-age Enya-type music, and looks at me. "Did you see the newspaper this morning?"

Oh heavens, when will I not learn something personal in the newspaper? "I'm avoiding it. Is there something I should know?" I really wonder what it must be like for families who actually talk and tell each other things rather than learn them in the gossip rags and society pages. Imagine what it would be like to hear your mother was a Hollywood actress from her, rather than in her obituary.

"I wouldn't have seen it," Poppy continues. "But I got into town early and read the paper in a coffee shop."

"You went to a coffee shop without me?"

"I had a green tea. Relax. I'll stop anytime you're ready if you want to ingest more poison."

I pull at the waistline of the pants Lilly made for me in "my size." That's a relative term, as in the last month I've put on a few pounds and apparently I am currently someone else's size. Someone who is distinctly bigger than me. I'm surprised Lilly didn't notice, but since she didn't, I have a feeling I'm going to be permanently tattooed with the waistline of these slacks.

"So what did the paper say? Am I going to jail? Is the tax man coming?" I try to laugh off any fears.

"It had nothing to do with the tax stuff. What's that about?"

"I don't know. I'll have to call my lawyer with the abs of steel." I start to giggle to myself. "He should have been a plastic surgeon." Mostly because he doesn't need an ounce of work himself. He belongs in Rome, cut from marble.

"Who should have been a plastic surgeon?"

"My lawyer. He's all clean-cut and pretty, like a plastic surgeon. Perfect teeth. I just don't think I can trust a man with perfect teeth."

"Maybe his father was a dentist."

"So how'd he get the abs? Is his mother Jane Fonda?"

"How do you know he's really a lawyer? Lilly said this was the guy at Spa Del Mar."

"He said my dad hired him after it was clear the government wasn't going to leave us alone and instead was deciding to pursue a lawsuit."

"Your dad hired a lawyer? And you believe that?" Poppy asks, a distinct tone of disbelief in her question.

"The charges are true."

"How do you know?"

"Daddy's getting a wife."

"It's about time, isn't it?"

"She looks sort of like Pumbaa with microdermabrasion."

"Oh," Poppy nods. "I see." And it's clear, she does. My dad is all about image, and he did not suddenly change overnight. Gwen clearly has some cash. I know it's awful to think such things about your father, but if there's one person I love, and yet still see the truth in, it's my dad.

"Did you look your lawyer up in the phone book?" Poppy asks.

"No."

"On the state bar website?"

"No."

"Did you even Google him?"

"No, okay, I didn't do anything. I lusted over his Bowflex bod and that was it. What more did I need to know? I'm shallow, and a wee bit desperate, all right? 'You've got a good behind, I'll follow you into court.' Is that what you want to hear? I was an idiot. Once again."

"Absolutely not. I'd just think if I was facing tax evasion charges, I'd be a little more serious. I mean, even that *Survivor* winner faced five years in jail for not claiming his million. I imagine your dad hasn't claimed a lot more than that."

"You're assuming he's guilty."

"I am."

"That's not like you, Poppy. What about his right to a free trial, and innocent until proven guilty? You're all about the 'peace first' effort."

"He's guilty in my book already for putting you on his business. You and Lilly have spent a lifetime answering to nana and your father. To the point that you're both scared to live. I'm tired of watching it, and tired of you both making excuses for your dysfunction."

"Dysfunction?"

"That's right. I'm surpassing 'issues' and 'fears' and going straight for 'dysfunction.' If your wedding history doesn't prove to you something's off, I don't know what will, Morgan. The fact that you've never had a full-time job, were engaged to a man you felt sorry for, and then one who conned you? If you're not seeing some dysfunction here, I can't help you. You're like a walking definition of *neurosis*."

"We may be dysfunctional, Poppy, but you're in the same pen as us. If we were dogs in the San Francisco SPCA, we'd be in the same chain-link box for our issues. Lilly with her little doggie Lysol can, you with your little hemp collar, and me getting 'fixed.'"

"I am a working chiropractor. I have a career. I have people who come to me for advice. I'm not dysfunctional."

"You haven't bought a new skirt in this decade. You smell like herbs rather than a woman, and the last date you had was probably when that skirt was in style. Am I right?"

"Unlike you, Morgan, I don't measure my successes in terms of men in my life."

"And that's a good thing, because it would make you a failure. I would assume you need men in your life to measure them. And cracking their backs doesn't count."

"I came up here to help you. Like Lilly, you're picking on my clothes. What is it with you two and my clothes?"

"If you have to ask, that's a problem. Listen, I'm sorry. I'm just tense. I suppose you have a balm for that."

"No, but I brought you some oolong tea. I'm wondering if I should have gone straight for St. John's Wort."

"What did the paper say this morning? Am I engaged to someone I should know about?" I might as well have it all in front of me before I go in and try to sell myself as the newest fashion maven.

Poppy doesn't answer me but instead drives for a long time until she gets to the edge of the Embarcadero past the Giants' stadium. She pulls over to the side of the road. The Bay's waves are lapping up against the docks, and occasionally over their edge, and I realize how much I miss the view. Here, when I look into the horizon, I feel like there's a whole life of adventure and opportunity out before me waiting to be lived. I'm not boxed in Lilly's windowless loft actively searching for something that may not exist. The truth is I've never had a better opportunity to sail off into the sunset than right now, and I certainly hope today's my day.

"There's a rumor circulating that you aren't really your mother's daughter," Poppy says in a low and serious tone. I imagine it's the voice she uses to tell someone they need surgery.

"Oh trust me," I laugh. "If I heard it once, I heard it a thousand times about my mother's poor abdominal muscles ripped to shreds by me, the enormous baby."

"It's just a rumor, Morgan; they got it from the Hollywood press."

I laugh out loud. "Next thing you know, I'll have sprouted from her costar chimpanzee if you believe what you read."

"I'm sure it's nothing. I just thought you should know about it, in case we run into anyone who might ask."

"What's the point of this?"

"I suppose it's to dispute your mother's fortune."

"Oh right, because *The Main Street Follies* made her so much cash. She wasn't Marilyn Monroe, Poppy. Traci Malliard's claim to fame was her halter-dress dance in a B movie." I scratch my head. "No, at best a C movie. She basically had a few bit parts in the *Alexander the Great* or *Waterworld* of her day."

"People don't realize that. I think they believe anybody on

TV is wealthy, and your mother did marry wealthy. But maybe we're assuming the worst—or at least the newspaper is."

"Where are we going first?" Even as I say it, I don't believe it. I loved my mother, and though she may not have been Mrs. Cunningham, she tried in her own way. She bought me painting canvases and tried to teach me to paint. I get the past mixed up with her illness, and by then the drugs had settled into her system. I don't know what her truth was, I suppose.

"I got you an interview this morning for a VP job of shoe purchasing at Ami's Boutique," Poppy says, pulling out a sheet of paper and turning towards San Francisco's fashion district.

"Oh, I love Ami's."

"Now, you're supposed to have shoe-buying experience, so you need to embellish a bit."

"What do you mean? I can buy shoes."

"You have to know about how many to buy in which sizes and such, and you have to purchase the shoes people will want, so it means being ahead of the trends."

"Poppy, look who you're talking to."

"I'm just saying."

"I am so glad I brought my Cole Haans up to Lilly's. I have to go back for my Donald Pliner's if I get called in for a second interview. Can you imagine showing up in cheap shoes?"

"Let's get through the first interview." She eyes me.

Poppy knows me well. "There's a coffee shop right there. I need a brew."

Poppy exits traffic like the proverbial bat out of the dark place and pulls into a twenty-minute parking zone. "Let's go."

Walking into the coffee shop, I sniff the rich scent of espresso and pop a few chocolate-covered coffee beans they have out for sampling. "Oooh, I feel a buzz coming on already." If you want to feel your humanity, try going without a steady diet of whatever your addiction might be. I'll tell you,

I never thought walking into a roasting company would feel like an extravagance, but here it is.

Poppy shakes her head. "I don't know how you can drink that rotgut, much less eat it in pill form. Do you know what it's—"

"Yes, I know what it's doing to my kidneys, and my liver, and all the other hosts of organs, and it's still worth it, so that ought to tell you something. Maybe your detoxified system is missing out."

She rolls her eyes. "I'll wait outside."

Once at the counter, I see the newspaper and the picture of me on the runway in the wedding dress. Isn't that the epitome of irony? I'm in the newspaper every day as a bride, and I've never been one. It really takes on a sickening hue of irony. If it were someone else, I might actually see the humor in it.

chapter 17

It's an odd feeling to walk into the behind-the-scenes warehouse of a boutique you've frequented. There are boxes everywhere, piled high to the ceiling as we walk along a dank hallway. Trust me, it's not the same high as walking into a carefully arranged shoe boutique where there are smartly dressed shop girls jockeying for your attention. Still, I'm mystified by the power of the box. Loving shoes as I do, I can't help but wonder what type of magic is within each box. The space smells like old books, though I don't see any, and I suppose I've never kept a pair of shoes long enough to find out if they do, indeed, eventually smell like books.

Ami Crittenden has several boutiques and has made a name for herself in San Francisco. I've never met the woman, but I've seen her in the newspaper. Which, I imagine, is one thing we have in common.

Poppy is behind me, praying loudly and asking for God to cover me with His grace as I go into the interview. Now, I'm all for praying, but Poppy sounds like she's having her own revival right here in the hallway. I turn and face her.

"Do you have to do that?"

"Pray? I thought you'd like it. I enjoy it when people pray for me."

"I do like it, but you know God has really good ears. We needn't shout."

"I want Him to know I mean it."

"God looks at the heart, Poppy. He knows you mean it. Are you coming into the interview with me?"

"No, I'm just making sure you get there. You have been known to chicken out at important events, you know."

I know Poppy means well, but sometimes, she's as bad as Mrs. Henry or my father. She watches me to the point that she hovers and makes me overly anxious. I'm going for a job interview as a shoe buyer; just how stress inducing can this be?

"I'd have been smart if I chickened out of Lilly's fashion show," I say aloud.

"Look at the good side of it—her gown appears in the newspaper almost every day."

I just gaze at her. "With me in it. Not really a highlight of my life, Poppy."

"Yeah, but it's Lilly's turn, Morgan. We're the ones always singing backup to your lead. Don't you love seeing Lilly be important to San Francisco fashion with all she gave up to get there? In college, we remember what it was like to see you in the Women of Stanford calendar in your cute little shorts. No one asked us to be in the calendar."

"Would you have been?" I ask.

"Of course not; my father would kill me."

"My father suggested it. I wore a San Francisco Jeweler's T-shirt."

"We remember, Morgan."

The only saving grace for my little calendar stint is that no one actually cared at Stanford. People went on with their lives, and the importance of a calendar to raise money for alumni was met with about as much interest as the girl's water polo team efforts. Maybe less than that.

I cross my arms to say something else, but I know Poppy is right. She's always been there for me, acting as a human Kleenex and putting her own needs aside as I went through one trauma after another. Most of them of my own making.

I can't really quibble with a friend like her. When the girls made fun of me for posing in the demeaning calendar, she was there to say to them that I had my reasons. Even if they weren't my own. When Poppy says to me that it's someone else's turn, I suppose she's right.

"Poppy, thank you for coming up here and for getting me this interview. I know I haven't done anything to deserve it."

"You bought me my first chiropractic table when the bank wouldn't lend me money," she reminds me. "You bought Lilly fabric so she could start her business. You've been there for us, too, you know. Now it's our turn."

But as she says it, it sounds like my father's money has been there for them more than I have.

My cell phone rings just as I reach the end of the hallway. I think about not answering, but what if it's Ami canceling my appointment? Maybe she saw me in the cheap shoes and my interview is over.

"Morgan Malliard speaking," I answer professionally.

"Morgan, it's Daddy."

"Hi, Dad."

"I need you to come home, princess. The lawyer just delivered the list of indictments against us. They'll be read to us soon before a grand jury. It's only because George is friends with someone that we got a preview." He stops for a long time, and I think I hear him choke back a sob. "It's not good, Morgan."

I feel panic for only a moment, then I actually wonder what it would be like to have a father who lost at something. Not a father in jail—I don't imagine that part—but to have a daddy who had time to listen to me because he hadn't cele-brated his latest win. A daddy who didn't have a meeting to attend or a city hall battle to create. When I hear emotion in his voice, all the possibilities come to mind, and mostly, I wonder what if my dad might ever share my faith. Granted, it's a huge leap from a speck of emotion to salvation, but as I've stated, I'm ever hopeful.

But my hope is quickly doused like baking soda to the flame.

"They're saying we owe more than I ever made. They'll ruin me, Morgan." His sense of entitlement is back with a wave of saliva. I hear him spit his words.

"Daddy, it won't be that bad. We'll pay them what we owe, and we'll start again. We can't possibly owe it all, and you know the diamond business better than anyone. That's never going to change."

"Morgan, I need you to come home. I have some papers we need to shred, and there's a litany of items we need to go through before we meet with that idiot lawyer."

For a moment I set aside the thought that my father actu-ally used the words "papers to shred." "I thought you said he was the best?"

"Which means he's a great white among tiger sharks. Still a shark. It's not a compliment. He's still a lawyer. He's still a leech making a buck off my money." I can hear the muffled words coming through his clenched teeth, and I can picture that vein bulging in his neck.

"Daddy, you're getting too upset. You need to calm down. We'll work this out. I'll be home after this job interview I have right now."

He starts to series-curse, stringing together a litany of swear words in something that sounds like Chris Rock's monologue. And then there's silence followed by a loud thump.

"Daddy?" I call. "Daddy!" I say more frantically. No answer. "Mrs. Henry!" I start to yell into the phone. "Mrs. Henry! Oh my gosh," I rake my hand through my hair and try to figure out what to do next. I'm just standing in the hallway, confused about what to do, who to call. I try to imagine my father is just playing chicken with me, to get me to do what he wants. He's just pretending, I tell myself while he shreds documents and my future. That's all this is. He's buying time to make me feel sorry for him.

But I continue to hear the deafening silence at the other end of the phone line, and I start to run back towards the door, grabbing Poppy's hand as I go. "Poppy, you have to get me home. Right now!" I hang up and dial back, but I only get a persistent busy signal. I pull Poppy along behind me down the hallway, hitting redial all the way. "Pick up, Daddy. Pick up the phone! Poppy, hurry!"

"Morgan, what can I do?" Poppy questions.

"I think something's happened to my father. He was screaming like he does, then it sounded like he fell down. We've got to get home."

We tear down the street to her car, and Poppy starts to shout-pray again, but this time I don't mind. This time, I know my father is in deep trouble, and it has nothing to do with his bank statements.

I continue to dial the house until it finally occurs to me to call 911. I dial and relay my fears to an overly calm operator, who takes my words down as though I'm giving her the weather report on a sunny day.

"Are you on a cell phone?" the operator asks.

"Yes! Yes, I am on a cell phone, but my father isn't with me. The address is what I gave you. Do you have the address?"

"I have the address, ma'am. The paramedics are on their way now. Do you want me to stay on the line with you?"

"No, no. Just get them to the apartment!"

I clip my phone shut and tap my foot against the floorboard of the car. I've seen the ambulances try to get through San Francisco. I've always hoped that I would never need their services, as the city dwellers can rarely be bothered to move over for emergency vehicles. They'd rather allow innocents to bleed in the street than be late for a personal shopping appointment. "Come on, come on. Step on it, Poppy!"

"I'm going as fast as I can," she says as we go airborne over a San Francisco hill, hitting the roadway with a hard wallop as we come down. Driving up Hyde, the cable car lumbers up in front of us, slowing traffic, and Poppy's right behind the old-fashioned trolley. As cars pass us to the right, I notice the tourists gaily taking pictures and pointing at the beautiful view I've taken for granted my whole life. Time seems to have stopped for me, but I can see by the enthusiastic expressions and cameras flashing that it does indeed go on. I hear my own heartbeat in my head, praying for my father to hold on, and wondering if a tourist will get home to Japan and see our Subaru driving erratically up Russian Hill, my frantic face in his viewfinder.

"Come on, come on, come on!"

As Poppy drives around the cable car, the first sight of my building comes into view, and I can see that the paramedics aren't there yet. Poppy drives the remaining block on the wrong side of the street, and we pull into the underground parking with enough force to bring the entire garage staff out to see the ruckus. I don't stop to speak with them. I just tear out of Poppy's vehicle and fumble for my elevator key, stabbing it into the wall of silver buttons. As the elevator climbs ever so slowly, it finally reaches the top floor with a subtle ding. I run into the penthouse to find the phone off the hook, but my father missing.

"Daddy?" I call and hear myself echoing off the travertine. "Daddy?" His papers are strewn about the floor near the phone, and I gather them up, stuffing them into a briefcase that's beside the phone. "Mrs. Henry?"

The elevator dings again, and two firemen stand there alongside Poppy.

"He's gone," I say. "He's not here."

"I'll check the hospitals," Poppy says, rushing to the phone and putting it back on its cradle. The fireman, always the first to arrive, check out the bedrooms, just to ensure that I'm correct.

Sticking out of the briefcase, I see the following heading on a long, ghostly sheet of legal paper: "UNITED STATES OF AMERICA VS. MORGAN MALLIARD. At all times relevant to this information, the defendant, Morgan Malliard, was a resident of California."

What? I search for my father's name on the papers, but instead find only count after count naming me as the defendant. My eyes scan the paperwork, falling on the number "$2,546,750." My stated income for the year. Hello? I definitely would have bought more shoes if I made that!

I feel myself fall against the couch and look up to see two men in suits enter into the penthouse, flashing some type of badge at me.

"Morgan Malliard?"

"Yes, do you know where my father is?"

"You have the right to remain silent. Anything you say or do—"

"What?" I ask, totally flustered, and yet partially relieved they aren't from the morgue.

"We have a warrant for your arrest for charges of tax fraud and tax evasion. You have the right to remain . . ."

As they spout their mantra, I allow the two burly men,

whom I can only assume are federal agents, to clip shut the handcuffs around my wrists. When I was talking about accessories earlier? This is not what I had in mind.

"Help me, Poppy!" I wail as I'm herded into the elevator while the cop continues to shout my Miranda rights.

chapter 18

When we arrive downstairs, it is to paparazzi snapping off pictures in rapid succession, shouting horrible questions at me. Clearly, they were forewarned about the agents' coming.

"Where's your father?"

"How much do you owe?"

"Where's the money gone?"

"Did you overcharge rent in Union Square?"

It's clear that the feds purposely parked outside the garage. It occurs to me that once again Lilly's clothes will be featured on the front page, and I'm starting to get suspicious. I wear her clothes, I end up in some scandal. This time in handcuffs. But I'm more numb than anything. I have no idea where my father is, or if he's safe, and that's my priority. The truth is I'd rather be seen in handcuffs than a wedding gown I haven't used for marital purposes. Neither event is a great Christian witness, but what's a girl to do? I imagine the handcuffs are doing nothing for my job prospects either.

When I'm hustled into a Town Car between the two agents, I finally speak. "Do you know where my father is?"

The man, a middle-aged suit without a speck of expression or emotion says, "No, miss."

"He's not under arrest somewhere else?"

The man shakes his head ever so slightly. I feel like I've been abducted and these aliens lack what we humans know as personality. "He will be arrested when we find him. You'll appear before a grand jury to have the charges read in detail."

My heart plummets in a freefall. At least if he were in jail, I'd know my father was safe. "Can I call my lawyer?"

"He's already been made aware of your situation. He'll meet you at our office."

"I'm not going to jail?"

"Not yet, miss. We have questions for you." I can tell the man is trying to be kind, as best as his type can, but white-collar crime is not something that speaks to the heart of the masses, and I'm already on shaky ground. I always wanted to be Martha Stewart but not really in this capacity. I was hoping I'd know how to whiten antique linens or something.

We drive to an ominous cement building, and I'm escorted out of the car with one man at each elbow. Once inside the building, the suit removes my handcuffs, which were apparently just for the pictures. It's the criminal's version of theme park photos of you screaming before the roller coaster thrusts you over its edge. Smile for the camera.

Inside the building, George Gentry is pacing outside the office I'm heading towards with my escorts. His perfect abs are covered by a well-made European suit, which tells me more than I want to know. Lawyers in good suits are expensive, and if I need an expensive lawyer, things do not look good. Of course, I imagine my name on an indictment and getting carted off in handcuffs should have been my first clue. *Well,* I think. *This is it. I truly can't sink any deeper now.*

George Gentry grabs me by the arm, ever so gently. "I'll need some time with my client." He pulls me into a room, and I focus on his perfect teeth. I wonder if they're paid for.

They're not horse-sized like the fake ones, but they are definitely white. Hauntingly so.

"I just had them whitened, is that what you're looking at? Too much coffee and late-night studying. On to the next thing, all right?"

I cover my mouth as I laugh, and I can only imagine from his frown that it's coming across as hysterical. Which, in fact, it is. "I'm in some major trouble here, aren't I?"

"Tax evasion is very hard to prove. The burden of proof falls on the government. Had I been hired earlier in the process, I don't think we'd be here. We can prove your innocence by a lack of motive and lack of knowledge of certain bank accounts. You just hired me late."

"I didn't hire you at all. George, my father may be sick. I know this is serious in terms of what kind of trouble I might be in, but my father's health is more important. Is there a way I can find out where he is?"

"I'll do what I can, but Morgan, we need to focus. I don't think I'm going to be able to represent both you and your father. I've looked over the paperwork, and I think if you are both listed, the burden of proof is much easier against your father."

"We didn't do anything wrong. Maybe my father made a mistake and took a write-off he shouldn't have, but people don't go to jail for mistakes."

"They do, Morgan. Every day. I think we need to separate these cases."

"Are you firing me?"

"No." He looks around the room. "I'm firing your father. Did you know about the offshore bank accounts?"

Now, how do I answer this without looking like a complete idiot? "Daddy gave me a Visa, and access to the Bank of America account. So I used an ATM. Is that what you're asking?"

He sighs huskily. "I need to know where these earnings went, Morgan. Over two million dollars last year alone. Where is it?"

I just shake my head and shrug. "I never made a salary that I know of, George. I spent money, and my father paid the bills. He kept money in my checking account, and I just never thought to ask."

"How did you get the car?"

"It was my birthday present last year."

"Is this your signature?" He shows me copies of the backs of checks.

"It is, but Daddy put it straight in the bank. My dad's not going to go to jail, is he? He wouldn't do anything illegal." Of course, as I say it, I think about the black-market incident that landed him in a Russian prison and put him at the mercy of Marcus.

"I think we need to worry about you, Morgan. Your father's lawyer will have—"

"You are my father's lawyer. He hired you, so I'm assuming you're the best. Take his case. I'll find someone else." I stand up, only to have George stand and press on my shoulder.

"Sit down. I don't know where you think you're going, anyway. You've been arrested. You just can't walk out of here." He pulls out my Visa statements, or rather copies of them, and there it is, in black and white. What I spend in a month totaled out for the year. Ouch.

"You spent nearly $148,000 last year, Morgan. There's a lot of money missing here for me to believe this story. You made over two million. Where is it?"

"I have the right to remain silent, is that right?"

"To the police, Morgan. Not to your lawyer if you want me to help you. Morgan, where is that money? It's imperative you tell me so I can get you out on bail and back home tonight."

I have no idea where the money is, none whatsoever. And if my father is lying in a hospital bed, I'm certainly not going to send him to jail over something as mundane as money. "I assume it's in some of my offshore accounts," I say emphatically, trying to sound like I have some idea of the offshore accounts.

George leans back, looking as though I slapped him. "I thought you didn't know anything about those accounts."

"I know Daddy believed in diversifying." In my brain, I'm thinking, *How can I get to my father's paperwork? How can I find out where he's hidden the money and pay it before any of this gets any worse?* "Is there an amount I owe? A number the government is naming?"

George rifles through the indictment and comes to the last page, where an amount is stated. "You alone owe $640,000 in back taxes, but the fraud investigation could net them more, especially with added fines. I'm sure the newspapers will be happy to let us know what that is. Your father owes a small percentage of that. But the chance of them letting you out of here when we don't know where your father is—" He shakes his head back and forth. "It's very slim. His absence makes you a flight risk."

"I have to get home, George. I'll find out where my dad is. Just make them let me out."

"What do you have for collateral?"

"I have the deed for the penthouse." I wither at this statement. "But it's in my father's name. Wait!" I lift up a finger. "I have the Beamer. It's brand new, all paid for, and the title is in my name."

George nods. "Do you have any cash to live on? If you're set free on bail, your accounts will be frozen."

"I'll be fine." I swallow hard at the amount they say I owe. I couldn't possibly owe that in the last year; I didn't even have a job. Never did, even though the paper trail tells an entirely different story. But I know Daddy wouldn't leave me out to dry like this.

Oh Lord, let him be all right so I can kill him when all this is over.

chapter 19

'm thinking I really deserve my own bed at the next Spa Weekend. George Gentry is bent over the mounds of paperwork, and he's loosened his tie and unbuttoned the top button on his business shirt. This is not what a person in trouble with the law wants to see out of her lawyer. I want him to look up and say, "Oh, big mistake. I'll get you out of here immediately."

No wonder our country is in debt. Did they really need that much paperwork to come after *moi*? The occasional sigh emanates from George, and he shows his frustration by gazing up at me and shaking his head in repulsion. He's not looking nearly so handsome at the moment. I'm just seeing him as annoying and somewhat arrogant.

Still, I'm glad my dad got me a gorgeous lawyer because he is the only thing to gaze upon here in this gray government office. How do people actually work in government offices? There is not one iota of personality in the building, and I'm thinking it explains why the feds are so stereotyped. They live in a colorless, bland world. They're the human equivalent of potato soup without cheese, cabbage stew without meat. Imagine what it would be like to not realize paintings or surroundings affect the personality. It's like *The Wizard of Oz* in here before the color part.

"Are you almost done?" I ask.

"Are you in a hurry to get to prison?" he shoots back.

Now that was rude. "You haven't even tried to call my father," I accuse.

"Morgan, I'm your lawyer; I'm not a babysitter. I don't know where your father is, and I don't have time to track him down. Have you noticed the size of your indictment? I have enough to do right here." He lifts up the mound of paperwork and drops it to the desk with a loud thump. "I've got a call in to the partners to take on your father's case."

"If your father was out there somewhere in the hospital, you wouldn't care if he was alive or dead? You seem to think I'm somehow not human here, George. This is my father, not some defendant." I start to pace the small, boxy room.

Another big sigh from George. "All right." He slaps his hand against the table. "I'll be back." He stands up and leaves me alone in my stark quarters. There are windows in the room that I can't see out of. I suppose this is an interrogation room. It would be really cool if I wasn't under arrest. I can picture myself in *Alias* mode, kicking some booty and crashing my way out of the building. *Yeah, that would be cool.*

They took my cell phone away. I can live with a lot of humiliations, but that one is beyond annoying. I feel absolutely powerless in this sterile room with no one here for support. I suppose that's their point. I should be more worried. I guess I just trust my father to get me out of this, even if the fact is he got me into this. I know he won't leave me or forsake me. He may not be the best taxpayer, but he'd never do something illegal. Not on purpose, anyway. There's a perfectly good explanation for this, and I'm just expecting my Bowflex lawyer to find it soon.

There's a knock at the door, and George comes back in.

"What did you knock for? Did you think I was in a dressing room or something? There's a window right there." I have to say I'm tempted to check my makeup in the makeshift mirror. But I refrain. I figure vanity will do me no favors at this point.

"I was trying to be polite."

If he was polite he would have found out about my father two hours ago. "Look, George, I don't mean to be ungrateful, but you know I didn't have anything to do with this legal mess. Can't you just get me home? I'll go to Lilly's if they're seizing the properties."

George sighs again, and I'm getting annoyed.

"I'm not stupid, George. My job consisted of going to events in certain jewels and making my father's store the talk of an event. It's not exactly in the classifieds for a job, but it was legitimate. I'm sorry it doesn't impress you."

"Ignorance is no excuse for breaking the law. These charges aren't going to just let you leave here and shoe shop when we're done, Morgan. These are serious charges, and quite frankly, you look guilty from the paper trail. Your signature is on everything."

I ignore his inference to my lighthearted lifestyle. "Did you find out anything about my father?"

"My secretary is working on it. I don't know anything yet."

I pace again.

"They want to interview you. Do you think you're ready for that?"

"Ready for what? I don't know anything. Have I not just been in the newspaper for being the most ignorant twit in San Francisco? What do you think has changed between last week and today?"

"You don't have to get mad. That won't help your case. I know you're not ignorant, Morgan."

I never thought you could go to prison for being naïve, but apparently that's not the case. Apparently, ignorance can get you into a whole lot of trouble. "I'm not mad, and only dogs get mad, people get angry," I remind him. "I'm powerless. Do you like being out of control, Mr. Gentry? No, because we're all control freaks at heart. Without a moment's warning, I just lost everything I knew to be my world. Try to have some sympathy, will you? I know I'm not your normal case, but maybe God's testing you."

He stares at me with hard eyes. I can tell he's summing me up, trying to figure out if I'm really naïve or simply a calculating vixen who has run off with an estimated two million dollars. I would think if he'd read the paper in the last two months he'd have his answer. *No, really, she is that dumb.*

"Why are you looking at me? You either believe me or you don't. If you don't, be gone and let me find a real lawyer."

"I don't think you're that easy to read, and you will allow me to have my assessment time. You're a beautiful woman, Morgan, and you've moved in some elegant social circles. I imagine you've learned a trick or two."

"And you're the poor, innocent lawyer next on my list, is that it? Will I grasp you in my clutches and make you powerless to escape? You'll have a hard time finding someone to feel for the lawyer."

He says nothing.

"I have a question for you, George. Why do you automatically assume because I am blonde and inherited my mother's looks that I am a schemer? What is it you think I have to gain by tricking you, my lawyer? Why do men always assume the worst of women?"

"I can't speak for all men, but are you familiar with Samson and Delilah?" He laughs and writes something down. "But you've got me all wrong, Morgan. I don't question your innocence. I'm just giving you a sampling of what you're going to hear in front of the grand jury."

His comment infuriates me and his profession of my innocence awakens something ugly within me. I've been accused my whole life of being the vixen. Only Poppy and Morgan ever gave me the benefit of the doubt. Why shouldn't I be Delilah? Maybe I wouldn't be in this ridiculous situation if I had a schemer's heart.

I bend over him, thankful Lilly's collar is high enough for any church girl, and I look him straight in the eye. I swallow hard and try to think like Delilah. My eyes want to fill with tears as I think about what George Gentry and so many others assume about me, but I force the feelings away. I draw even closer to his face, so close I can feel the heat from him. I see his lower lip moving slightly, and I try to copy what I saw my mother do so often at birthday parties and fashion shows. I lean my elbow on the table, only to have it slip off and I nearly whack my arm on the table. I reassume the position.

"Maybe Delilah was fighting for her life, too."

He takes a sharp breath and pulls away from me. Then he slams his folder shut and stands up. "You think this is a game, don't you? You think your beauty, your grace is going to just let you walk out of here scot free, don't you?"

I sit down, feeling the sting of tears, their warm stickiness falling down my cheek. "No, George, I don't think I'm going to go free. If anything, I feel like I'm trying to accept my fate. I think my father could be out there sick, or possibly even dying, and I'm in here playing cat and mouse, and I don't even care. You want to lock me up? You go ahead, but tell me that my father is all right."

I stand up straight and walk across the room from him, allowing his eyes to fall on my figure. "You're just like all the rest. I'm guilty by association. After all, a woman who spent nearly $150,000 last year can't be good. She can't have right intentions." I pull out the Visa bill from his pile. "Read it."

"Read what?"

"Where my money went, read it."

He starts to list shoe boutiques and Nordstrom's, but then he comes to more. Lilly's fabric: $7,000. The spas with my Spa Girls: $4,300. World Vision: $58,000. And my church: $24,000. And suddenly he looks up at me, questioning everything he knows to be true.

"I am not selfish, Mr. Gentry. I may not be an intellectual like yourself, but I am not selfish. I'm only wealthy and I don't answer to you, or even the U.S. government. I answer to God, and I know in my heart my motives have been pure. If He chooses to land me in jail, that's His choice, not yours."

"I might remind you that the government doesn't care if you were generous with their money."

I flinch as though I've been hit. George's lack of belief in me only reminds me I'm a bad judge of character. It will do me no good to prove anything. People believe what they're going to believe. "I suppose you think I've had it pretty good all along, and now I'm getting my just desserts. Is that right? For someone who supposedly believes in me, you have a funny way of showing it."

He looks down at the paperwork again. "I'm not here to judge you. I'm here to defend you." But he won't look at me. Maybe I am naïve, but I do think he believes me. If I had to put money on the situation, I'd say he was trying to avoid the chemistry that is so obvious between us.

"So defend me, and let's leave the personal judgments alone. I would have traded every cent to have a father who loved me."

"I'm sorry, Morgan."

"Forget it." I wipe my face with the back of my hand. I

don't bother to dab my eyes daintily the way I was taught.

George comes alongside me in my chair and kneels beside me, staring deeply into my eyes. His face rises to a mere inch from my own and we both use every ounce of self control to avoid the obvious—that I want to forget where I am and be kissed by this lawyer like I've never been kissed before. The heat between us generates like a steam engine gathering speed. I close my eyes, hoping to feel the warmth of his lips on my own, but after a time with my eyes closed, I open them again, only to see he's pulled away.

"Do you want me to say I believe you, Morgan? Because I'll reiterate. I believe you had nothing to do with this, and it's my intention to prove it in a court of law. If you are a conniving woman, I see none of it." He laughs a little. "As a seductress, you're not very good. No offense."

I start to giggle through my tears. "I'm not?"

"I knew from the first moment I laid eyes on you at Spa Del Mar you were innocent. I never questioned it once, not even through that pathetic come-on. I'm a good judge of character, and I trust what I see."

I start to blubber. Not a pretty, graceful cry that my mother practiced with flair, but a heaving, ugly sob that leaves me completely emotionally naked before my lawyer. I put my hands over my face and try to control myself, but the tears burst forth, and I feel myself shaking. It shouldn't mean a thing that some guy believes me. Not a thing. But for some reason, his faith in me is exactly what I needed today.

"It's all right, Morgan," he says softly into my ear. "It's okay." He comes closer once again. I feel him press his lips to my forehead. "I'll get you out of this."

I pull away and look into his intense brown eyes, believing with everything in me God has truly sent me an angel with a six-pack tummy.

But of course, I've believed that before. The first time I ended up with a dead fiancé. The second time, I ended up with a Reno annulment. Now I'm sitting here with a United States indictment, and this time I don't know what to believe. Except I know that George believing in me is the whisper from heaven I needed.

chapter 20

First rule of law: the U.S. government is not in any hurry. I mean, I actually wonder if these people could afford espresso, would it get any quicker around here? Probably not. I wonder if you crushed up some No-Doz in the cafeteria food would we see some action. But the last thing I need is to be caught thinking about how to drug federal agents. Not really a great Christian thought, and besides, even if they worked at lightning speed, it would still feel like eons. The wheels of justice turn slowly, and although I've been interviewed again and again, I feel no closer to going anywhere.

Truthfully, I think they believe me. I suppose the dumb-blonde bit has been well-publicized of late, so it's not exactly hard to believe.

They're giving me a break now, and because no charges have actually been formulated, they're allowing my first visitor. So I'm tapping on the table waiting for Poppy to arrive and tell me how blessed I am. I have no idea for what at this point, but she'll find something. She is an eternal optimist.

The door opens, and Poppy stands in the doorway, her luxurious red hair a mass of flyaway split ends. Her "vintage" (a nice word for "used") peasant skirt has shrunk from multiple washings and now lands above her knees, showing her moccasin-style boots (that really should be burned) coming to about midway up her calves. She is a walking fashion nightmare. But I look great, and I'm going to jail, so apparently, I'm not one to give advice.

"Did you find anything out about my father?"

She nods slowly.

"Tell me, Poppy!" I jump up and grab her hands and I search her brilliant blue eyes, hoping for some sign of peace.

"He's resting comfortably in the hospital."

"The hospital?" I put my hand at my heart, silently repeating the name *Jesus* over and over again.

"He had a stroke, they think. He's having trouble speaking right now, but the doctors feel his speech will come back rather quickly, because his other functions have been restored. You'll appreciate this—he's trying to yell at them, but his voice won't work properly."

"You didn't tell him where I was?"

Poppy shakes her head. "I thought it would upset him. I just told him I was going to you, and that you loved him and to get better."

"Thank you, Poppy. I owe you big time."

"I met his girlfriend."

"And?"

"Bad energy."

"Wicked bad? Or just unhealthy bad?" I cannot believe I'm asking this question, but Poppy does have a discerning spirit, and she really can sum people up rather quickly. Even if she does couch it in her "energy speak."

She lets go of my hands and sits at the gray plastic table. "She loves your father. She's not in this for money."

"Well, that's good because there might not be any. Or is that not obvious by my location?"

Poppy lifts her eyebrows at me and continues. Nothing

fazes her. "But Gwen does want to control him, not to share him." Poppy takes a long, cleansing breath like she's been known to do in the oddest of circumstances. "I think she'll want you out of the picture."

I look around at the stark interrogation room. "I think my father might have actually taken care of that for her." I try to avoid the obvious thought that my father managed to use me as a human shield in the court room, but I'm beginning to wonder if there's any other conclusion.

I put my chin in my hands and look around again. I've never actually been in a room with less character for such a long stretch of time. I would be willing to bet the carpet doesn't have six hundred knots per inch.

"I feel like I'm living in an elevator. Only the bad music is missing."

"Shh," Poppy puts her forefinger to her mouth. "Don't give them any ideas; they might use torture. The Muzak version of Beyoncé or something."

Again we laugh. "Poppy, how do you know who Beyoncé is?" I ask, totally in disbelief that she pays any attention at all to pop culture.

"She's Jay-Z's girlfriend."

I nod and Poppy goes on.

"I'm not totally a hermit," she explains.

"Wonders never cease. Poppy Clayton knows who Beyoncé is."

"And I watch *Survivor*. And *The Amazing Race*."

"No, no more. Next thing you'll be telling me you're into *American Idol*, and I can't believe my beloved Poppy would stoop down with the rest of us Americans."

"I only watched the one with Barry Manilow on it. He's my favorite."

I start to crack up. "Now that is the Poppy I know and love."

She starts to croon "Mandy," and I groan.

"You know," I shake my head, ruffling the cuffs on my shirt. "You're right about one thing. Being on the front page in a con man's arms is really nothing compared to losing your freedom. I need to quit whining, because it only gets worse. I need to look for the joy, for the contentment in every day."

She shrugs. "You'll be out of here soon." She rummages through her oversized tapestry bag. "I brought you some essential oils. This is lavender for relaxation." She places a bottle on the table. "And this is ylang-ylang for stress and anxiety."

I gather up the bottles. "Thanks, Poppy, but I'm not sure how the feds feel about essential oils in the pokey. I imagine they'll just get confiscated." But I do open them up and take a long, cleansing breath of them. The sweet, floral smells remind me of Spa Del Mar, and for a moment I imagine myself floating away into a hot-stone massage. "I wish I was at the spa."

"You're not going to prison. Your lawyer is waiting to hear what bail is set at in your arraignment. After that, I'll take care of it."

I laugh out loud. "Poppy, they've frozen my assets."

"They haven't frozen mine."

"You don't have any." Now I may be a little slow, but I know that whatever my bail is set at, if they consider me a flight risk, there is no way Poppy has the money to pay it. "Even if bail is set at a fraction of what they say I owe, there's no way."

"There's a way. My parents' house is going to be collateral. I inherited it fair and square, and I can't think of anything better to use it for. I went to the bail bondsman, and I found out how everything works. It's really quite fascinating. You're entitled to your civil rights," Poppy chirps happily. "I love

America."

While I'm thrilled the justice system is exciting to Poppy, I'd rather she just watch *Court TV* than get too involved. Of course, she'd have to get cable for that, and that isn't likely to happen anytime soon. TV has bad energy or something like that. She's just learning that Beyoncé exists in the world. I don't want to stretch her too far, too fast.

The door opens, and George comes walking through the doorway. His tall stature fills the room with his presence, and I feel it in the pit of my stomach.

"Morgan, you're free to go home," George says.

"What do you mean, I'm free?"

"They're not going to arraign you until Friday. There are a few last minute details they're needing. You're not a flight risk any longer because your dad is incapable right now of signing anything, which means you can't run off with any significant funds. But there is a small catch. This is my request, not the court's."

"Name it, what is it?"

"I want you to stay away from your father. You can call him and talk to him all you want on the phone, but I'd rather you not be seen with him, so we can show that you are not involved in any kind of underhanded dealings."

"Oh." I think on this for a moment. "Not see my dad? But he's sick in the hospital. What kind of daughter ignores that?" I'm thinking to myself, *What if he dies and I never see him again?* "I can't possibly."

"Your father's fine, Morgan. I made sure of it. My secretary has been on it since I arrived."

Poppy nods in agreement.

"One visit could cost you your future. Just please listen to me on this."

"Can I go to Spa Del Mar until then?"

George looks at Poppy and then to me. "Will you have your cell phone?"

"The whole time," I cross my heart with my hand. "I promise."

"You'll be back by Thursday night?"

"Thursday night, early."

He opens his wallet, takes out five crisp twenty dollar bills, and counts them for me. "Can you live on this until Thursday?"

"I can live on less than that," I say, handing him back his cash. I'm offended. I mean, what do I do to give off this lameness factor to people? Wait. I don't think I want the answer to that question.

Poppy is gathering up the bottles of oil she's brought, and she looks at George, and then to me, and backs out of the room. "I'll just wait outside."

As I stand face to face with the telling eyes I've grown to trust so quickly, I feel the root of my issues rear their ugly head. I am so quick to hope, so willing to believe that every man in front of me is my hero, my rescuer, that I never change. I play weak, and even dead to get what I want, and it's pathetic. And I'm done in that role.

As I stare at George with the money in his hands, I don't even want to say what it makes me feel like. A flush of anger rises within me, like a fountain that's just been turned on. He's getting paid to do his job, and that's all there is to it. If George didn't have access to my father's payment for his services, I wouldn't have George, and that's the harsh truth.

"Keep your money," I say.

"Morgan, you might need it. How will you eat?"

"I'll sponge off my friends, like normal people do." I think of the freeze-dried noodles at Lilly's and shudder.

"At least let me take you to dinner. It's been a long day and you need to keep your strength up."

This makes me laugh out loud. Keep my strength up? What am I, Oliver looking for some porridge? Honey, I was living on coffee long before you started law school.

In George's honest brown eyes I see exactly what I saw in Andy: a rescuer, a knight in shining armor who has come to take me away from everything. And finally, I see the pattern. Men only compound my problem, which must, as Poppy would put it, be at the cellular level or I'd be brighter by now. As I sit on the cusp of entering federal prison, I realize that perhaps trusting another man is not the best course of action.

"You don't have to take care of me, George. I am not a child, and I do not need to be fed. Whether you believe it or not, I am capable of finding myself dinner. I can still go back to my father's apartment, can I not?

"Did you want to do that?" he asks, blinking in what I can only assume is mock innocence.

"If I did, am I allowed to do that? From the government's point of view, I mean. Your legal opinion?"

"You're free to go, Morgan. Do whatever you wish. Just be back in town on Thursday night, and I'll go through all these allegations before then and make sure we're prepared. If you are charged officially, you won't be able to leave the county without permission, so I think now is a fine time to go to Spa Del Mar."

"What's my defense?" I ask, wondering if there's a chance under the sun I might beat this rap. My lawyer may be optimistic, but perhaps all that ab work has gone to his head.

"That you didn't have anything to do with this. You're innocent. Right?"

"Of course I'm innocent. Do you have to ask?"

"You're upset. It's been a long day, Morgan. Go home and relax. I'll make sure your expenses are covered at the spa."

I'm upset? Well, isn't my lawyer the genius. And discerning too! "I don't want you to make sure of anything like my spa stay being comfortable. You're my lawyer, and I don't need to go to the spa, George. I want to go. I'll find a way, and if I choose to stay home, I will."

"Morgan, why do you insist on fighting with me? Why are you so afraid to let me do my job?"

That's a good question, isn't it? "No offense to you, George. But I've learned my lesson about putting trust in people too quickly. I'm sorry if you're bearing the brunt of that, but I'm done trusting people." Especially of the male persuasion, I add silently.

"If it makes you feel better, you're paying me well to care for you."

"Not really, no. So money is your motivator—do you have a wife somewhere who doesn't treat you right? Are you misunderstood? Frustrated? Doesn't she listen to you?"

George slams his folder into his briefcase. "You're way too young to be so bitter, Morgan. So you've made a mistake. Welcome to the real world. You've been hurt; doesn't that make you special? I have to say it's better to be hurt than bitter. Bitterness is like a well gone bad. Heartache crushes the spirit. I've survived it, and I'm here to tell about it, and God gave me the greatest blessing from that suffering."

"Thank you, Billy Graham." I gather up my purse. "In fact, I am planning to trust you. So don't let me down."

chapter

21

Poppy drives me back to the penthouse, and I decide I'm going to grab as much paperwork as I can find and stuff it into my Coach overnight bag. I want to know exactly what I'm accused of and just how much I may actually be guilty of. Maybe I'll be like those men who get their law degree in prison.

"I like George," Poppy says as we reach the apartment.

"How nice for you. He's single—do you want me to set you up?"

"As if."

"As if, what?"

"As if a guy in a European suit is going to be interested in me. He has good energy, though. You might keep that in mind, Morgan. In case you ever get interested in the male species again."

"Really? Good energy?" I say with too much enthusiasm.

"Seriously good energy. I just wanted to reach out my palm and feel it."

"Oversharing, Poppy. Don't scare me. I can put up with only so much of the weird talk, okay? When you start feeling for people's energy, you totally lose me, and I think sanitarium."

"In the beginning, God created light. Light equals energy, God's first building block."

"You scare me. Seriously, sometimes, Poppy, you sound like you worship at one of those transcendental schools of enlightenment."

She shakes her head, "Absolutely not. I'm a Christian through and through. I just believe God created the body to heal itself for the most part. We need to be quiet and listen. The body tells you so much if you only listen to it. But you know, when you get out of whack, it's harder and harder to hear."

"Enough, though, all right?"

"It doesn't matter if I'm interested in the hot lawyer anyway, because George has eyes for no one but you. Did you notice he looks at you like Max looks at Lilly?" She shakes her hand. "I felt it. Seriously hot. Now there's some energy."

"He does?" I almost want to tell Poppy what happened in that interrogation room, but I know better. My friends have heard from me and my false-hope handbag way too often.

"Listen, I'll pick you up in an hour. I called Lilly on the cell phone, and I'm going to pick her up. She has to work while we're at the spa, but she's coming and bringing her sketch book and a gown she has to finish."

"Perfect. Give me at least an hour."

I rush into my father's office while Poppy goes back down the elevator. I start to go through more of the paperwork he left strewn on the floor. There are countless receipts and bank statements from a bank in Caicos. *Lord, I don't even know where that is! Have mercy on me.*

I look over the statements, and my stomach churns. There is more money in these banks than I ever thought possible. I always knew my father had money. I just had no clue how much. One particular copy of a check shows my signature for our mortgage, which is made out to a bank in Bermuda. This does not look good.

One thing is certain, the diamond business means noth-ing to him. It's a front. I look at all the bank accounts, and my name is on at least half the statements. I know my father thinks he was protecting me, helping to ensure my future. As it turns out, my future may be life without parole.

"What are you doing?"

"Ah!" I turn around to see Mrs. Henry standing over me, her fist resting firmly against her full hip.

"Did you find what you're looking for?" She goes for the paperwork and starts to stack it.

"Mrs. Henry, what are you doing here? I thought you'd be at the hospital with my dad."

"It turns out his lovely Gwen is taking fine care of him and doesn't want me around."

"Do you know I've been arrested?" I ask sheepishly. I mean, she could have called the feds herself for all I know.

"The men were here for you earlier."

"And you told them when I'd be back?"

"I did no such thing, Miss Morgan. They obviously came back."

"Thanks for the warning. I do still have a cell phone."

She picks up more of the paperwork. "What have they charged you with?"

"Tax evasion and fraud."

She nods knowingly.

"You don't seem surprised."

"Why would I be? Your father's been making mysterious trips for years, and he pays me way more than seems fitting for what I do. I've learned to not ask questions. I figured there had to be some sort of bribe involved. But since it's putting my grandson through college, I hardly saw the need to ask about it."

"What will happen to you if we go to jail?" I ask her, just to see if she's concerned.

She's not. "I imagine I'll retire. I've been squirreling away money since I started here. Your mother left me a small stipend when she died. Well, that's not true—it was quite healthy for the times. Reaganomics, you know. It was the best of times, it was the best of times."

Mrs. Henry has always been somewhat of an unknown to me. I can remember her sopping up the sweat from my mother's forehead, crushing the many pills, and putting them in homemade cheesy-mashed potatoes. Much to my mother's dismay. Although she weighed about eighty pounds during her illness, Traci Malliard was so worried about gaining weight it was a chore to get her to eat.

Yet in all her concern for my mother, I can't remember a single thing Mrs. Henry ever did that was kind for either me or my father. She did a lot. Just none of it out of the goodness of her heart. My memory is riddled with her cool and aloof demeanor, her absolute inability to speak to me in a warm way, and her apparent anger, always simmering under the surface. I was afraid that any step I made might tip her to boiling over, and so I stayed clear. It was as though even looking at me was a chore for her.

"But you never questioned anything my father did?" I ask.

"I never thought your father would do anything illegal. I still don't, Morgan. He's a businessman. He always put money ahead of anything else, there's no doubt about that, but he's about playing the game, not cheating it. You'll be fine. You always are."

"Let's hope that's the case."

"I never expected to hear that out of your mouth."

Neither did I.

"Why have you stayed so long?" I get up from the floor

and find my way to the leather sofa. "You obviously never liked my father or me."

"It's not that I didn't like you, Morgan. It's that I saw what your father did to your mother, and I have a hard time forgiving, I suppose. She was a fragile lady, your mother. But I know that she would have wanted you looked after, so I just kept to myself."

I start to laugh. "You're saying you stayed for me? You, who never gave me a moment's attention or a word of kindness? You stayed for me, is that right?"

"Morgan, things are often more complicated than they look from our own perspectives. I was never the motherly type—you can ask my own daughter if you don't believe me—but I did see to it that you always had three square meals every day. And when your father tried to talk you out of going to college, it was me who pushed you into Stanford."

"I thought you were trying to get rid of me."

"I was trying to make sure you had a life of your own. That's what your mother never had. She didn't have the education or the talent to make it on her own. She was beautiful, there's no doubting that, but she lacked the star quality on the screen. She was always going to be second rate in terms of acting, and I think she understood that. That's why she married your father in the first place. She thought he'd care for her."

"He did care for her!" I insist. "He made sure she had round-the-clock care." But as I voice my contradictions to her tale, I'm only prodding to hear more. I always thought there was more to the story, but I was too afraid to deal with the truth. If I have to deal with a low-security, federal prison, I imagine this will be a walk in the park.

"He didn't really care, Morgan, not in the important ways."

This comment gives me pause as I think about my mother and her screeching voice calling after my father. But there's one scene I'm seeing as if for the first time, and it's my mother yelling at my father's back.

"Did he pay attention to her?"

"Not after the first year. By then, she was like a worn toy to a child. He'd moved beyond being interested."

I feel the tears sting my eyes as I think about hearing anything negative about my father. "I saw what he took from my mother. I saw what he endured. And he never abandoned her, Mrs. Henry. He made sure she had the best care her whole life."

But even as I say it, I don't fully believe it. The memories are coming back more vividly now. My mother crying after my father, begging him not to go to a meeting, and him slamming the door on her while she sobbed.

Mrs. Henry smiles condescendingly at me. "Sometimes, Morgan, people can be physically present and yet they still have abandoned you."

I can't speak. In my subconscious, I know what she says is true. My home has always had a layer of frost on its walls.

"I have something for you." She exits my father's office, and I start to rifle through all the paperwork, and I see my name on nearly every sheet. I am in so much trouble, it's not even funny. As he lies alone in that hospital room, I have a hard time feeling anything toward my father. I search for the excuses that he had my best interests at heart, but right now, they're not ringing true.

I look at the paperwork, and the shredder sitting behind it, and I cringe at the thought. For about one second I think of shredding everything. Not because it's evidence of my guilt, but because it's evidence that my father is not the man I have always thought him to be: hard-nosed and lacking emotion, but always, always the one who had my best interests at heart. Even when he wanted to exploit my publicity for the store, it was so my inheritance might grow. I know my father.

Mrs. Henry comes back and sees me hovering over the shredder. "Don't do it, Morgan. Besides, the government has already been here. If they wanted it, they have it."

I pull the papers away. "I only thought of it for a moment. I wouldn't have done it." And really, I wouldn't have. God did give me a conscience.

Mrs. Henry hands me a pretty envelope in pink linen that reads "Mrs. Traci Malliard" in raised letters in the upper left-hand corner. My name is scrawled across the front. I run my fingers over the letters.

"Where did this come from?" I ask, knowing full well it's my mother's handwriting. Even though I was ten when she passed, I remember that much. Is there anything more personal when someone's gone than her handwriting? Or her voice on the answering machine? It's haunting, and yet you can't bring yourself to erase it.

"I'll leave you alone." Mrs. Henry exits the room and shuts the office's double doors behind her.

I stare at the envelope for a long time, wondering what my mother might possibly want to say to me all these years later, and why Mrs. Henry would keep it for so long.

Finally I jump up from the sofa and follow Mrs. Henry into the sterile kitchen, its granite countertops freshly gleaming, the strong scent of the polisher lingering. "Why now?" I ask, holding up the envelope.

"You're finally ready to hear it. I hoped that day would come. Independence Day, I'll call it. I needed to know that you saw the chink in your father's armor."

I look down at the envelope, and I say a small prayer. I can't help but wonder what was behind my mother's stunning façade, and if perhaps this holds the key. I want to tear into it, and be done, but I'm so worried I'll be disappointed that I stuff it into my coat pocket. "I'll read it at the spa."

"You're going to that spa? Again? Morgan, you have an obsession."

"I do." I square my shoulders, just to show her I mean it. The spa is the one place on earth I feel free.

She shakes her head as she walks away from me. "You're your mother's daughter, all right."

"I think this is the kind of letter that should be followed with a hot-stone massage chaser."

Mrs. Henry rolls her eyes, and I forage through her heavenly leftovers in the refrigerator. George is living in a fantasy world if he thought he could feed me better than this. I sigh dreamily.

"What's the sighing about?"

"Do you think I'll ever get married, Mrs. Henry?"

"I sure hope so, Miss Morgan, and I hope all these test runs you've taken have taught you a thing or two your mother never learned." She doesn't say this with a hint of loving-kindness or concern. It's more of an attack. Sort of the equivalent of, "If you can find someone stupid enough, sure you can get married."

Mrs. Henry shoos me out of the way and prepares something for me while I sit at the kitchen island wondering what kind of relationship my parents actually had. I thought Mrs. Henry held the key to my history, but it's clear she's not about to share it with me. My parents' icy realm frosted all who lived here, apparently.

It's really no wonder my father picked diamonds as his business. They are the hardest substance on the planet, and I imagine he feels a certain kinship to them.

chapter 22

Before we leave San Francisco, we go by the gym and pick up my Beamer. I think if you're going to go to prison for extortion, fraud, and tax evasion, you should definitely go in a high-end German car. It shows that at least you have good taste and appreciate fine engineering. So we arrive at the Spa Del Mar in style, and let's just say they aren't surprised to see us. I'm struck by something I learned back in my church counseling days (when I actually thought I should be counseling, rather than realizing I was more the counselee). Addictive behavior is a cycle. Something negative happens, it triggers a response in us, and we need instant gratification. And so we fill ourselves with whatever that gratification is, be it alcohol, caffeine, marriage proposals, etc.

Lilly is addicted to Lysol. Apparently, bad smells are her trigger.

Poppy is addicted to good, clean living and natural oils. I have no idea what her deal is. But I have a feeling it's related to endorphins.

I'm addicted to needing someone, like your standard orphan puppy. My trigger is loneliness. I hate to be alone— and yet, generally speaking, I've always been alone. There were always people around, but no one ever paid much attention.

My mother didn't want me, and my father was too busy for me. Somehow I've always thought being married would solve this cycle, and my loneliness. But right now that seems like an exceptionally stupid way to go about things. Especially when I could've always just gone to the spa for fulfillment.

Or perhaps I should have just gone to the pound and gotten a little toy poodle to cart around in my bag at all times, like all the movie stars. Perhaps then I might have avoided the bad-engagement phase of life, which led to ignoring what my father was up to and the necessity of getting a job and moving out of my dad's penthouse. To think a dog might have solved it all.

But the important thing in the addictive cycle is to break the response. So when I was completely tempted to kiss my lawyer? I didn't. I fought the temptation with all that I'm made of, and I'll continue to do so. This is what we call progress!

I'm addicted to Spa Del Mar, too, because this is the one place where I know my friends will always be here for me. Cell phones stop ringing (they don't usually work out here, although once in a great while we get lucky–or unlucky as the case may be). I know that when I speak here at the spa, some-one will listen. They won't be running off to their next meeting, unless it's a papaya facial, and I can totally forgive that. No one has anything more important to say than, "It's time for your papaya facial."

"I am pathetic, you know?" I toss my Coach overnight bag onto the bed.

"Sure, we know that. The three of us are pathetic. I do believe that's what made us friends in the first place," Lilly offers.

"I've discovered I'm addicted to people," I say. "I can't be alone."

"Like a codependent?" Poppy asks.

"Sort of, but I can't really find anyone to be codependent with, so I think I'm just dependent. 'Insert current boyfriend here.'"

"You should get a dog," Lilly says.

"That's exactly what I was thinking!" I answer, amazed that my friends and I think so much alike.

"You might want to wait until you find out about the charges, though. They don't let dogs in prison."

"Lilly!" Poppy chastises. "Ixnay on the isonpray."

"I may not be concierge material, but I do know my Pig Latin, Poppy."

She laughs. "We really should have taken a language at Stanford."

"Obviously."

"So what are you going to do about this addiction to people?"

"We all have addictive behavior, Lilly. You're addicted to Lysol, and maybe success, too. Poppy's addicted to clean living, and getting everyone else to live her way. She's a control freak of sorts."

"As I said, now that you've figured us all out, what do you intend to do about it? And I don't really see my Lysol addiction as all that upsetting, actually. Bacteria-scented rooms are worse. And how is Poppy running 10-Ks and living clean bad? I mean, have you seen the girl's body lately?" Lilly looks over Poppy and lifts her skirt above her knees. "Now, if we could only get her to actually show that body off a bit." Lilly sighs. "That's her addiction—bad clothing. She's got the body of Jessica Simpson in Daisy Dukes under the style of Whoopi Goldberg. That ain't right."

Poppy sighs and rolls her eyes. "No one wants to see me in Daisy Dukes."

"No one wants to see anyone in Daisy Dukes," Lilly says.

"What about your inability to commit to a good man, for fear you might miss the success boat?" I ask Lilly pointedly. "As if getting married will get in your way?"

"I'm not afraid to get married," Lilly says, dismissing me, because clearly she doesn't want to talk about Max. "Poppy, at least let me make you a pair of jeans. You would rule the sidewalk in a pair of my jeans."

Poppy shakes her head. "Too stiff. I don't like denim."

"Oh no, my jeans are like butter. They will hug you and your curves like buttah, I tell you." Lilly raises her eyebrow and rethinks her strategy. "Natural fibers. All-natural fibers, and you look good, too. How bad could it be?"

"You're avoiding the subject Lilly. I'm on to you."

"I'm not avoiding the subject. I'm changing the subject. I just don't understand what your delving into addictions has to do with me. Let's focus on why you have to have a boyfriend, all right?"

She looks at me and sees my frustration, and I can see her guilt well up on her expression. "I'm sorry, Morgan. You're addicted to people. That's a good step for you to figure that out. We just need to find you a decent person to be addicted to."

"I think I'm going to stick with my faith from here on out. I wonder if being an evangelical Christian, I'm eligible to be a nun."

"Nuns don't get pedicures every week," Poppy reminds me.

"It's that whole living simply thing," Lilly agrees.

"I might be living more simply than the nuns if the feds get their way."

"Would you stop?"

"We're here for you Morgan. This could be your—" Poppy cuts herself off.

"You can say it. My last shot at freedom. My last visit to Spa Del Mar for a very long time." I put my head down. "Well, you know Martha Stewart lost weight in prison; maybe that will happen for me. I'm going to be an optimist. Maybe I'll meet a cute prison guard."

"Martha wasn't a six to begin with, Morgan." Lilly shakes her head. "And aren't the prison guards women?"

"How would I know?" I pull the pink envelope from my jacket pocket. "I have a letter here from my mother."

After a moment in which both Lilly and Poppy blink at my non sequitur, Lilly shakes her head. "Oh, be careful with that. My biological mother came to visit me, and I only got abandoned all over again." She takes the envelope from my hand. "Do you want me to read it to you?"

"Will you tell me what it really says?" I ask.

"Maybe." Lilly opens the envelope carefully, and I watch as her eyes scan the contents. The letter is short, and when she's done Lilly looks up at me with tears in her eyes. "Your mother experience is better than mine."

"Let me see it!" I grab the letter from her hands and allow myself to focus first on the beautiful script my mother had. "She was such an artist," I say. It's so strange to think after all these years my mother had something she wanted to say to me.

May 7, 1985
Dear Morgan:
If you're reading this, most likely the cancer finished its job, and I am on to the next level of living. I have asked Grace Henry to give this to you when she thinks you are old enough to hear it. There is so much I want to apologize for, so much I should have done for you, but I suppose this is the way it's supposed to be. Your father will marry again, and find another woman to fill in where I

was so inadequate. I wanted to be a good mother, but there was nothing in me, no reserves and no motherly instincts. Everyone told me that I'd find them, they were there dormant in me, but I found that this wasn't true. Being a mother involved offering something of myself that simply wasn't there.

You probably remember that your father and I had a combative marriage. We were not in love when we married, but I thought his care of me would fulfill something I'd been missing in my own experience. He thought he might train me to be the right kind of wife who would be accepted into his world. For the most part, I think we achieved our goals, but the crack in our great plan was you. We could fool the whole of San Francisco, but we could never fool you, my love. You saw who we really were. I wish that I'd taken the time to grab you up in my arms and hug you with all my strength. It's what I wanted to do, but it was too late for you. You were afraid of me, and I can't say I blame you.

I've asked Mrs. Henry to make sure you get an education, and I have prayed that if there's a God, He will hear my prayer and not let you make the same mistakes. You are a beautiful treasure, Morgan, the best thing I ever did in this lifetime, and I want the path to be easier for you. Get an education. Make your own money. Know that I loved you, even if I didn't know how to show it. I will always love you, Morgan. When I think of some of the things I've said to you, I feel the cancer in my bones, and I think I deserve it and more. Be love, Morgan. Don't let them break you.

All my love,
Mom

My friends are flanking me, their tears as apparent as my own, but my first awful thought is, *This is a day late and a dollar short! Get an education? Be independent? Thank you, Mrs. Henry, for handing this to me after the Feds came with my less-*

than-independent name attached to a grand-jury hearing.

My friends hug me from each side. "I think Mrs. Henry gave this to me a little late. I could have used the 'make your own money' advice a little earlier in the process."

We all laugh through our tears.

"Let's drive into town and see a movie," Lilly says.

"And eat at that fattening steak place," Poppy adds.

We both look at her, surprised that she'd not have a lecture for such a suggestion.

"Vitamin B12," she says, and we giggle. "And vitamin B6."

"That is not going to help you detox tomorrow, during your facial and massage," I remind her.

"No, it's not," Poppy admits. "But we're about breaking our addictions this weekend, aren't we?"

I grab my friends' hands, and I praise God for their friendship. As I stand on the verge of legal uncertainty, I have to say that they are my constants. They remind me that God is up there, and He is listening.

My emotions are in full tilt as I discover just how much my mother and I were alike, and how we both looked in the wrong places for love. Actually, in the same man. My father may not be evil, but he is certainly not a reservoir of love. His well ran dry a long time ago, and he filled the coffers with gold instead. I've thought about calling him a million times, but right now, I'm so confused I'm just happy for the respite.

"So? Steak?" Poppy asks.

"Steak," I answer, feeling a bit like I'm enjoying my last meal. But the thing is? I'm going to enjoy it.

My mother loved me. She had an odd way of showing it, but in order to break this addiction, I have to show it, and build on this letter of encouragement.

"I love you gals!"

"What's not to love?" Lilly asks.

We get dressed for dinner, and I allow Poppy to dab my wrists with essential oils that will lead to calmness. This definitely beats buying shoes, and it fills a far deeper need. The words of my favorite hymn come to mind: "Here's my heart, O take and seal it, seal it for thy courts above."

In my mother's way, that's exactly what she was trying to say: share your heart with the right people, and seal it from harm. Okay, maybe I'm taking liberties. But my mother loved me. Right now, I could sit in prison with this thought. It changes everything.

S teak. Filet mignon, to be exact, and it was only the beginning. We indulged in Caesar salad, minestrone soup, and tiramisu—all served with several glasses of Diet Coke. Literally, they could have rolled us out of the restaurant, like Violet Beauregarde out of Willie Wonka's factory.

"Let's go to the movies!" Lilly says when we exit the restaurant.

"Chick flick." Poppy agrees.

"Poppy, what's gotten into you? What about detoxing to purify our systems before tomorrow?" I ask.

"So we'll get acne after the facial. Big deal. We survived puberty, we can survive this. It's not like any of us have dates, except Lilly, and she doesn't even care."

"Are you not feeling well?"

"No, just ready to have some fun." Poppy claps her hands together. "Let's boogie."

"What is going on?" I ask. "We know your type of fun has nothing to do with eating badly and watching a chick flick. You do realize we'll have to get popcorn and candy at the theater."

"It's the rule," Lilly adds with a shrug.

"I want to break my addictions, too. Why should you guys have all the fun? I need my own issues, don't I? I don't want to be left out. Besides, I'm practicing to get on *Survivor*."

"The TV show?"

Poppy nods.

"No offense, Poppy, but I think what you eat now is closer to what they're going to give you on *Survivor*. Don't go getting taste buds now. It will totally harm your chances."

"I can't imagine who would want to be on that show. I mean, unless you're looking to lose weight, what's the point?" Lilly adds.

"It's about facing your fears, struggling against the elements, and winning, proving to yourself you can do it," Poppy says enthusiastically.

"To prove what? That you can live on bugs? When are Americans going to actually need this skill?" Lilly asks.

"I think that's *Fear Factor*," I clarify for Lilly.

"Still, don't you wonder what other countries think of us and our entertainment? We want to watch people eat disgusting things. How weird is that?"

"It's strange," I agree.

We get into the Beamer, which is currently being tracked by the feds according to George. He told me they would, and also that I won't be allowed to leave the county without permission. This is before anyone finds me guilty, I might add. This is after the charges are read. So much for a free country and innocent until proven guilty. I fear I'll be bidding good-bye to Spa Del Mar, and I think that's why I was so anxious to get down here for one last hurrah.

We're just arriving at the theaters when Lilly's cell phone rings, and we all groan. Apparently, the phones work out here, and I have to say, being free and gorging ourselves on fattening food was a very liberating experience. It was like I was flying! (Of course, now I feel nailed to the ground by fat calories, but that's another story.)

"Lilly Jacobs Design," she says into the phone. "Uh-huh. Yes. Right." More waiting. "I'll be back soon." She clicks the phone shut and stares at us, the lights from the parking lot highlighting her face and her flattened, pomaded hair. Lilly is under the distinct impression that big hair makes her less professional. In actuality, the pasted look is not for her. Max has tried to tell her that, as have we, but daily she applies a litany of flattening products on her hair. At least she's not going to the salon for straightening anymore. She learned her lesson when her promotion went to someone else the last time. I guess we all take baby steps, don't we?

"Who was that?" I ask.

"Max. I didn't actually tell him I was leaving town."

"Are you nuts?" I squeal. "Why not?"

"His mother came to town by surprise. I think it was good timing that I left."

I just shake my head. "You know, how about if I show up at Max's house and claim to be his girlfriend, because I'll tell you, I'd have that man to my father's store before he could finish his next column."

"Come on, the movie's starting," Lilly says.

"Not for us, it's not. We're going to the spa. I'm going to see if they're offering a hot-stone massage and lobotomy session for you, Lilly."

"Why are you so anxious to get me married off? What if Max's mother disowns him? Won't you feel bad then?"

I laugh out loud at this. "Lilly, you would never allow yourself to fail at anything you set your mind to. We're going home, and you are going to meet Max's mother. What's wrong with you?"

"Well, I didn't exactly have a stellar experience with my

own mother. What makes you think Max's will like me?" She drops her head in her hands, "Oh gosh, guys. If you only knew."

"Max loves you, and it behooves a mother-in-law to like her daughter-in-law. The daughter-in-law is the key to unlock the grandchild door. If you didn't love him that would be one thing, but you're just completely warped. We're going to fix your addiction, change it from Lysol to a view of the Bay. A view you can only get in Max's house."

"Why is it such an issue for you? You should be more worried about Poppy trying to get on *Survivor*."

The truth is it's easier to worry about Lilly's garbage. Lilly's stuff can be fixed. Mine is completely out of my hands. "Do you know how the frog in the water gets really comfortable, when in fact he's sort of reaching the boiling point?"

"I've heard that story."

"That's what you're doing, Lilly. You're boiling over in your own filth, and spraying Lysol isn't fixing the problem. You're like a walking bacterial infection, and you won't take Max, the antibiotic."

Poppy shakes her head. "It would be a good analogy, but you shouldn't take antibiotics. They're making infection impervious to the antibiotics."

"Do you mind? It's an analogy. Not medical advice."

"It's not a very good analogy is all I'm saying."

"It's good for Lilly; she hates bacteria. I'm trying to show her she's becoming what she hates because of fear."

"I thought we were going to the movies."

"I thought when you let your hair go natural, you were fixed, but I can see by the shellac currently on your hair you're not quite comfortable in your own skin at the moment."

"Morgan, I appreciate your worrying about me, but Max and I are fine. You're creating trauma where there is none.

Relax, will you?"

But of course, if I relax, I have to think about all my own garbage, and I don't want to go there. "Max is your man, Lilly."

"I'm not arguing that. I'm only saying his mother might become a serial killer when she finds out I've trapped her son."

"If there's a serial killer present, it's Nate. Freak of nature. Who would put up with a smelly dog like that? And how he's always hovering ready to offer a word of encouragement while he treats his own girlfriend with contempt? What do you see in him as a friend?"

"He loves Charley," Lilly immediately comes to Nate's defense. "Nate accepts people and dogs for who they are. He doesn't expect anything more of them than they can handle."

Please. "Is that what this is about? You think Max wants more out of you?"

"I know his mother does."

"You don't know any such thing. You've never bothered to meet the woman."

"Life is good. Why do I want to mess with it?"

"I didn't mess with it, and look where it got me. Ignorance is not bliss. Ignorance is fifteen years to life."

"You're different—you trusted too many people. I don't trust anyone. Right now, it seems to be to my benefit."

"Until you lose Max."

"I can't make Max stay, Morgan. If he wants to leave he's free to go, but there's more to our story. It's just not the right time to be talking about it."

Her words cut me to the core, not because of her great strength, but because of my own great weakness. I don't just want to be married. I want a man to look at me like Max looks at Lilly. I know Poppy said that George did look at me that way, but I am probably just a human wallet to him. If he gets into my good graces, and even if he doesn't, he comes out a winner. I could be headed for prison, and a substantial portion of my money is still headed for George's wallet.

"I think you're crazy," I say quietly.

"I'm sure I am. One does not get raised by my nana and turn out normal," Lilly laughs. "Are we going to the movies or not?"

"Not," Poppy and I say in unison. "Let's get back to the spa and go in the hot tub," I add.

After we drive back to the hotel, I make excuses to the girls and walk into the courtyard under the lit jacaranda tree. Smelling the strong scent of the eucalyptus trees, I think twice about what I'm about to do, but I do it anyway. If I'm going to break my addictions, it's going to take something stronger than Diet Coke. I take out my cell phone, which by some miracle is actually getting a signal, and I punch in George's cell phone number.

"Morgan," he says when he picks up. "Is everything all right?"

I look at my cell phone and see it's just shortly before eleven p.m.

"Everything's okay," I say. Not adding that I just wanted to hear his calm voice. That I just wanted to know he was there, on the other end of the phone line when I called for him. If I were to explain any of this, he'd know just how pathetic I am. That it wasn't an accident I have been a staple in the *San Francisco Chronicle* for the last month.

"Do you need anything, Morgan?"

I'm silent. I can't think of a thing to say. Why on earth did I make this phone call? And what happened to the days when you could just call a boy and hang up? Stupid caller ID.

"No, I don't need anything," I finally say.

"Morgan, do you need me to come get you?"

"No, I'm at the spa. We drove down this afternoon. It's been a long day. I'm sorry I woke you."

"You didn't wake me. I'm working on your case."

"I'm not guilty, George."

"I know that, Morgan."

"It might not make a difference, true?"

"It makes a big difference."

"I'm sorry I called. I don't know why I did. A week ago I was looking for a purpose. Now my purpose is to stay out of jail."

"I'm glad you called me, Morgan. I hope it means you trust me."

Oh heavens, I hope it doesn't mean that. Because I haven't known George nearly long enough to trust him.

"I should get back to my friends."

"This is a long road, Morgan. The trial probably won't happen for a year or more."

"They won't put me in prison until then?"

"No, but in some ways, they might as well. They'll tap your phone, they'll give you a probation officer who can turn up at any time, and they'll freeze your assets. It won't be a party, regardless."

I sigh and say good-bye before standing under the trees and chastising myself again for calling George. For hoping a man could solve my problems and take me away on his white steed. The addictive cycle has started again. I knew better. But I called him anyway, and he calmed me down. Just like Andy's voice used to do, just like Marcus's used to do. I need help. There has to be some twelve-step process for this kind of pathetic.

Pathetic is easier to see on friends, though, and I am so missing the hot-stone massage to get Lilly back where she belongs. If she gives me any trouble, meeting Max's mother is going to be the least of her problems.

chapter 24

W here are you?" My dad's gruff voice is "business as usual." If there is any weakness, he does not let on. "My lawyer thought it best for us to stay apart. He thinks it will help our case."

"Our case is his problem. You're acting like we're guilty, Morgan. Gwen has been telling me it's simply not right to have my daughter absent at the hospital. What will the paper think when they get word? I'll not have it look like you've abandoned me. You get down here."

Gwen says? Gwen can't even dress herself. Don't get me started. "Dad, have you seen the indictment? We do look guilty. There's no sense in giving them more than they already have. Caicos, Dad? Our money is in some foreign country and I don't even know where it is."

"There's nothing wrong with banking offshore and what did I send you to Stanford for if you weren't going to learn where Caicos was? The government tries to make you sound guilty for sound business investing, but I sheltered my money legally. They'd take everything if we let them."

"Our money," I correct. "If I'm named in the proceedings the least you can do is call it ours."

"I used your name for your own protection, Morgan. That

way I could do our taxes together, and that saves us money in the long run. I did you a favor. There's no death tax if it's already in your name."

"It feels like the death tax now. How's your health, Daddy?" I think about him lying in the hospital room, and my heart rises in my throat. For all he is, he's my daddy, and I love him like I always have. Even if I do want to throttle him at the moment.

"I've been better. When will you be home—to the town home? Gwen is getting nervous about you being out in time for the contractors to enter the apartment. You do realize you'll have to move for them to come in."

"You just hired designers." There is no way they can possibly have work approved and permits ready. "Besides, did you ever think maybe this wasn't the best possible time for a remodel?"

"I'm not guilty, I'm not going to act guilty. You don't understand money, and we can't stop living while the government gets its act together. They'll understand what I did was legal, and we'll have a new penthouse. It's part of the game, Morgan—you can't let them see you sweat."

"Dad, our assets are going to be frozen. You couldn't find a contractor or a bank to sign on to this right now if they lacked business in San Francisco. And they don't."

"You let me worry about the money."

"Yeah, that's seemed to work for me. I understand my name is on a lot of banking paperwork, and that makes me responsible. I know that much. I have a right to be nervous." I feel my jaw tightening. Isn't that just my dad's way? To tell me not to worry my pretty little head while the guys in suits come get me. I honestly don't know which feels worse: being dumped publicly, losing all my money, or knowing my dad just doesn't care about any of it. No, that's not true. But I know my father's bristling effect has shocked me for the last time.

"Don't worry about things that don't concern you. The lawyers and I will handle this. Just keep to yourself and attend the parties like you would normally do. George's partner is handling my case, and it's their job to worry about it. Not ours, Morgan."

"I'm not going to any parties, Dad. I'm the laughingstock of San Francisco, and I would prefer a low profile at this point. I'm looking for a job, and I'll stay at Lilly's if that makes Gwen happy."

"You can't let them talk you down, Morgan. If they do so, they win, and we are not about to go down without a fight, all right? What job? You don't need a job. If you get yourself a job now, they'll say I didn't provide for you."

If I ever had any fight in me for the social scene, it's long since gone. Numbed by seeing myself in a wedding dress every day, attached to the scoffing headlines. "I'm getting a job, Dad. I was looking for one when I found out about the charges and your illness."

"You don't worry about me. It's going to take more than a stroke to bring a Malliard down."

More than a stroke.

More than an extortion case.

More than a flurry of embarrassing headlines.

My dad is a stronger Malliard than me. Any one of those things, and I'm ready to throw in the towel and beg for mercy.

I twist the gargantuan blue diamond on my hand. It's really a disgusting display of cash, but when I reach to pull it off, I find it's wrenched on like Drusilla's foot in Cinderella's shoe.

"Daddy, I don't ask for much, but please don't rip apart the penthouse right now. George tells me we're going to be on house arrest of sorts until this is through. 'Grand-jury indictment' is a phrase the newspaper loves to use, and it's going to become synonymous with the Malliard name. At least let us have our sanctuary."

"I'm going on with my life. They're not going to have their way with me. Gwen is right beside me all the way, and I think she's right about you having a place of your own."

"Just like a good, loyal breed."

"What did you say?"

"Nothing, Daddy. Frozen assets mean we're not going to buy any real estate soon. Listen, I'll call you every morning and night, but I have to get to work finding a job." And getting Lilly to meet her future mother-in-law.

"If you go looking for a job, they're going to think we're guilty. Are you not hearing me?" he says in a tone that usually has me acquiescing.

We are guilty, I think to myself. The government only has to prove it. "Be that as it may, Dad, I need something to stimulate me. Since I can't spend money, I might as well earn it."

"They can't freeze the offshore accounts. Do you need money?"

They can't freeze them, but he can't bring the money into the country either. A fact I'm sure he's going to figure out soon enough. "No, Dad. I'm fine." Thinking to myself, *They'll freeze it if we bring it into the country.* Or am I imagining things? "Please don't transfer anything until all this is over. You'll just get us in more trouble."

"If you want a job, make sure the Red & White Ball is covered for jewels this year. All right? Anything worth over $25,000 in the store needs a security guard, but we need to prove that San Francisco's Jeweler is still on top, still number one. Give us presence! I've ordered a whole array of rubies and garnets for this year, but remember, the money is in the white. Sell the diamonds. It's a pity it's not the Blue & White Ball with all those blue diamonds I bought."

"All right, Daddy."

"I raised you to get back on the horse, didn't I?"

"You did."

"So climb back on, Morgan. This is just a hurdle; you can jump hurdles. What were all those pony lessons for if you can't jump hurdles? Get your jodhpurs on and get out there."

I think about the letter from my mother, and I feel strength rise up within me. I think about how my life might have been different if my mother had had the strength to tell me she loved me. I swallow hard and say what needs to be said. "I love you, Dad."

"So you'll get to the store?"

"Did you hear what I said?" I ask.

"Morgan, I'm not going to die, there's no reason to get blubbery with me."

He hangs up on me, and I look at Lilly and Poppy, who won't meet my gaze. They know everything they need to about the conversation. It's really quite surprising I'm as normal as I am. I should have been fitted with a diamond-encrusted straitjacket a long time ago.

"Does Max know we're coming?" I ask. We had Lilly get a facial this morning while we quietly packed and snuck every-thing into the car. Then we talked about breakfast, got her into the car, and we're on our way back to San Francisco. I guess I've got a little of my father's deviousness in me after all.

"I called him when we stopped for coffee." Lilly rolls her eyes. "He thinks meeting his mother is a priority for me now. He's going to be sure to be available when we get home."

"Isn't that sweet?" Poppy says and means it.

"Let's stop and get his mother a gift before we go," I say.

"A present isn't going to help." Lilly crosses her arms like a small child about to throw a tantrum. "I'm still the wrong religion. Still not good enough for her precious son. She's going to kill us."

"Let's give her a spa package!" Poppy shouts. "We can talk about how we're the Spa Girls and how our friendship has grown with the spa, and make her feel like one of us. It's too bad we didn't think to get her a Spa Del Mar robe when we had the chance."

"Oh goody," Lilly deadpans. "She'll love knowing I have an expensive spa fetish that her son will have to support."

"That's a great idea! I have those essential oils you gave me. That would be perfect to throw them in there."

"Maybe while we're at it, we can get her some diamonds from your dad's store, Morgan, and let her know I like those, too."

"I'll stop by Blooms," I say, mentioning a local spa.

"I can't afford Blooms."

"You can't afford to buy your mother-in-law something cheap."

"What's my goal in buying her off?"

"Your goal is to not end up alone like your nana for all those years, and to find a man who is willing to put up with the Lysol thing. We don't play around when men find our weirdness cute. Am I right, Poppy?"

"If I found a guy who thought it was sexy that I could crack his back and maneuver him like a pretzel with ease? I'm so there."

"You two sound absolutely desperate," Lilly scoffs.

Need I remind her we met at a social that no one but us came to? Need I remind her we are all nearly thirty (Lilly *is* thirty) and none of us have a hope on the horizon of getting married but her? If that doesn't tell her we are, indeed, desperate, I don't know what will.

"You say desperate like it's a bad thing."

"Oh, I give up." Lilly brings out a baby can of Lysol from

her purse. But she wiggles it and shows me it's empty. "I was just throwing it away."

"Don't you dare spray that stuff in my Beamer! It may be all I have left when the U.S. government gets through with me. You'd think they'd have more important things to worry about."

"It's stuffy in here," Lilly whines.

"Only because you don't like the topic of conversation."

As we reach San Francisco, it's nearly lunch time, and Lilly cries hunger, but we're onto her game. We know she never eats and could probably last a week on a Cup O' Noodles, so we drive her straight to Max's house. I think Poppy and I are as curious as Lilly. Probably more so.

I look over at Lilly, and I can see her hands trembling and her finger on the Lysol trigger. She is as nervous as a new kitten.

"You really don't want to go?"

She looks at me with her eyes propped wide like the peaks of the Golden Gate.

"I'll take you home."

She just nods, and I steer the car towards her loft. It's not Max's mother Lilly is afraid of. It's Max, and we have to figure out why before she ends up designing her life away and collecting cats.

She could be heading home to my house, after all. To the house where the hearts are as unbreakable as diamonds.

chapter 25

"All right, Lilly. Out with it," Poppy grabs Lilly by the back of her shirt and doesn't release her as we reach the street in front of her loft.

"What?"

"When have you ever been afraid of anything? Besides bad hair, of course. You stood up to your nana. You overcame Sara the nightmare boss. What's this about? You're not afraid of marriage any more than Morgan is, and she should be afraid."

"Thank you," I say. "Could we leave me out of this?"

"First the weird, 'Oh I'm afraid of meeting his mother' thing, and now the lack of Lysol. Show me the second Lysol in your purse, Lilly."

She can't do it, and we're both stunned, but Poppy clearly notices more than I do.

"You didn't sneak a Diet Pepsi all weekend. Why not?" Then Poppy turns on me. "And don't think I don't notice you hanging out at the jacaranda tree by your lonesome, you and that two-liter bottle. What's going on?" Poppy narrows her eyes and looks directly into Lilly's wide-eyed, innocent gaze. Or, I should say, she tries to don this innocence, but she is the worst liar on the planet. I think all that Lysol infiltrated that part of her brain, and it's like truth serum—she cannot tell a lie.

Her expression contorts like a circus gymnast. "You're going to kill me."

"Lilly," I plead. "It's us. What could you have possibly done that you can't tell us? We knew you when you spied on that Colin creature in college and dropped your notebook in front of him, when you paused the VCR to kiss Johnny Depp's luscious lips on the TV screen. Heck, we knew you when—"

"Just never mind. I'll tell you, I'll tell you. No need to torture me." She nibbles on her lip. Her hair is in full frizz mode today. She didn't bother with the laminate she normally uses, and she's like one big puffball of hair. I suppose that's how Poppy figured out she's not being upfront with us. Lilly's issues are all in the hair. If the hair is bad, Lilly is feeling it. I wish I'd been more attentive, but I was too lost in my own world.

"You're going to be mad. I'm a little mad."

"People don't get mad. Dogs get mad—"

"People get angry," my friends finish for me.

"So you've heard it before; why don't you fix it?"

"We like to disrupt that prep school girl in you. It's endearing," Poppy says.

Lilly mats her hair down with her hands and sucks in a deep breath. "I can't believe I did this."

"Did what, Lilly?"

"I sort of pulled a Morgan. And I've been lecturing her, so I knew that I was going to get lectured, and I already know what I did deserves a lecture. I just haven't had to face the consequence yet like Morgan has."

I feel my brows lower, "Lilly, what did you do?"

"Max and I took a little trip late one night. It was the most gorgeous sunset that night, and the sky was just pink and purple and—"

"Lilly! Back to the story."

"So we sort of hopped in the car and headed towards South Lake Tahoe."

I cringe at the thought of Nevada. Home of my ever-so-brief marriage and my infamous annulment.

"And you gambled?" Poppy asks.

"Sort of. We got married."

"What!" I have never known Lilly to do a spontaneous thing in her life. Everything is calculated and exact and planned to the hilt. This is completely...Well, this is completely like me.

"Lilly!" Poppy says. "What on earth moved you to get married?"

"Max and I, we had a great arrangement as boyfriend and girlfriend. I'd go over there, I'd sketch. He'd watch TV for work. All was well and good until that one sunset." She pauses as though remembering the colors. "I just noticed his eyes, and we sort of . . . Oh, I don't know, we were like magnets. We just rushed each other. And all the while I know my nana is downstairs and she can walk up at any minute. I looked at Max, and I said, 'Baby, we gotta get out of here before we do something we'll regret or be held accountable for.' So we leave, and I'm thinking we're going to go get ice cream or something to cool off—even though it's a San Francisco summer night and freezing outside."

"Get to the wedding part," I say, grabbing Lilly's hand.

"So we get into the car. And remember that brooch he gave me of his grandmother's?"

"Sure, my dad said it was the highest quality," I offer, but from the looks I get, no one really cares.

"The engagement ring matched, and he had it in his pocket."

"So he asked you to marry him in the car?" Poppy asks.

"That's not very romantic," I offer.

"He said he knew the first time he saw me, and from being around my nana because of all the wonderful things she thought I was. And, um, go figure. But anyway, he said we were just wasting time. I thought about that six years I spent in finance, and that it really was a waste of time, and I thought, *Do I really have the time to waste? Who is coming along who is better than Max?* So we drove to Lake Tahoe, found us a wedding chapel, made out on the beach, and found us a hotel. The end." Then her face contorts. "Sorta."

My mouth is agape. I have been trying to get married for eons. Eons, I tell you, and Lilly just happens into it like it's buying a losing lottery ticket. There is no effort, there is no exchange of dowries. She just finds herself a rich, sexy husband by drawing dresses in the guy's house. Because conveniently he lives over her nana.

If my dad rented out a place, the guy would inevitably be at my house because he was short on rent or moving back with his mother. Life is so unfair.

But I couldn't be happier for Lilly.

If not insanely jealous.

"None of this explains why you are living in your loft with Morgan. Did you get married for a one-night stand?" Poppy steps back, and several horns honk behind us while we await the answer. It's a fall day, the best San Francisco has to offer, and we bask in the warmth of the rare, bright sunlight.

"Max has been trying to get me to move in as his wife, but we aren't quite sure how to break it to people. My nana is going to kill me for running off, and my mother-in-law is going to think I trapped her son for his money. When I found out she was coming, I thought moving in could easily happen after she visited. I designed her gown for the Red & White Ball next month, so I thought I'd use work as an excuse. I certainly have enough to do."

"Well, you have to tell them, Lilly."

Lilly clucks her tongue, shaking her head. "One night, we're looking at the view, and the next I'm a married woman."

"Where's your ring?"

"Max is getting it sized."

"You didn't take it to my dad?"

"Um, no, I didn't. He would have told everyone in San Francisco."

"My dad may be a lot of things, but indiscreet is hardly one of them."

"He would have told you," Lilly accuses.

"True."

"Let me get this straight." Poppy shakes out her long red tresses. "So you're not living with your husband because your nana's going to be mad you got married without the big wedding."

"That's part of it," Lilly explains. "The other half is that Max's mother is going to have to explain how to announce this to the society pages and ensure it's not a shotgun wedding. I still had the lease on my loft, and a lot of work to do, and we just sort of let things slide."

"Lilly, no one's going to think any such thing as a shotgun wedding. In nine months, they'll know better."

"Here's the funny part," Lilly says, kicking the sidewalk and looking at the street. "I am actually pregnant. Wedding-night baby, if you can believe that."

We're speechless. Even Poppy has nothing to say. Nothing to add about energy, good or bad, and she can't even work up something about the need for proper nutrition for baby.

I run through the spectrum of emotion. First, there's anger that any best friend of mine should get married and deny us a wedding. There's a deep envy streak growing by the minute as I think of Lilly, not even looking for love and it's found her doorstep. Then, there's the betrayal. How could she not tell us?

After a few minutes of goggling, Poppy tries a response. "Lilly . . . Wow, that's amazing. Congratulations!"

She starts to hug our friend, but Lilly groans and pushes her away. Again, she pats down her hair. "It's not amazing! It's humiliating, actually. I can't get a design business started for six years, but I can get pregnant on the very first night? Do I have the weirdest life or what? And just imagine what Max's mom is going to say. If there was any hope of a big wedding, it's definitely out of the question now. I doubt we can pull off what Mrs. Schwartz expects before I begin to show."

I finally find my voice as I decipher what she's told us. "Are you nuts? So you're not sleeping with your husband, but you're carrying his baby?" I'm astounded. I know Lilly has always done things relatively backward, like getting a finance degree and then a master's because she couldn't announce to her nana that she hated all of the above, but this takes the cake. This is her living our pathetic lives out when she has an actual choice.

"I'm not living with Max, but I'm taking my prenatal vitamins. And who said anything about celibacy? We have our ways. Besides, this way if I have any morning sickness, he won't have to deal with that."

"Good for you, Lilly. Make sure you're drinking plenty of no-sugar-added orange juice as well. Fresh squeezed is best," Poppy says. "And don't buy cheap prenatals; they put cheap binders in them. I'll get you the best."

"Oh, that sounds great, Poppy," Lilly nods.

I'm still trying to process all this. "There is no way on earth we're supporting you in this. We'll tell Mrs. Schwartz ourselves. It's only going to get worse if you put it off."

"So just how long have you actually been married?"

"A little over a month. I just found out about the baby the

day before yesterday. We didn't make it very long after the fashion show. I just never realized love was such a strong motivator. And I sort of lost my head, and we ended up in Tahoe before I knew it. Even with his broken leg." She gets a secret smile on her face. "It was worth it, though. He's worth it."

"Lilly, I can't believe you, who wasted all those years on the wrong degrees, could be so impulsive."

"Have you seen Max lately?" Poppy asks.

Translation: does he know about the baby?

"So now we get no bridesmaid's dresses? No Lilly Jacobs wedding gown for the town to behold."

She shakes her head. "None of the above. I haven't seen Max lately—well, not since he was here—and you're not getting bridesmaid's dresses. Just the satisfaction of knowing you are my maids of honor."

"Well, it's over now, but you've got to move in with your husband, Lilly. This is just weird."

"It is," she admits.

"What did you wear?"

"I wore a pair of jeans and flip-flops."

My best friend got married, and I wasn't there. There seems to be no justice here, and I'm still in a bit of mourning. "Why wouldn't you tell us? We would have come at any hour of the night, you know that."

She nods. She does know it, but apparently friends are no match for Max Schwartz. What irony—the purr of traffic above our heads from the freeway overhead, and Lilly's explaining to us that she's living my life:

She's married to a wonderful man.

She's having his baby.

She's not going to jail.

What the heck happened? Where was God when I

mentioned how desperately I wanted to be married and out from under my father's grip? I mean, did he just miss with the bolt of lightning and aim at Lilly by accident? I ask myself all these questions, but of course, it does me little good. I'm thrilled for Lilly. Really I am. But I feel more alone than ever. Just like when you're in a movie theater by yourself for a romantic comedy, and the couple in front of you is making out. It amplifies one's pathetic-ness.

There's a rumble above us, and the main apartment door opens with Kim rushing out the door, her half-opened suitcase thrown after her. It hits the landing, exploding the contents down the front steps in a waterfall of bad clothing behind her.

"And stay out!" Nate is at the doorway, and he slams the door with vigor.

I knew something was awry in that house. No woman puts up with a dog who smells like that without something festering beneath. Kim looks at us, trying to maintain her sense of dignity as she picks up the clothes. Lilly and Poppy both bend over and begin helping, but I'll admit, I'm too mesmerized by the scene to do anything but watch it unfold, like a roadside accident. I see Nate in the window beside the doorway, surveying his damage with a smug and yet grim smile. So, apparently, asking how Kim is feeling is probably not the best course of action.

Kim's ending with Lilly was no different. Kim decided she was moving in with Nate and left Lilly to pay the rent for that month. Sure, she helped her sew things for the business, but if Lilly's boss had found out, Sara Lang would have pulled funding faster than you could say tattoo. And yet, I don't know what Kim's story is, or why Lilly seems to care, but Lilly never abandons her. It seems no matter what this girl does, including living with the man who kissed Lilly full on the lips, Lilly just picks Kim up, dusts her off, and sets her back on course.

I think we have just witnessed the true Nate. The one who keeps Kim around as he needs her, and feeds off others to tell him how fabulous he is. Lilly still seems to think he's a fabulous person, and I'll grant her he's a very charming personality. But charming people generally don't vomit their girlfriend's stuff onto the sidewalk. However, Lilly's continuous support of Kim fascinates me in a sick sort of way. The entire codependent threesome needs to move on.

"I take it you're moving out," Lilly says.

Kim purses her lips and keeps stuffing her clothes into the suitcase.

"I could have told you he wasn't going to put up with your dating other guys. He found out?"

"Lilly, enough with the words of wisdom, okay?" She looks to Lilly with those eyes, and I can tell she's going to ask to stay in Lilly's loft, which is a bad idea on so many levels, so I step in front of Lilly.

"Listen, if—"

Kim holds a palm up in my face, "Listen, princess. I got nothing to say to you. Go back to Snob Hill and leave us poor vermin to our lives."

"Kim!" Lilly yells. "Do you mind? That's my best friend."

Kim looks back at me, and her hard expression softens. "Sorry, Morgan. I suppose you and I have more in common than I'd like. Men throwing us out on our ears and all that." The corner of her mouth turns up in a sly, devious way. "Can I crash at your place, Lil?"

"Morgan's staying with me right now. Besides, it wouldn't be good with Nate upstairs. You need to give him some time to cool off."

"I didn't think he had it in him," Poppy muses. "But his energy has always been draining."

Kim rolls her eyes, "Would you tell Hari Yogi to be quiet? I've just been dumped."

"Do you need a few days off?"

"Yeah, Einstein, I do."

For the life of me, I cannot understand why Lilly puts up with Kim. She's just bad news all the way around, from the scattering of tattoos evident all over her body—more readily viewable due to the lack of clothing she employs—to the plethora of body piercings. Now, I've lived in San Francisco long enough to know not to judge on the exterior, but what I've always noticed about Kim is her quick temper. Her inability to see the best in people, but to always assume the worst and speak of it rather than hold her tongue. How she managed to overlook Nate's many shortcomings in favor of picking on Lilly remains a mystery. But I guess charm goes a long way. It worked for Andy, so who am I to judge?

Kim tries another tactic and softens her tone, "I finished the Red & White ball gowns tonight. Mrs. Sheen will be picking hers up on Friday and Mrs. Schwartz is coming into town tomorrow, and she'll get hers then. I imagine you can just take that one to Max's. It's up at Nate's."

Lilly nods, and my hearts jerks just a bit as I hear about the Red & White Ball. This year's ball coverage will only remind me that the life I knew is over. Even if I manage to get in with my father's jewels, I'll be the laughingstock of the entire event. I'll be witness to everyone I know, dressed in their finest, snickering behind raised, cupped hands. I wonder if I'll even have access to the jewels or if those will be frozen, too. Frozen ice. If it wasn't so dismal, it might be funny.

"Where are you going to go?" Lilly asks.

"I thought maybe I'd go to Max's."

Um, I don't think so. If Lilly lets this woman anywhere near Max, I will personally hurt both of them.

"You can't go there," Lilly says. "His mother is visiting."

See how nice she is? I'd have told her, "You can't go near another one of my men, you pathetic tramp," but see, Lilly has grace and she's a much better Christian than I appear to be. And I was trained in such niceties. Doesn't say much for me.

"Kim, you can't keep living my life. Max is not going to take you in, and you can't ask him to. You should have figured this out before you decided that Nate was expendable. You're not going to keep taking from people I introduce you to."

"Lilly, I didn't cheat on him, you know I didn't. I love Nate."

"Then you've got to quit playing him like this. You purposely made him think you did."

"He won't marry me, Lilly. I thought if he thought I might go somewhere . . ." Suddenly tears are rolling down her cheeks and Lilly is rubbing her back.

Mental note: the dramatic someone-else-wants-me trick doesn't work either. Marriage is going to solve none of Kim's problems, and with striking clarity, I realize it's not going to solve mine either.

chapter 26

oppy's taking Lilly to get her hair cut and styled at my hair salon. She is treating her to the salon as an engagement gift. We want her to look her best when she meets Max's mother. I wish I could go, but I'm not inclined to show my face at the moment. I could use freshened highlights, but I have to find out where the money will come from.

I know that when faced with Mrs. Schwartz's prying questions Lilly will bounce back, and she'll stand firm. She always has, just like the Weebles. She wobbles, but she gets right back up again.

I unlock the latches at Lilly's loft, and I notice Nate at the stairwell.

"Lilly's gone," I say to him in a sharp voice.

"Did she take Kim with her?"

Do you care? "I don't know, Nate. I just know Kim's not staying here." I allow the keys to dangle from one lock, and I turn to face Nate. He's handsome, in an innocuous engineer-type way. Put it this way—he's no Orlando Bloom. He and Kim couldn't make a more opposite couple. He looks straight out of grad school with a perfect-part boyish haircut, and Kim looks as though she was kicked out of a rock band for too much partying. When I look into his eyes though, I see what she sees in him. There's something about Nate; he's always there when you need him. That steadiness is attractive, even when you know it comes with a cost and it's more an illusion than reality. Consistency doesn't have blowups that force your girlfriend's stuff onto the street. Consistent people don't find satisfaction in such theatrics.

I walk over to him, and when I think of what he did to Lilly, I want to punch him in his clean-cut face.

"Why do you and Kim do this?" I ask.

"Do what?" Nate asks with a breathy laugh.

"Emotionally zap those around you like a faulty lamp."

"I beg your pardon? If we're discussing relationship issues, I don't exactly think—"

"No, you don't exactly think, Nate." I push at his chest, and he wobbles back slightly. "You two think all this drama makes you both so desirable, but you look pathetic to the outside world. You do realize that? When you kissed Lilly and came to her rescue with computers and sewing machines, you got to play the big hero, didn't you? But look at you."

"Where were you, Morgan, when Lilly needed you?" His words hit like a fist. "At the Black & White Ball? Or wait, was her crisis during the start of the opera season?" He puts a finger at his chin. "I can't remember, but I know one thing. My loft was always open to Lilly. I made a mistake when I kissed her. I told her that, but unlike you, Lilly has a forgiving soul."

Looking at Nate, I'm so very grateful Lilly is married and free from his many "rescues," which only looked heroic when Lilly was drowning. I hope she sees now that he was only an anchor, pulling her down into his world—a world that appears bright and gleaming like his fancy espresso machine but is really just a façade. That's our precious Nate, saving the world one espresso at a time.

As I sit here judging him, though, my resolve weakens slightly and I don't want to answer his return volley.

"I was there for her when I knew she was in trouble." I grab the keys again and open Lilly's door. "But anyone can study my flaws; the newspaper makes it easy."

Nate gives a disgusted huff. "If Kim stops by, tell her to come over. We need to work this out."

"Right, because a woman who has just had her entire life thrown onto the front steps really should come back for more." I roll my eyes, thankful my conversation with Nate is over and that I have nothing more to work out with him.

Perhaps I haven't been the friend of the century to Lilly, but I'll tell you one thing, I won't make that mistake again with my Spa Girls. In my new reality, men are going to take a backseat to those who love me. Including my own father, who loves me in the best way he knows how. Why do I say this? Because when I look at Nate and Kim, I'm embarrassed to say my life isn't all that different from theirs. And yet I've been a Christian for years. Granted, I may not have slept around like Kim, but I squandered my emotions just as cheaply.

Inside Lilly's loft, I pick up the scraps of fabric she's left all over the floor and I set her desk to rights. I even find a hammer and hang a picture she's had sitting on the floor since I remember her moving in here. When I run out of "honey-do" items, I plop on the futon and waste time flipping channels, bouncing between Oprah and the cooking channel. I don't know why I find it so fascinating to watch people cook—I'm not actually sure how to work our stove at the penthouse—but it's one of those mundane pleasures that makes you feel so homey.

After a few hours of useless, mind-numbing television, I gather my sweater, climb into the cowboy boots Lilly bought me, and walk the short path to Lilly's church. I have no idea what my plan is, or why I expect anyone to be there at five p.m. on a Wednesday, but somehow my feet just keep stepping in front of each other. Perhaps it's the cowboy boots, and like a horse near the barn, I'm finding my way to the one world I know doesn't care who I am or what I've done this week.

When I get to the warehouse building, the door is propped open with an old music stand. I hear the faint music of a guitar, but when I wander in, the music stops suddenly. Kyle Keller, the man who seems to look right through me, is now looking directly at me.

"Don't stop on my account. I was enjoying it."

He doesn't start again, just taps at the guitar and keeps his gaze on me.

"Am I annoying you?" I ask.

"I'm practicing," he claims. Though it sounds eerily quiet. All right then, practice, little buddy.

"What are you practicing for?" I ask, hopeful there's some raucous, raging Christian party tonight to take my mind off the lawsuit and my lawyer's abs.

"Mid-week Bible study tonight. Do you want to join us?"

I shrug. "Oh I don't know. It's been a long time since I did a formal study." I was really hoping for more of a potluck of sorts. I rub my belly, wondering if I too will start to be as thin as Lilly living with her.

"Maybe if you hadn't let up on the study, you might have known your country singing star couldn't actually play the guitar."

"You know who I am."

"I'm not oblivious to the world. Plus, I take offense to people who claim to be musicians, like your former boyfriend. Real musicians work hard at the craft."

"You were oblivious to me the last time I came in."

"Lilly made us promise we would be. She called ahead on

her cell phone and made us agree. A six-foot blonde who looks like you walks into a singles group and no one pays attention? Yeah, that could happen." He starts to laugh and begins to pluck a few chords on his guitar.

"Lilly." I shake my head, not feeling nearly as guilty that I didn't go with her to Max's house. "She told me it was my clothes."

"I'm glad she did it. Everyone deserves the right to be unnoticed—to fly under the radar, as it were, once in a while. I imagine it's not easy for you."

"I'm only five foot eleven. Not six foot."

He laughs again. "Yeah, that makes a difference. So, you coming to Bible study tonight?"

"That depends. Has everyone been warned to ignore me tonight?"

"Hmm. Not yet. Do you want them to be warned?"

I think about this for a while. I mean, what girl doesn't want to be noticed? But instantly, I remember all the things I am currently known for. "Yes, I do think I'd like to be ignored again. Can you work your magic?"

"You know, I hate to break it to you, but no one here really knows who you are. It's the fact that you're a six foot—excuse me, a five foot eleven—blonde and single that actually grabs our attention."

"You knew who I was."

"Do you know who I am?" he asks.

I look at him intensely. He does look vaguely familiar, and I probably should know him, but I have no idea who he is. He's got a subtle look to him, not someone you'd necessarily notice in a room, but most pleasant. "Should I?"

"What kind of music pastor would I be if I told you not to stay at Bible study?"

"Oh, you're a pastor?"

That didn't come out right.

"Don't believe what you hear. We don't bite. Besides, I'm a lay pastor. I work during the day as a. . . ." He pauses and sits back in his chair. "You don't remember who I am?"

"Should I?" I ask again.

"I worked for your father many years back. I collected rents for him while I went to college."

"Oh!" I point at him, "Now I recognize you. Wait . . . don't tell me. Kyle."

He smiles, "You do remember."

Kyle is about ten years older than me, and truthfully, I remember him from my youthful fancy. He was the one with the money. At the time, I didn't know the checks he brought were my father's—I just thought he was rich as Solomon, and his appearance meant more inventory for the store. But I remember him coming in each week and my father mercilessly counting the checks in front of him, eyeing him as though he'd stolen one.

"So what do you do for a living now?" I ask, curious to know what one graduates to after working for my father and garnering his wrath when the checks weren't exactly right.

"I'm a CFO for a small start-up. Your father taught me to be careful to ensure you always get what's coming to you. I suppose I learned it well from him. I'm a glorified accountant, but I do all right. My wife says—"

"Oh, you're married. Not that it matters or anything; I was just surprised."

"Yes, I'm married with two little girls."

Knowing he's married brings me some comfort, and I find a folding chair in front of him and sit down. I wonder what Kyle thinks of my situation right now, having once known my father as the untouchable boss counting checks. I wonder if he thinks it's poetic justice for our sorry lot.

"I'm in the news again, you know. Being sued for fraud and tax evasion."

"Hmm," he nods. But he says nothing. I imagine anyone who actually worked for my father and paid attention wondered what he did with his countless funds.

"It doesn't surprise you."

"There was a time, Morgan, as a young man when I thought your father might be like Ebenezer Scrooge and see the error in his ways, pass out geese to the poor. But, you know, I ceased praying for him a lot of years ago. When you were back in the newspaper, I remembered. He's part of the reason I became a pastor. I give out financial advice, and I'm reminded every day that money does not buy happiness." He strums on the guitar. "Your father was never happy. Once in a while he might have been less than annoyed, but he was never happy."

I think about my steam shower with a small window overlooking the Bay, my lovely shoe collection, and my brand-new Beamer, and then it's quickly overshadowed by thoughts of the lawsuits, my future stepmother, and a father in the hospital. "No, you're right. It can sure fool you for a long while, though."

"Are you still looking for work?"

"I am. How did you know?" (The shoe interview disappeared when I didn't show up. Some people are so picky. I had a good reason!)

"Lilly put it on our prayer list."

I nod. "She's a good friend."

"My wife is looking for some help with the girls. It's just part time, and I know it's not exactly your expertise, but just to hold you over until you find something better, it might work out."

I swallow hard. "I don't know anything about kids, Kyle. I don't even remember being one myself."

He shrugs, "Like I said, it was just a thought." He stands up and puts the guitar in the corner. "My wife will be there. Jenna just needs a hand."

"I'll do it," I hear myself say. Now, I have never even changed a diaper or helped a child with her homework. I have no idea what I'm doing, but I can't explain it. I just feel the need to say yes. I knew I shouldn't have watched those nanny reality shows. What business did I have judging anyone's parenting skills?

Oh, I know this is going to come back to bite me. I just know it.

chapter 27

stayed for Bible study. What did I have to lose? It's not like I had anywhere to be, and I imagine God thought I could use some fulfillment. We were in Hebrews, and I think God picked out the verse for me especially: "Anyone who lives on milk, being still an infant, is not acquainted with the teaching about righteousness. But solid food is for the mature, who by constant use have trained themselves to distinguish good from evil" (5:13–14 NIV).

Yeah, it's that whole distinguishing thing that gets me into trouble. I've called Lilly and Poppy and they're coming to get me at the church, and we're heading to Max's house to meet his mother. I've met his mother before, and she's an interesting lady. The epitome of elegance, yet she speaks whatever is on her mind. When she lived here in San Francisco, she was voted one of the ten best-dressed women in the *Nob Hill Gazette*, and the one to most likely tell you the truth. I have to laugh, because she pulls it off with such flair and style, one almost looks forward to her callous speeches. Of course, one was never directed at me before. Or my best friend.

As I'm waiting outside the church, my cell phone rings, and I have to say I'd almost forgotten I'd carried one. I seem to be on the Most Likely to Not Call list.

"Morgan Malliard," I say very professionally. See, I am so ready for the job market.

"It's George." From the sound of his voice, I wasted my greeting. His call might be good news if he weren't my lawyer and I wasn't most likely sending his future children to college with my case.

"Hi, George. Beautiful night, isn't it?"

"I wouldn't know. I haven't left the office. Listen, I have a proposition for you."

Okay, I'm embarrassed at how completely good that sounds to me right now. Was I not just in Bible study? Lord, the flesh is weak.

"I'm not that kind of girl," I say in my best coquettish voice.

"What?" George asks, clearly confused.

If by all accounts my mother was gifted in the realm of flirting, it's definitely not a gift she passed on genetically. I'm shot down like a duck over a hunter-infested bog.

"Just a little joke."

"Right. Listen, can we meet? There's a lot we need to discuss, and this is going to be hard to understand."

Okay, not appreciating the "You're stupid" implication. "I'm quite bright, George. Went to Stanford. I think I can handle it."

"No, actually, I don't think you can, because it's a complicated case, Morgan. The U.S. marshals don't come after just anyone. There has to be proof and a victim. They claim both."

"Who is the victim?" I ask, knowing full well my father's schemes may be elaborate, but he would never harm someone.

"Your dad sold some property on Union Square and held the mortgage. That's where the wire fraud comes in. The mortgage owners are the victims."

"Are they complaining?"

"No, actually, they're getting a better rate than the U.S. banks would give them, but that's hardly relevant to mortgages being held offshore. It's still illegal what he's doing—and you're doing."

My head is swimming. Normally, this is the point where I'd run to Bloomingdale's and buy myself something really fabulous, but of course, my credit cards will be denied like a homely girl at the Viper Room.

"I might have found a job," I inject. "I have an interview tomorrow morning."

"Morgan, that's fabulous. Do the people realize that you'll be at the government's beck and call for a while?"

"No, but the job is part time. I imagine I'll be able to do it and work around the trial. It's just helping an overwhelmed mother out for a few hours a day if she likes me."

I wait for awhile and he says nothing. "No comment about me being a nanny?"

"So tomorrow after your interview, can you meet?"

"I can. Say lunchtime?" Okay, I know this is pathetic, but I am starving for some stimulating conversation and a fabulous restaurant ambience. A girl like me just can't be expected to give up everything cold turkey. I mean, the credit cards were bad enough, but I cannot be expected to live on Ramen noodles forever. I figure George has access to my money and he's like calling in overdraft protection.

"We have a lot to discuss. How about if I bring something to the penthouse?" George asks.

My excitement withers. "Can't we even meet at the club? The health club?"

"Morgan, I know this is hard on you, but we really can't. Everyone will recognize you, and this is really private business. Any word that gets out, and it could be worse on you and your father."

"What could possibly be worse, George? I don't have any part of my life any longer."

"Jail could be worse, Morgan. You'll have your meals regularly then and they won't be the fine dining you're craving."

"Point taken." I look down at the cowboy boots, and I have to say, I've gotten used to these shoes. Sure, I look like Daisy Duke or Ellie May come to San Francisco, but I'm comfortable. Precisely because for the first time in my life, no one really cares. No photographers are stalking me, as they clearly have yet to figure out where I'm staying, and I'm not attending any fabulous dinner parties to be seen. So for now, the boots work.

"So I'll see you tomorrow at noon. Your father's place," George says curtly.

"George, when are my credit cards going to work again?"

"I'm working on it, Morgan. I told you to take some cash. It may be a while before we can access any of those accounts."

"No, I don't need cash. I can do this a little longer," I say, more for myself than George. "Can you do me a simple favor, though?"

He sighs. Clearly, his clients are usually far more savvy than me and probably less high maintenance. "What is it, Morgan?"

"Can you get me a Starbucks card? I think I could deal with a lot if I had caffeine in my system. Lilly has this weird neighbor with an espresso machine, but that isn't going well. I sort of gave him a piece of my mind today, and I think he's not apt to share anymore. But if I had espresso, then I wouldn't remember that I don't have Bloomingdale's or fine restaurants or even my hair highlights."

"Done. Anything else?"

Well, since he's asking. "Maybe some Godiva chocolate?"

"Would you like a butler to deliver it?"

Now that's not nice. "You asked if there was anything else."

"I'm your lawyer, Morgan, not your personal shopper. Need is generally not associated with chocolate."

Spoken like a true male. "I should think for what you're charging me an hour, you'd be whatever I want you to be." Oooh, I sound like Potipher's wife here. I start to apologize before realizing I am spending a small fortune on defending something I didn't even do. Technically speaking, anyway. "Besides, don't you have a secretary or something?"

"What, are you living in 1950? I can't ask my secretary to go shopping for coffee and chocolate. It sounds like I'm having an affair."

"Then I'll ask her. What's her number?"

"Fine. Those two things, but any other luxuries, including hair products, are your own responsibility."

"You'd be content to see me using cheap shampoo, wouldn't you? Well, George, if you ruin my hair during this trial, I'll blame you publicly."

He laughs at this. "Now that's a new one. I've been the victim of many a threat as a lawyer, but hair ruination is definitely original."

"This is California fog country. I bet you'd be held liable too."

"I have a question for you."

"Yes."

"What is the difference between me giving you cash and you doing your own shopping, and me picking up your—" He stops for a moment. "Ahem, your necessities."

"Cash makes me feel cheap and tawdry," I announce.

He laughs again, "Morgan, you are anything but cheap, and tawdry women eat Russell Stover's chocolates. They don't hold out for Godiva."

"Very funny. I'll see you tomorrow at my dad's place. Bring the chocolate."

"The Feds have been through the house and may be back."

"I understand." I cannot help but wonder if Homeland Security is this thorough. I mean, we have no real victims, and look at their stealth handling of this case. Granted, my father probably didn't exactly play by the rules, but that whole innocent-until-proven-guilty thing comes back to haunt me. How exactly am I innocent here if agents are trudging through my bedroom?

"Morgan Malliard." I turn. Standing here in front of the church, a female flashes her badge at me and reminds me she's my parole officer. As if I'd have trouble remembering that fact. You know, I may not be the sharpest knife in the drawer, but women assigned to follow me I remember.

"I have to go, George." I snap my phone shut and concentrate on the officer—who clearly has been endowed with healthy-sized implants. I wonder if that helps stop a bullet.

"Yes, are you here to search me?" I say, rolling my eyes.

"No, I'm just checking your whereabouts."

"I've been to church, and I'm going to a friend's house tonight. Tomorrow I'll be on a job interview for a nanny position at a pastor's home. I'd appreciate it if you didn't follow me in. You might scare the children."

Her eyes narrow at me, and I can't help what comes out of my mouth. "You should really use eyeliner. It would make a big difference in the appearance of your eyes. They're quite pretty."

After a look of disbelief, the woman nods. "Thank you. Keep out of trouble." She swings her badge shut, just like an episode of *Law & Order: SVU*.

She's way cool. I wonder if I would be a good federal agent.

"I haven't gotten married in the last twenty-four hours, so I suppose I'm doing pretty well," I quip.

"Keep up the good work."

Man, I need a spa treatment. Not just a measly pedicure or a pink-and-white nail fill. I need the full treatment: an enzyme peel, a moisturizing facial, a cucumber mask for my puffy eyes, a hot-stone massage, and maybe even a diamond treatment (where they put diamonds on pertinent acupuncture points). Poppy turned us on to this one (I know—it really should have been me).

I know all of the above are just habits I've gotten into— more of my costly addictions. My life of purpose was really summed up in spectacular grooming, and I suppose that's not really a purpose at all. Unless you're a chimpanzee.

Tomorrow will be different. Tomorrow, I'll interview for a job and eat at home with Mrs. Henry. Maybe George will bring me some takeout with my Starbucks card. *Oh heavens, I do hope Mrs. Henry is still there.* I imagine if they've frozen our accounts, she's not being paid, and that usually doesn't go over well with the hired help. Even if they have been around forever.

Poppy and Lilly pull up in my convertible, giggling. Lilly's hair is now highlighted with gentle streaks of strawberry blonde.

"You look fabulous."

"At least I don't look pregnant," she says as I climb into the car.

"Mrs. Schwartz is going to be a piece of cake, Lilly. It's your nana I'd worry about," I say. Lilly's face contorts into a new look of anxiety and Poppy gives me a "What are you doing?" look. Sorry, can't help it. I know just how Lilly feels. It's always the curve ball that gets you. You're looking straight ahead, and bam!

chapter 28

M ax's house is all lit up like a Christmas tree as we get there. He's obviously more than expecting us. He's guiding us down the runway like a DC-10. I have the distinct feeling that if he could have rented a spotlight to beacon us there quicker, he would have done so. I hear Lilly taking deep yoga breaths, with Poppy whispering calming mantras to her: "This is the way things in my life have been written. God loves me. Jesus died for me. I'm married to the man I love, and I will love his mother. Even if she doesn't welcome me with open arms, I can run to you, Father."

"Poppy! Would you cut it out, you're making *me* nervous."

She shakes her head at me to let me know I'm interrupting their Zen.

"Poppy, we're here," I tell her. "She's meeting her mother-in-law, for crying out loud, not facing the firing squad."

"She's facing her nana, too," Poppy reminds me, and at that remark Lilly stiffens. We all see the comparison is easily made.

"Let's go home!"

"This is home, honey. You're married now." I get out of the car and allow Lilly to exit from the backseat. I should have let her continue to drive after they picked me up, but I was worried we'd end up at Spa Del Mar instead of here. If there's one thing the spa has taught us, it's that while lying under a pile of sweet-smelling papaya plaster, the ugly realities of life just drift away. Farther and farther, until waking up is like a newborn being slapped as he's brought into the world.

Nana's apartment on the street level of Max's house is pitch dark. Which can only mean one thing: Nana is up there as well. Together the three of us look up at Max's brilliantly lit house and then to one another. I know what we're all thinking. We're all thinking that Lilly's regular Diet Pepsi fetish and pickles sound pretty good about now. Too bad she's on this recent health kick for the baby. Here, Poppy thought she'd suddenly cared about her health. It was just mother's guilt.

We're like three kids at the haunted house, each one of us wanting to run for our lives, but we're here gaining strength from each other and it's time to get this over. Yet we can't seem to move.

When I first met Lilly, I thought she was kidding about her nana driving down every weekend to check on her at Stanford. Lilly was a grown woman, but somehow that message took a long time to take root in Lilly's brain. (I suppose I wasn't much different, except for the fact that no one cared to check on me unless I did something unworthy of the Malliard name.)

Lilly's nana loves drama and direction. She's been watching *Days of Our Lives* since its inception, and she can relate anything that happens in life to something Marlena or Bo went through. Actors always say they want to direct, but Nana just does. She's been choreographing Lilly's life since her son (Lilly's father) was killed and Lilly's mother abandoned her daughter.

Nana is the Fred Astaire of the Italian set, and Italian weddings are apparently a big deal. Therefore, getting married without her nana's approval and wedding coordination is about as rebellious as Lilly can get. It's worse than her rejecting the Stanford degree Nana paid for to be a fashion designer. This drama tonight has a starring role for Nana, and she doesn't like surprises, nor parts she can't control. All I can say is let's hope Marlena handled this well.

Before we slam the door on the car, Max is on the porch on the second level, and I watch as he bounds down the steps like an overeager puppy. He gets to the iron gate that separates him from the world, and he zeroes in on Lilly. He doesn't notice her hair; he's far too manic and I suppose it is rather dark under the orange street light.

"What took you so long?" Max wonders.

"I got my hair done," Lilly says, waiting for her compliment. "And Morgan went to church. I didn't think I should turn away my friend's spiritual enlightenment." She looks at me, and we both smile.

"Are you ready for this?" Max asks.

"I brought backup. Did you prep them?"

"I told her you were after my money and poorer than a church mouse."

"Great, that should help. Did you warn her about my hair?"

"Your nana has stuffed her full of lasagna. I think she has less fight in her than an hour ago."

"What about Nana?"

"She is buzzing around like a springtime bee spreading her sunshine. She thinks we're announcing our engagement tonight." Max reaches for Lilly and kisses her cheek. I'd like to say she dissolves into his warmth, but she's a nervous wreck, and his kiss only causes her to weaken until her knees buckle.

"Just think how excited they'll be that we've already taken

care of the details for them," she says sarcastically, matting down her hair out of habit.

"You're denying Nana the chicken dance and hiring an accordion player. It's every Italian grandmother's dream to have an accordion at the wedding. She told me so."

"Max, you are not helping," I say.

"You know, what is your nana's maiden name, Lilly? I always thought it was weird your last name was Jacobs. How Italian is that?" Poppy asks.

"It's Puccinelli, actually." She raises her eyebrows to Max. "Does that scare you?"

"Not if she taught you to make lasagna like that." He pats his stomach.

Lilly purses her lips. "You eat lasagna like that every night, and you'll look like Pavarotti. Is that your goal?"

"I'm a TV writer. It's almost expected that I be a couch potato."

Lilly eyes Max's strong, muscular body and wiggles her eyebrows. "As if I'll let you get away with that. I did not marry eye candy for nothing. My papa did not live a long life, Max. Remember that when you're going for seconds."

The two of them smile and zone into each other, grasping each other's hands. I'm disgusted. I mean, do I really need to be witness to this? It's like my lawyer having abs of steel. What is the point of that? God says He'll never send me a temptation I can't stand under, but you know, I do believe I am reaching my weight limit.

"Can we get this over with?" I hear it come out of my mouth, but I'm as stunned as anyone I said it. I am usually the epitome of decorum. Something is not right here. I think the fog is affecting my brain. Of course, there is no fog tonight, but maybe the invisible stuff is worse for you.

Poppy and I follow Max and Lilly, feeling completely out

of place, but silently hoping there's a little lasagna left. It's just what I need to make me feel better: abs of veal.

Mrs. Schwartz is at the doorway, and in a split second, I see her gaze scan Lilly's frame and come back up with a warm, albeit fake smile. I'd know that princesslike you-can't-tell-what-I'm-thinking smile anywhere. I have perfected it.

"Lilly Jacobs, aren't you just beautiful?" Mrs. Schwartz grabs Lilly's hands, pulling her from Max's grip. "Well, you just must tell me how you met my son."

I have been friends with Lilly too long to not know what she wants to say. What she wants to say is that she hog-tied him and poured alcohol down his throat until he confessed his love. I see her sly smile towards Poppy and me, and we start to giggle. Sometimes, it's really not a good thing to be so in tune with your warped friends.

"There's not much to tell actually. He rented the apartment to my nana, and we just got to know each other over time. When he broke his leg at the hotel, I helped care for him."

"Isn't that sweet? Just like Florence Nightingale." Mrs. Schwartz looks to me and Poppy. She focuses in on me and drops Lilly's hands. "Morgan Malliard, is that you?"

I nod, biting my lip.

"Max, I didn't know you were friends with Morgan." Mrs. Schwartz walks away from Lilly and stands before me. She's wearing a flawless diamond the size of a bottle cap, and it completely distracts me from her face. I know how much that diamond is worth, because I can see all the facets, all the light and colors gleaming under the dim light and there's not a spot to be seen.

"Perfect," I say aloud.

"Mr. Schwartz bought it for me in Barbados. It is perfect, but then, I'd guess you'd know."

I pull my gaze away from the diamond and focus on her

deep brown eyes. They're so much like her son's, only far more critical. I see that Max and Lilly have one more thing in common. They were both raised under the watchful eye of female hawks.

"Mrs. Schwartz." I nod pleasantly. "Lilly and I went to Stanford together. She helped me with my studies."

"You might have taken a lesson from her in dating. She appears to be more accomplished in that arena."

That was below the belt.

"Not all of us can attract the attention of Max Schwartz. There's only one of him, after all." Fake-princess-smile right back atcha.

"Mom, Nana." Max claps his hands and forces everyone's attention toward him. He walks over to Lilly and puts his arm around her. "I know you're all expecting an announcement of sorts, but I think what we have for you is not what you're expecting."

"I don't like surprises, Lilly and Max." Nana drops a wooden spoon she'd been drying and wipes her hands on her apron. Her expression softens. "Unless of course, you're going to tell me something I've been waiting to hear."

Max draws in a deep breath, sticking his chest out. "Lilly and I have lived our lives alone for a long time. I'm thirty-five, she's thirty, and we're people who know what we want."

I wish I could crawl under the sofa about now. Lilly's hands are trembling, and the two elder women do not look like they're willing to hear whatever's about to come.

Mrs. Schwartz lifts her chin and gives a tight smile. "What is it you want, Max? I would think your lives are both very successful and that you should take time to be grateful." Her smile fades. "You're not going on one of those ridiculous mission trips, are you?"

Max laughs. "No, Mother, God hasn't called us to the

mission field—although I wouldn't rule it out just yet."

"Us?" Mrs. Schwartz asks. "Did you get a pet, my dear?"

Max gets fed up with the constant barrage and blurts out the truth. "Us, Mother. My wife and me. Lilly and I got married over a month ago. We went up to Tahoe and did it because we didn't want the fuss. All right?" He tightens his clasp on Lilly, who looks ready to faint.

Poppy and I stand there looking from Max's mom to Nana, waiting to see who takes the first strike. Since Nana seems to be momentarily stricken with apoplexy, it falls to Mrs. Schwartz. Her face tightens and a muscle starts to tic in her jaw, but she waits until she's paced the length of the room before she speaks. "I see," she says quietly. "I must say I'm surprised." She looks at Lilly. "If for nothing else that you design wedding gowns for a living, and yet you eloped to Tahoe."

She's looking at Lilly as if she's the ultimate betrayer. I suppose Lilly was nice enough when she wasn't a part of the family.

"Max, you're one of San Francisco's leading bachelors. You're just going to walk away from that with no fanfare whatsoever? How am I supposed to explain this?"

"I imagine you'll do it the same way you told the world I wasn't involved in the family business. I'm the black sheep."

"Lilly Jacobs!" Nana's found her voice. Poppy's and my heads swing to her like we're watching a tennis match. "Lilly Jacobs, this had better be a joke." Her face is as red as a ripe tomato, and all sense of peace has left the room. Both she and Mrs. Schwartz are now pacing, but when Max's mother sees her own reaction is the same as Nana's, she halts in her steps.

With a nod at each other, Max and Lilly split to their respective fights. Lilly takes her nana to one side, and they begin to whisper in loud, ugly tones. I see Mrs. Schwartz sit beside her son and pat his leg. The one he broke in three places and still limps on. Her expression has softened, but I can't help but wonder if it's only because she doesn't want to be associated with Nana's behavior. But I literally witness the fight leave her as she looks at her son and pats his leg again.

"She's a sweet girl," Mrs. Schwartz says while watching Lilly defend herself against Nana. Truthfully, I'm not sure she means it, but it's obviously a way to get through to her son. "I think you'll be very happy. You might want to find Nana a new place to live, though."

Mother and son laugh. Max pulls back and says, "Do you mean that?"

She smiles. "I want what all moms want. I want my son to be happy, and if Lilly Jacobs—excuse me, Lilly Schwartz—makes you happy? That makes me happy. But if you're still into praying, I'd ask that you get your father an heir. He was worried you might be gay, so I imagine this will come as a pleasant surprise. That's why he sent you that beautiful Russian girl. Once you rejected her, he was convinced."

I see Max considering telling the rest of their news and deciding to wait. He laughs out loud. "She is gorgeous, isn't she, Mom?" he says, watching Lilly, whose hands are flailing as she talks to Nana.

"Did you give her Grandmother's ring?"

He nods. "It's being sized."

"I knew it was coming, once you gave the matching brooch, so I'm not completely surprised."

"How will you tell your friends?"

"Oh please, everyone's kid is living with this person or that. They'll be more mortified you got married. It's so old-fashioned."

I watch mother and son giggle together, and I try to remember when I ever had such a conversation with my father.

Even watching Lilly with her Nana makes me long for what they have.

"At least you didn't marry that flighty Malliard girl."

The two of them stop speaking and look at me.

Poppy takes my hand. "Well, pleasure seeing you all. Morgan and I have to run. She's got a big job interview tomorrow. Big job interview."

"No, I don't have to rush off," I say, unwilling to be bullied by restless talk.

Poppy looks at me. "Don't you think we should leave?"

I shake my head, "She's got a right to her opinion. We're here for Lilly."

At the sound of her name, Lilly looks up from her conversation and puts her arms around her Nana. "So we're going to have a small wedding gathering for friends after the Red & White Ball."

Nana is still beet red. She starts cleaning up pans (loudly) in the kitchen.

"So, thanks for coming, girls!" Max says, giving us our path out, for which we are grateful.

We give him and Lilly hugs and polite good-byes to Mrs. Schwartz and Nana and then Poppy yanks me from the room. I clutch my hand into a fist, feeling the blue diamond around my right-hand ring finger.

"That Mrs. Schwartz is a piece of work. Max would be lucky to have you, Morgan, you know that?"

"It's all right, Poppy. It's nothing I don't know. If it makes you feel any better, I don't think her husband got any sort of deal either."

"What do you care what that elitist crowd thinks anymore? One good thing about being poor, you won't have to hang out with them anymore."

Poppy opens her despicable tapestry bag, which looks

like it's from a carpetbagger during Civil War times. It's just as old, and just as ugly. "We got you something." She hands me an envelope.

"For what?"

"Because you need it, and that's what we do as Spa Girls. We stick together no matter what. You seemed depressed, and you didn't get your spa time this morning when we rushed Lilly home. She felt bad."

I rip open the envelope and it's a gift certificate for Blooms. My favorite spa in the city. "Oh Poppy, how on earth did you have time for this?"

"We have our priorities straight. I know you don't need it right now, but I didn't want you to be stopped by what's going on if you need it in the future."

"Isn't that just what a girl under federal indictment needs—a facial?" I cannot believe my life has come to this. My friends buying me charity spa treatments.

"Yes, actually it is just what a girl needs. That's why we bought it." Poppy closes up her dirty sack, and we're on our way. The two single Spa Girls on the town.

chapter 29

I t didn't really bother me at the time that Lilly's mother-in-law dissed me. If anything, I thought, *Good, this takes some of the pressure off Lilly.* But the more I thought about it the more ticked I got. To say she's happy her son didn't marry me? In front of me? I don't know what charm school she hails from, but she left the charm there. If I've learned anything about society it's to maintain an image publicly. Maybe she's just old and cranky, I don't know, but I hate how everyone's declared open season on Morgan Malliard. I have feelings. I have struggles.

But of course, we created this image. We only wanted people to covet my father's latest piece, not actually find out what I felt.

Regardless, I'm glad I have this job interview this morning. I wonder if all this stuff happened when I was in the penthouse, and I just never noticed.

At the moment I'm focused on what to wear to the interview:

Chloe is out.

Gucci is out.

Prada is definitely out.

Even Lilly Jacobs' designs are not necessarily right for a

nanny position. This would be a good job on the clothing budget, and considering that I don't have one right now, I think that's a good thing. From what I understand, it's dirty work—lot of climbing around on the floor and flung-food avoidance. Lilly and Poppy found it hilarious that I was going for a nanny position, but I really don't see what's so funny. I was a kid once. I had a nanny. I know how things are supposed to go.

I rifle through what Lilly has for me and finally choose the pair of jeans she made me and a flowing sage green shirt she made from scraps. With the cowboy boots, I am completely ready to shine. Mary Poppins, eat your heart out.

I arrive on the doorstep of Mrs. Keller and the house is quite luxurious. It's in the Pacific Heights part of town, and backs up to the Presidio. As far as addresses go, I must say, the CFO business must be pretty good, even in start-up mode.

I brush my hair back after ringing the doorbell and shake out my shoulders, rolling my head around and cracking my neck. I'm so nervous. This is an actual job interview. Granted, it isn't the job I thought I'd be going for with my Stanford degree, but I'm here, and I'm excited.

Mrs. Keller answers the door with two little girls at her feet, each yanking on her for attention. They both look up at me suspiciously.

Their mother's weary expression is evident. Mrs. Keller is tall and lithe, albeit a little emaciated; her tiny frame looks worn and haggard. I wonder when her last good meal was (Mrs. Henry could fill her out quickly). She doesn't have a stitch of makeup on, and her long light-brown hair is in tangles over her shoulders.

The little girls, in contrast, are perfectly dressed in matching knit dresses with coordinating bows at the crown of their heads.

I bend down to greet the little tow-headed blondes, and they run behind their mother.

"You're Morgan?" the mother sighs.

"I am," I say as I stand and stick my hand out to meet her.

I see her blow her bangs up with her breath and close her eyes, shaking her head. "I'm Jenna. Come on in," she says without any actual welcoming. "Clear yourself a path and have a seat."

"Is this a bad time?"

"Did you actually meet Kyle?"

"I did. At church. Why?"

She sighs again. She's big on the sighing. "I can't hire you. Sometimes my husband doesn't pay attention to the obvious, if you know what I mean."

I really don't. "Why not? I can be good with kids. You haven't even given me a chance. Look, they'll love me, won't you girls?"

The two little blondes study me for a while and finally the oldest nods at their mother. "Pity," the eldest mutters. I'm assuming she means "pretty," but I think "pity" is much more appropriate.

"It has nothing to do with you and the kids." Jenna sits on the sofa, covered with laundry that needs folding, and the girls climb up into her lap.

"What then?" I mean, I know I'm not exactly known as being a domestic, but I can learn. "If you don't mind telling me, I can take it. In the past day, I've already heard my bank accounts have been frozen and that a mother is glad her son didn't marry me. I can take what you can dish out, really. I mean, no one will hire me, and I'd love to know why. I may not have a lot of job experience, but I'm not inept."

"Morgan," Jenna says gently, patting my hand. "Kyle is a pastor. I know he's a CFO full time, but he's still a music pastor, and as such, the church watches what we do very closely. That's why Kyle wants a nanny in the first place." Her eyes sweep around the room. "We're not exactly set up to invite the masses to dinner. I'm afraid my Martha qualities are very well hidden under a loving Mary façade."

The house is atrocious, but clearly Jenna has her hands full. "I can just come in and help you clean if you're worried about me being seen with the girls." I'm desperate here. As chaotic as this home appears, it feels like a home. An actual loving environment that I would just love to witness in action. There are crayon drawings on the wall, toys askew, and two very darling little girls. "Mrs. Espinoza, my father's house-maid, taught me how to scrub a sink so there is absolutely no ring of anything anywhere. I can even speak a little Spanish because of it."

This memory sets off a little sadness, as I realize how pitiable I was, following the maid about because she was the one person who always had a hug for me.

Mrs. Keller smiles while the girls climb up onto the back of the sofa. They're both staring at me as though I'm some kind of zoo animal. "Morgan, I don't how to say this. It's not politically correct, I realize."

"It's the federal indictments that scare you. I'll pay taxes on anything you give me; you won't even have to keep track. I'll make sure the social security gets taken out and every-thing. I'm very good with accounting. I've done a lot for my dad. Well, before . . . I mean—"

"Morgan, stop. It has nothing to do with that, though Kyle did forewarn me. It's that you're a six foot blonde, and you bear a striking resemblance to a young Christie Brinkley. He sort of forgot to warn me about that."

"She's back doing makeup ads, did you see that? Christie Brinkley, I mean."

Mrs. Keller nods slowly. "I did. The church wives, their tongues wag. They can't help it, but they watch their pastors closely. It's bad enough we have money and that I need help with the two girls, but I do. I'm not one of those mothers who can instinctively get everything done. It's shameful as it is for me, Morgan, and if they see you, it will be even worse for me. And for Kyle."

"Then I'll help you. You name the hours. No one has to know I'm here."

"It's Nannygate. It's the whole Jude Law thing. My husband is a well-off pastor and a nanny doesn't look right, but a nanny who looks like you is definitely out of the question. I can't believe Kyle didn't notice." She laughs a little. "I guess I should be grateful." She puts her hands through hair that clearly hasn't been washed or styled today.

"Can I at least stay until you've had a shower? No charge." In Jenna, I see my mother. I can't help it, but when I think about how Kyle saw his wife drowning, and his desire to help her, I can't help but want to be a part of that. It's so completely foreign to what I know.

Seeing Jenna, I see a great lesson that I should have learned a long time ago from Lilly. People have needs, and I don't often notice them. Yes, I did finally notice that Lilly was drowning financially, and I helped her with credit, but not before Nate and Kim came to her rescue. What does that say about me?

"I don't want things to be this way." She lets out a long, haggard breath. "But they are this way and I am an inept homemaker."

"I had it!" one child screams as she jumps off the couch.

"No, me!" The other one flies off as well.

The two girls are locked in a battle with the intensity of animals, their little blue eyes turning dark and treacherous while an innocent Dancing Elmo takes the brunt of their anger.

Mrs. Keller falls back on the couch, the back of her hand resting on her forehead. "Have at it, girls. Fight to the death over Elmo."

Seeing their mother is not involved in their fight, they both release the doll and let it tumble to the floor. Crisis averted.

"Bath. I want a bath."

"No, I want a bath."

"How old are they?"

Jenna beams over her daughters. "Fifteen months and almost three. Hospitality may not be my gift, but my husband and I have no problem with fertility. He seems to look at me, and I get pregnant." She rubs her belly and nods.

"Another one? When?"

"March 18 this one is due. Kyle is hoping it's his boy. I'm just hoping I can get through the next few months and maybe get a nap once in a while."

"I won't wear makeup. Will that help?" I ask.

She laughs. "I'm not asking you to be ugly, Morgan. I'm only saying that I know what we're in for if I hire you, and it's just one more thing I can't handle. So you see, even if you help me at home, I'll have to deal with it at the church."

The girls have now climbed on top of a plastic house that would normally be in a backyard but is prominently displayed in the dining room. Seeing the girls and the way their mom looks at them, with doe eyes and a proud smile, leaves me wistful. I know I can't go back—that for some reason this wasn't the childhood I was meant to have—but I can see how it's supposed to be done.

"This is a crappy job." Jenna continues, her own blue eyes watching her girls. She walks over and easily whisks them off the plastic roof. "I mean, I love it, I wouldn't be anywhere else than with my daughters, but raising a family in the city is a hard business, and as a pastor's wife nearly impossible. I need help watching them on outings, and getting them dressed so we can actually have an outing once in a while." Then she looks out the window, and I hear her silent anguish. "He's never home. Between work and the church, it's just constant."

"Kyle?"

Okay, my first thought is, *Sheesh, he's home enough to get you pregnant,* but that's hardly kind and completely irrelevant.

"Why would you want this job?" she asks me, and I can see she's weakening.

Looking around at the messy house and the granite countertop I can't see and the floors with little feet marks on them and the walls with scuff marks that are in need of those Mr. Clean erase markers that I think Mrs. Henry owns stock in, I can't imagine why I want the job, but out of my mouth comes the truth: "I want to know what it's like to be in a normal family. I know that's weird. I promise I'm not like *The Hand That Rocks the Cradle* or anything, but I really want to know what's the glue that holds families together."

"*Mom* is the glue. Don't let anyone ever tell you differently."

If that's true, that would explain a lot. There was nothing to hold us together in our house. We were like a popsicle-stick construction.

"I can help you, Jenna. No one even has to know. You have your private shame, I have mine. We can do this together. Please." I never thought I'd find myself begging for a job, but I stand here realizing if I have any pride left, I forgot where I left it.

"Kyle told you the pay?"

"He did," I nod.

"That's barely enough for weekly lattes."

"They make me fat anyway."

She grins. "I need a self-starter. If you're looking for direction from me, you're looking in the wrong place."

"I've watched enough maids and nannies in my lifetime. I know the drill. I'll do my best, and you can tell me if it's not good enough. Let's just agree for the week if it scares you."

"You're hired."

I look around the room for something that should be a priority, and I decide to clean. Jenna wouldn't feel nearly so out of control if her house was put together. "I'll get started in the kitchen."

As I look at the previous night's dinner dishes in the sink, I feel this incredible peace wash over me. For once in my life, I feel completely necessary, and for fifteen dollars an hour, that isn't a bad deal.

chapter 30

After a morning of joyful drudgery, I drive to the penthouse giddy yet completely ignorant as to what I'll find in my former home. I do know I'm going to have to find a way to pay the rent on Lilly's loft, since I imagine she'll be moving in with her husband now. I can't imagine what possessed her to do anything differently. Hmm . . . House in the Marina overlooking the Golden Gate with a man, or unkempt loft in Cow Hollow. Hmmm, what would I do?

I arrive at the penthouse, and pulling my Beamer into the parking garage feels like every day of my previous life. Like I've just come home from a luxury luncheon or a pedicure appointment. In actuality, today I scrubbed ages-old macaroni and cheese off of granite countertops and threw science experiments away from an odiferous refrigerator. No, today is the first day of my new reality, and so far, it's disgusting, but not bad at all.

For one thing, I made a new friend. Jenna doesn't care what kind of car I drive, nor does she care what bling my father gave me to wear today. She just wants to know her daughters are well cared for, and I was actually a help. Amber and Anne are sweet girls, but they are a major handful. They're both extremely bright, and they seem to take pleasure in finding what trouble they can mix up while Jenna turns her back. Just my extra set of eyes was enough to ward off several impending disasters.

As I enter the garage beneath the apartments, I watch the bellman look down. Even though I pull my car up obnoxiously in front of the closet he calls an office, he promptly ignores me. I honk the horn because, well, because I've just spent all morning scraping food particles off of places they had no business being. This doorman isn't going to give me any garbage.

He doesn't look up when I honk.

This is fun. I honk again. I just took on two toddlers all morning; just try it, buddy.

Finally, I see him slap down his clipboard, giving me the satisfaction that I have indeed annoyed him to the point where he's roused from his nest. Or perhaps lair is the better term.

"Can I help you?' he asks with his spindly arms crossed in front of him.

"I still live here." I shake my hair out, with my hands still gripped to the steering wheel. I'm trying to maintain a sense of authority, but I'm not feeling it. "Daddy still pays your tab, and don't let the newspapers fool you, I am a part of this co-op."

"For now." He rolls his eyes. I suppose watching me being taken off by federal agents did nothing for my reputation, but we still own the deed on this extraordinarily priced house, and until our neighbors work up the gusto to force us into a sale, I expect to get my money's worth. Watch out, world, Morgan Malliard is a doormat no more! "I wouldn't be so certain of your stature here," he continues, his dark eyes meeting mine in challenge.

I hone in on his nameplate, "Mark, regardless of what my neighbors think, you still work for them and me, so check yourself." A time not so long ago, I would have been totally put out by this sniveling dork and been apologizing to ensure I didn't offend him or the co-op board. But those days are gone. When you answer to God and the U.S. government, bellmen and snooty neighbors no longer hold power over you. We, I might remind them, still own the penthouse, and until Uncle Sam says otherwise, I can dish it out, too. I'm not my father's daughter for nothing.

I throw my keys at the bellman. "Not a scratch, do you understand?"

He mocks me, mimicking what I've just said in a small, whiny voice, and I head upstairs to the penthouse. As the elevator opens, Mrs. Henry is sitting on the living room sofa with her feet on the antique French empire table, watching *All My Children*. She scurries to remove her feet and turn the television off.

"Don't bother. What do I care?" I ask her, dropping my purse at the foot of the table.

"You look tired. Where have you been? At the spa for a few days?"

"I took a job, actually."

"Doing what?" she laughs.

"I'm a nanny. Do you have any idea how hard yogurt is when it dries?"

"I do. I used to know someone who ate it in the bathtub."

"That was a long time ago," I defend myself.

"It was still an odd thing to do. Mrs. Espinoza used to go on in Spanish forever about it."

"How's my father? I haven't called him today."

"He's got his voice back," she sighs heavily.

"I heard yesterday. You would have never known anything was wrong with him."

"He called to tell me all that had to be spit and polished

before he returned. I heard from the store. They've heard from him, too."

"I see you took him seriously." I shake my head.

"He wouldn't know clean if I rented an industrial floor polisher and gave him a sponge bath with it."

"Why did he call then?"

"To make sure everyone he's paying is still working."

"I see he was effective," I laugh. Then I slap my own forehead. "Oh that's right. I forgot I'm supposed to pick out pieces for the Red & White Ball."

"You're not really going to that?"

"Why not?" I shrug. "I've already lost all sense of dignity. Why shouldn't I go play with the brats in the sandbox. It's been a long time since I had reason to dress up. And red is my color."

"It hasn't been that long since you dressed up."

"I don't care about the ball. I'm just going because Lilly will make me a gown, and everyone can say how scandalous I am in red. Any publicity is good publicity. It worked for Paris Hilton."

Mrs. Henry purses her lips together in that way she has that makes you feel about two feet tall. "Gwen is coming over with Frick and Frack, the designers, this afternoon."

I groan. "My lawyer's going to be here. Can't you tell her to keep out?"

"She's good for your father. He's determined to make it long enough to get her to sign a prenup. Gwen gives him a reason to get up each day and battle that stroke."

"I'm going to see him this afternoon. I don't care what that lawyer says." When I think about my father, I see this poor helpless lump in a hospital bed who longs to see me, but I know that's a mythical and thoroughly wrong view. I'll go in, he'll ask me about the store and the lawsuit and send me on my way. Ah, the father-daughter bond.

"That lawyer is a nice-looking boy." Mrs. Henry says, looking for more information from me.

"I hadn't noticed."

She laughs. "Morgan, you have man radar like I have never seen before. You can walk into a room of four hundred married men and find the finest, richest one in half a second. You'll sell them a piece of jewelry for their girlfriend and then go find the poor, helpless loser in the room for yourself."

"Those days are gone. I'm learning to be independent."

"As a nanny? Honey, that salary couldn't pay for your monthly gym bill."

"Then I'll have to join another gym. Or maybe I'll just run up Telegraph Hill once a week."

"You're going to work out without some gym rat hanging around and barking at you continuously?"

"If I have to." I mean, I do possess a certain amount of vanity. Okay, an inordinate amount. I am my mother's daughter as well.

Mrs. Henry smiles, and I see the warm side of her. Every so often, there are the days she defrosts just a tad and let's me see into the side of her that cared for my mother. I never heard a harsh word from her mouth to my mother, and there's something innate in humans that when you see that warmth and comfort in a person, you long to make it your own.

"Your mother used to say that, too, about working out. She always had to be the thinnest woman in a room."

"Luckily, I'm friends with Lilly, so that isn't possible and I have no false hopes."

"Your mother was a shapely woman. It wasn't good for her either."

"How come you are so sweet when talking about my mother?"

A grin graces Mrs. Henry's face as she talks of Mother. "Because I knew a Traci Malliard no one else got to see." Mrs. Henry gets up and starts to clean imaginary dust from trinkets around the room.

There's so much I want to ask her, but the doorbell rings, and it's like the foghorn. Life is clouding up, and my transparent view to the future is about to get muddled. It's time to go back to the lawsuit and back to an unknown world.

I open the door to George, and my heart beats just a little faster. He's wearing a wool jacket the color of his eyes over a business shirt with no tie and a pair of jeans. One advantage to jail is that when I get a visitor it's going to be this hottie. There are worse things.

Of course, a better thing would be that this hottie would actually be a good lawyer and get me out of this mess.

"George, it's good to see you," I say.

"Hello, Morgan," he nods back like I'm one of his mother's friends or, worse yet, just a client. He walks straight to the dining room table and plops his briefcase there, pulling out files.

"Can we do this at the kitchen countertop? That's a French antique." I'm cringing for Mrs. Henry, who is beside herself, eyeing George as though he's the devil himself. Being handsome is one thing, abusing the antiques she cares for quite another to Mrs. Henry.

George stuffs his briefcase again, pounding on the table as though it's a voodoo doll of Mrs. Henry, who flinches and aches with his every harsh move. He moves to the counter, slams the folders onto the granite, and opens them before me. Mrs. Henry rests on the sofa, her hand over her chest.

"I've run the numbers, and you're entitled to this much salary as a partner in the business." He points to a number I must say is a little less than I was expecting. "Your credit cards will still be frozen, so you have to learn to live within this number."

"Do you think I'll have difficulty with that?" I give a light-hearted, tinkling laugh, wondering how the heck I am going to buy highlights with that paltry number. I am not about to leave Franco, San Francisco's highlight guru. I mean, the gym I can give up, the fancy eateries, but a girl has her pride. I am not going with boxed highlights for any amount of money.

He scans me, my unkempt nails, and I close my fists around them, very aware that my hygiene is not up to Malliard standards. "You're used to more than this, I would think."

"I can live with that."

"Good. You can't sell any assets at the moment. Your car is under surveillance, and the penthouse will be put up as collateral."

My stomach twists as I think about our home being used in this way. But before I can comment, Gwen comes bounding through the elevator doors.

"Dad gave her a key?" I ask Mrs. Henry across the room. She nods.

"Mrs. Henry, do get my bag," Gwen drops her Coach duffle bag, one exactly like mine (oh the horror), at the door. "And we'll need something to eat when Sven and Jackson get here."

George stands up. "Excuse me, but who are you?"

"My father's girlfriend," I explain.

"Fiancée," she corrects. "I'm meeting my designers here. We're ready to gut this place and bring back its elegance."

Fiancée. As if. Where's your ring? I mean, is it just me or does my father specialize in diamonds and you're not wearing one?

"Well, I'm sure you're concerned for your fiancé's future

but we are in need of some privacy here," George says with such grace.

"Apparently, we don't have enough animal print," I say under my breath.

"Why is she here?" Gwen points to Mrs. Henry.

"She might be indicted as well. This concerns her." Mrs. Henry's eyes get round, but George winks at her and she relaxes. I'm not prone to lying, but it's a selfish plea. I want Mrs. Henry's cooking.

"Gwen, why don't you and Sven and Jackson meet in the foyer to go over the designs," I say.

"Absolutely not." George stands up. "This home is up as collateral to the government. There will be no redesign nor anything done to the home until the lawsuit is over."

"Well, when is that?"

George shrugs, "It could be years."

"Well, I'm not going anywhere." Gwen parks herself on the sofa, and I see George's eyes flash. I rest my chin on my hands. Let the games begin.

chapter 31

Y ou are going somewhere," George says this in the same
tone as Bond, James Bond. And I have to say, his confidence is quite appealing. I know, I know. He's my
lawyer, and as far as buoyancy options, all I've got to save me
from drowning. Nothing is going to happen, but if I live in
this imaginary place in my mind, where George Gentry
rescues me from certain death (or in this case, federal prison),
life is just easier to deal with. Why shouldn't I live in a
fantasy? What else do I have?

"Do you realize who I am?" Gwen stands up straight,
though there is very little difference in her potato form. "I am
Gwen Caruthers."

"According to the paperwork I have here, your name is
nowhere on this deed, and this concerns the people with
rights to the properties. I'm doing what's best for you, Miss
Caruthers; I'm working on showing the U.S. government this
property and all the others have been paid for accordingly.
Now, I hate to be rude, but I will call the police if you don't
vacate the premises immediately."

Gwen's mouth drops. "You wouldn't dare!"

George is all business. He doesn't care an iota about the
drama of my father's girlfriend. He's thinking billable hours,

and this woman is in his way.

I sit back in my chair, confident that if my lawyer can take on the U.S. government, Gwen and the frat boys are no competition. But she surprises me.

"Do you have a key to this penthouse apartment?" she asks, crossing her long but substantial arms. I must say if they got into a fight, I think it might be a draw. George has the abs, but Gwen clearly has the pure brute strength on him.

"I have better." He pulls out a sheet of paper. "A copy of the deed that's being fought over. I suggest if you ever hope to live in this apartment, you'll leave me and Miss Malliard to our business of saving Mr. Malliard's hide. There's not a government agency in San Francisco that will approve permits for a house being held as collateral."

Meow! You go, Georgie.

Gwen huffs off, lifting her Coach signature bag with such force that it slams into the wall sconce and breaks the light. "Mrs. Henry!" she shouts, as though her temper is the light's problem. And I suppose it is.

Mrs. Henry rushes over with a broom she managed to get so quickly it's like it extended from her arm or something and starts to sweep up the glass on the floor.

"I'll meet Sven and Jackson downstairs. Call the lobby when you're through with this ridiculous business." Gwen focuses her steely gaze on me. "Don't think I don't know where this started, Missy."

Before I even have time to protest my innocence or stick my tongue out at her, she's gone. George dives right back in and continues to tell me all the places I can have access to, and where I'll need to cut back, and where I'll especially not want to be seen spending money, what will raise red flags for the government, etc. Blah, blah, blah, blah.

"Do we get to the keep the apartment?" There's this dark

side of me that would rather get rid of it than watch it fall into the hands of Gwen's designs. "I mean, when all this is over, and it's not collateral anymore."

"Morgan, we haven't even heard the indictments read. A lot will depend on the grand jury they've called, and their reactions. You have to know, your recent history in the paper can go either way. Either people will feel sorry for you, or they'll think you're only getting more of what you deserve— that you feel entitled to act any way you feel, so creating that emotion in the jury will be crucial."

"What do you think?"

He slams his stylish Mont Blanc lawyer pen on the table. "Why are you always asking me that? Do you want my legal opinion? Or do you want to be pacified?"

"I want to be pacified. Duh."

"Then life will go on, Morgan, with a few kinks."

"I can't read you at all, and you fascinate me because there are so many things that don't make sense. Like why do you have a twelve-dollar haircut and Bowflex abs? Why do you wear a European suit and yet walk into a steam sauna with it? Why aren't you married?"

Did I just say all that out loud?

"Why do you want to know all that?"

Why not. "Would you stop lawyering my questions with more questions, and answer me? I have a right to know."

"You really don't. Legally, anyway."

"But what reason do you have to keep it from me? I figure, why beat around the bush? You know every square inch of my financial history; why shouldn't I know why you work for those abs of steel and yet share them with no one? You're not gay."

"How do you know that?"

"You don't want to know."

"No, really, I do."

"A gay man would never notice my figure. That day at the spa, you did. Then again, at the health club. A gay guy might notice my clothes, or even my accessories. He might hone in on my daddy's latest bling, but never, never . . . " I put my forefinger up for emphasis. " . . . would his eyes scan me up and down, and then pretend to not notice. I saw your Adam's apple move when you finished."

"I beg to differ with you on that. I think anyone would notice your figure." He clears his throat uncomfortably. "Anyone."

I smile a little self-satisfied grin. Of course, I don't admit to him that I'm noticing his abs right now, and the tuft of hair that's peeking from the collar of his unbuttoned business shirt. That's extremely pathetic and sexist. Besides which, a girl has to have a few secrets. "So you're not answering my final question: why aren't you married?"

"I was engaged once," he says, still scanning the paperwork as though he's not really participating in our conversation.

I know he had to break it off. No one in their right mind would walk away from George Gentry. "Why didn't you marry her?"

"She had a thing for another guy. I suppose you'd say she just wasn't that into me."

"She had a crush on another guy?" I ask.

"Actually, a little more. She had a little fling with the stripper at her bachelorette party." His face gets red, and I see the humiliation flood his senses. I hadn't meant to make him feel that way.

Ick. "She had a bachelorette party?" I have always wondered about the fascination with bachelor and bachelorette parties. To me, if you need one, you really might want to think about getting married in the first place. Of course, I may have fared better with the stripper. I'm kidding.

"Did you have a bachelor party?" I ask, wondering if she was only exacting her revenge.

"I went golfing with my friends at the Olympic Club. One of the partners got me in and we had a wild day on the links." He shrugs. "I think she needed a little more excitement in her life."

"Why did you think she was the woman you wanted to marry in the first place?"

"I didn't really think at the time. I thought it was the point in my career where I should get married. She was a legal assistant in the office, cute, and it just seemed right. She was—" He pauses, unsure of what he wants to say. "She was stupid, quite frankly, but very attractive, and she had the partners wrapped around her finger. It seemed like a good career move at the time."

I smile and cover his hand with mine. "Thanks, George."

"For what?"

"For reminding me that I'm not the only one who makes mistakes and being honest enough to tell me the truth."

"What if I just reached for a storyline from *Dynasty* years back during law school?"

"Maybe since we've had such incredibly bad taste, we've learned what we're supposed to, and God will clear the path for the right person."

"See, I don't think it's just that. I think it's that we're optimists, Morgan. We see the best in people, when really we might want to delve a little deeper to see the reality."

"I can't believe you said that. I'm totally into reality right now." Okay. That just sounded incredibly teenlike. "What I mean to say is I'm working on my dose of reality now. God seems to be helping a little with this whole poverty-stricken realm."

"I heard you were a Christian. I'll admit, I sort of found it hard to believe with what the newspaper said about you."

"Would that be the same newspaper that thinks paying the homeless is a good idea?"

"That's the one." He grins and my heart bumps.

"You don't laugh much, do you?"

He looks up from the papers, and lights me up with a view of his freshly whitened teeth. "I did once. But a laughing lawyer isn't exactly a strong suit. If anything, I should practice my poker face."

His smile straightens out, and I'm so tempted to reach out and bring it back again, tipping up the corners of his mouth with my fingers, but I refrain. If I've learned anything these past months, it's that self-control goes a long way.

"Actually, today, there's not a lot to laugh about."

"Because my case is so bad?"

"No, I think you'll be fine. I thought it would be better to split your cases up and have you testify against your father. I had this great strategy, and I told the partners about it last night."

"I would never testify against him."

"That's what the partners said. They also cited quite a few test cases they thought were more applicable, and you're better off sticking together. The government has more burden of proof that way."

"So that's good news, right? I mean, beside the fact that you were wrong. We didn't go forward with it, so no harm, no foul."

"Except to say that my law firm and I are parting ways. Lemur will be by this afternoon to be introduced to you. He's taking on your case. Your father will have one Lemur, and you'll have the other at your disposal."

My smile disappears. "What does that mean exactly? Is there a reason you're just now relating that you're not my lawyer anymore? What are you even doing here?"

"I was fired, but quite frankly, I don't know if your father had anything to do with it. So I'm here until I've been dismissed by you. I'd been in a little heat after the secretary-stripper fiasco anyway. When I broke the engagement, she filed a sexual harassment suit that made it hard on the firm."

I feel the cool air hit my tongue as my mouth dangles open.

"I made a mistake on your case, and they claim it was that of an amateur, and therefore not only will I not be promoted to partner, but I'll be finding out what it means to collect unemployment for a while."

"Why are you here again?" I can't believe someone would be here when they had just been fired.

"Because I said that I would be. I didn't want you to open the door to Lemur's stark face and think your lawsuit was in the toilet. They're right, and they'll handle the case with perfection. I just didn't want you to think I'd abandoned you, Morgan. You're entitled to select your own lawyer, and quite frankly, I'm here hopeful you've made your choice, and you're satisfied with it."

"I don't want Lemur and Lemur. They sound like an exhibit at the San Francisco Zoo, not a set of lawyers."

"They're the best, Morgan. Your dad is a big client, and they won't let him falter." George stands up, and I'm face to face with those abs again—well, really just his business shirt, but my imagination flourishes. What is wrong with me? "That's not true. I'm the best."

He starts to pack away the papers. I stand up and meet those forested eyes as he dons his matching jacket.

I want to say a million things. I thought George was a part of my life for the next year at least, and now he's telling me that I have to make the choice. Haven't I made nothing but wrong choices? And my history wasn't even as salacious as a stripper and a sexual harassment suit. I'm just too afraid to make this decision on my own. It's too big. It means too much, and trusting this man . . . this man who showed up at my doorstep when he knew he wasn't really retained by me. . . . It sends chills up my spine.

"Will you come to the indictment hearings tomorrow? I'm not ready to make a choice. I'll pay you to be there. I don't know how, but as a consultant. My father won't be there. I just want to know someone's on my side. Lemur and Lemur can't say anything about my hiring a consultant as well as them."

"I wish I could Morgan, but you have to hire me on your own or this is considered stealing a client. I can't be with you tomorrow."

"Why not?"

"Lemur is your attorney now. Any witnesses won't be allowed to have an attorney present, so it's a small group. Maybe about twenty people on the jury and the FBI witnesses. It will be over before you know it, and I just think you're not guilty, so you're better off facing the jury than forfeiting your rights. The grand jury will have to approve any charges. Since the prosecutor has already charged you, tomorrow is a preliminary hearing. Lemur will get the opportunity to defend you." He slides the last folder into the briefcase. "Don't leave the apartment today. Lemur should be here soon." I nod, my eyes closing, and I feel his palm come to my cheek. I put my hand over it, holding it there briefly. All I have to say is that he's hired, yet I can't get my mouth to form the words.

"Thanks for all your work."

George's phone rings, and he answers it immediately after seeing the number. His expression immediately changes. "I have to go." He runs from the apartment.

I walk into my bedroom and slam the door. Just once in my life, I want to meet someone who doesn't turn his back on me and leave me to face the consequences alone. I suppose that's entirely too much to expect from a lawyer.

chapter 32

"H i, Daddy." I see my dad lying in the hospital bed, and my first thought is how strong and perfectly normal he looks. But as he speaks it's a different story.

"Princess," he moans. I reach over the bed and kiss his forehead.

"How are you feeling?" I ask him, careful to not show any sign of emotion other than the crisp kiss he requires.

"I thought you were warned not to come here." His full voice is back intact now, and I stand back.

"You're my father. I'm not going to let a lawyer tell me I can't see my father."

"I hired us the best firm in the business. You're going to do what they tell you. Now go on, get out of here. If George told you, that's good enough for Lemur and Lemur."

I stand up straighter. "No, I'm not going."

"Morgan Malliard, this is not a joke."

"Am I laughing?"

"You need to go home and be with Gwen. She has the designers coming over, and I'm sure she'd like your input on the changes."

I'm sure she would. "Daddy, there won't be any changes. The lawyers said the penthouse will be up for collateral if these indictments come down. We're not going to be able to do anything to the house. And we can't buy anything else and move, so we should brace for some harsh treatment by the co-op board. George quit, you know. The Heffers, or whatever they're called, are handling the case."

"That's true about the co-op. I'll tell Gwen when she visits. I had that kid fired. Do you know he was trying to get you to turn on your father?"

I literally start to tremble when he tells me this. I'm looking at this man who is a total stranger to me. He's lying there in the hospital bed, and I see just another patient. I'm trying to remember to breathe. My father is drowning under a sea of his own dishonesty, and rather than setting me free, he's pushing me under to get himself air.

Narcissistic, selfish, greedy monster who cares only for his own image.

"I am made in Christ's image. Not yours," I say, practically spitting the words through my clenched mouth. Not probably the best way to use Scripture, but I'm struggling here. "You're the one who fired George?"

"He's just a kid. Thinks we're better on our own, but that isn't the case. They're more likely to go after one of us that way."

"You think they'll go after me?" I ask.

"Morgan, we don't want them going after either one of us. One for all, and all for one."

"A cord of three strands isn't quickly broken," I say, quoting Ecclesiastes.

"Right. Right."

"The third strand being God, of course."

"No, no," he holds up a palm. "I am not getting into the religious discussion again. You believe whatever you want, I won't bother you, but you leave me out of it."

"If only you'd been so kind to me." It's the first time I can remember ever really attacking my father and it leaves a sick feeling in my stomach.

He wrinkles his forehead, "What?"

"I am not your property, Dad. I never was, and as for this lawsuit? I'll give away whatever I have to give to make it right with the government, but I didn't do what they're accusing me of. I won't turn on you, Dad, but I won't take the blame either."

"You're not going to have to give anything back. It's mine, Morgan. I earned it fair and square."

"It's yours? Or it's ours?"

"Ours. You know what I meant."

I look into his eyes—the dark, empty eyes of a caged animal—and I wonder how I ever thought this man cared about me. Just like Andy, I only saw what I wanted to see, and my troubles started long before a fake Christian rock star. They were all about the fantasy of creating a father who actually loved me.

Parents love their children. It's just the way it is. Unless those parents love something far more deeply. Sometimes it's drugs. Sometimes it's another woman, or money or power. But sometimes, parents love themselves so much they are absolutely incapable of seeing people as anything more than an extension of themselves—a rung on the ladder to lift them ever higher on their own great throne.

My expression falters, and I think about the words my mother wrote to me: "Get an education. Make your own money. Don't let them break you."

"You haven't broken me," I say to my father.

"That's right. We Malliards get right back on the horse."

"And we get thrown, yet again."

I go to the nearby sink, and I wet my hands, applying

soap and lathering my fingers full of antiseptic bubbles. I manage to pull off the precious blue diamond ring, and I set it on the sink while I dry my hands, and then the ring. I approach my father's bed, and my heart is in my throat as I think about life as I know it being over. The money being such a very small part of it.

I hold out the ring to him.

"What am I supposed to do with this?" he asks gruffly.

"Give it to your fiancée. I understand she doesn't have a ring yet."

"I was going to give it to her Saturday night at the club, so everyone could see it." He starts to get excited, thinking about the spectacle. "The women at the club will turn green when they see what I've got in store for Gwen, and if at least 25 percent of the men there on Saturday night aren't in my store by Monday, I wish them the best going home to their wives."

I keep holding up the ring, but he's pushing it back towards me. "Take it, Dad."

"I can't take it Morgan. I'm in a hospital."

"I'll give it to a nurse then. I'll bet one of them would enjoy it." I start to turn from the room.

"You can't give it to a nurse. It belongs to the store. We can't just write off that kind of money." He starts to get agitated, and I worry I've upset him too much. I grab the ring in my hand.

"See you at home, Dad."

"Yeah, yeah. And don't go acting crazy because you think the sky is falling. I know the tax laws like the back of my hand. The back of my hand!"

He's still shouting it at me as I leave the room.

When I'm able to notice my surroundings again, I'm face to face with the hospital white board, with patients' names scrawled haphazardly in the lines. I stare at it absently, until....

My focus hones in on the name "George Gentry" and my heart begins to pound. I look up the room number—248—and I start to walk down the hallway, feeling the wall as I take in each room number.

252

250

248

The door is closed when I get there, and I wonder what possible excuse I might come up with if I walk into this room and discover an old man who may or may not be George Gentry's father. He did get an urgent phone call. What if it was about something bad and George's father is in serious condition, like my own father?

After a few paces back and forth outside the doorway, I close my eyes, whisper a short prayer, and knock on the door.

"George!" I say, seeing my former lawyer hugging a child, who seems about four, with wispy blond hair, cherub cheeks tinged with color, clear blue eyes, and the unmistakable expression of Down's Syndrome. His eyes are red from crying, and he takes sharp intakes of breath and cuddles closer to George.

"You came to see your father," George accuses.

I just nod.

"I knew you would. You don't seem the type to take direction very well." To my surprise, he smiles.

"What are you doing here?" I ask, certain it's none of my business.

"My son had a little accident."

"Your son?" I feel myself swallow hard at the thought that George Gentry surprised me yet again. There are a thousand questions racing through my mind, not the least of which is "Huh?" But I see from the steel in George's eye as he watches my reaction that now is not the time. So I just take a breath and nod. *A son*, I say over and over again in my mind. *He has a son.*

George loosens a bit and smiles down at his boy, who's still holding on tightly. "This is George Gentry the fifth, so if you think my mother isn't very creative, you're really going to have an issue with me."

"Is he all right? What happened to him?"

"He's a bit clumsy sometimes, and he took a little tumble. His bones are fragile, so they brought him here as a precaution, but he's just scared. He is a trooper, aren't you, Georgie?"

The little boy nods, and the sight of the two so obviously in awe of one another makes my heart leap.

"He's in daycare?" I ask, wondering how on earth George manages a career and his son.

George looks down. "My mom watches him during the day. She went to get some coffee. You just missed her. I think Georgie gave her the scare of her life today. No more jumping off the landing, right?"

I come closer to little Georgie, and take in his sweet expression and babylike features. "He's gorgeous." I allow my hand to touch his cheek, and I'm rewarded with a toothy grin. "Just like his father."

"You see what I mean about being an optimist? Sometimes, our biggest mistakes give us our greatest rewards."

"The fiancée?"

He nods and stands up, lifting Georgie onto a table. "They're just about to check us out of here. You up for some dinner?"

"Me?" I put my hand on my chest.

"The four of us: Georgie, my mom, and me and you, of course. We'd love to have you if you aren't too busy, and now that I'm not your lawyer, you can get that good meal you've been craving."

"I'd love to."

"We'll celebrate me losing my job."

"And my last night of true freedom."

I slide my father's ring back on my right hand so I don't lose it, and then I ask if I can pick up Georgie from the table.

"What do you think, big man? You want to see Miss Morgan?" He warns me, "He's getting heavy to hold."

Georgie grins widely, and I pick him up, "I can handle it. All that time at Square One wasn't for nothing." I stare into the most beautiful, innocent blue eyes I have ever seen. I feel my eyes prick with tears as I think about his purity, and the depth of love George so obviously has for him.

"He likes you."

"I bet he's like his dad, and probably sees the best in most people."

George's mother comes back into the room, blowing on her steaming hot cup of coffee. She looks like George, with dark brown hair tinged with gray and dark brown eyes. She pauses in surprise when she sees me, but when she notes my emotion, she smiles warmly.

"He's just like his daddy. Goes straight for the pretty girls, don't you, Georgie?"

"Mom, this is Morgan Malliard."

"The lawsuit girl?"

The fiancée girl, the spinster of death, the daughter of denial, the ice princess . . . take your pick. I just nod and she does the strangest thing—she grabs a lock of my hair.

"You're much prettier in person. The papers don't do you justice."

I just laugh.

"I loved that wedding gown. You have to tell your best friend she's a heck of a designer."

"She is, isn't she?"

"You hear my son got fired today?"

I nod.

"Did you have anything to do with that?" She narrows her gaze.

"Probably. I sort of attract trouble like a lint roller."

Mrs. Gentry puts her arm around me. "Good, then we'll get along just fine, honey."

George takes his son from me and sets him on the table, tying his shoes. The act is so simplistic, yet so beautiful all at once. When he's finished, I reach out my hand to him, saying with my eyes how hopeful I am. Laying out the fleece, and wondering if he's been feeling the same thing as me. He clasps my hand tightly, and we look into one another's eyes. This time, it's not my imagination.

The three of us walk out of the room, following his mother. I don't take my eyes off of George, and I think to myself, sometimes our biggest mistakes give us our greatest reward.

"Y ou know that I'm unemployed, and I live with my mother." George's words make me laugh out loud, and his mother purses her lips.

We're at Denny's. Fine dining and Georgie are not a good match, but he's partial to the chicken dinosaurs with a side of ketchup, and I can't say there's anywhere I'd rather be at the moment. Tomorrow holds so much trepidation for me, and being in the mundane environment of Denny's makes me forget I'm special. Either as a former diamond heiress or a possible grand-jury defendant. Tonight, I'm just Morgan Malliard eating a Swiss-mushroom burger at Denny's.

"You think unemployment scares me? Hah! As long as you've got under two wives, I think we should talk."

"This isn't funny," Mrs. Gentry says calmly. "You two think this is funny?"

George and I meet each other's smiles and laugh all over again. "Hmm. No job, living with his mama. You sound just like one of my former fiancés." I shrug. "Is there a problem? Of course, you do realize that I'm under federal investigation, and am facing twenty-eight years in jail for wire fraud and illegal offshore accounting?" I raise an eyebrow.

His mother is shaking her head, "Could we eat our dinner

without this? You're both giving me indigestion."

Georgie is happily marching his dinosaurs across the plate, then biting their heads off with vigor, leaving little headless chicken nuggets askew.

"I'm sorry." I breathe in deeply. "I'm just nervous, I suppose. Hearing your name associated with the term *grand jury* is a little daunting."

She puts her hand on mine, "I'm sure it is, honey."

No one knows what will happen tomorrow. I know my father's lawyers won't allow me to separate myself from him and the charges, for fear he'll be sent up the river for a long time, and I just don't think I could do it anyway. I don't care how my father has always treated me, he doesn't deserve to be abandoned.

"You're thinking about your father," George says seriously.

I nod, looking over my half-eaten hamburger, but having forgotten my appetite.

"I think we can get your case separated, Morgan. Plead ignorance." George dabs his napkin in water and wipes it across Georgie's ketchup-laden mouth.

"It's too late. The grand jury is meeting tomorrow, and Daddy's already planned his defense. Our defense. I can't just let him take it alone."

George slams his hand on the table. "Why not? Why can't you let your father take the rap for doing what he did? It was illegal, Morgan. If he pulled the trigger on the man, would you take the blame?"

I open my mouth, but I can't find words.

"Come on, Mom. I've got to get home. I'm preparing a case for Morgan Malliard."

I don't get up from the table. "Don't do it, George. It doesn't matter."

"Look at you, Morgan. You're beautiful, you're fabulous

with kids, and you have more love for that stone of a man than I can possibly imagine. Do you know what that says about your character?"

I smile up at him, "It says I'm an optimist."

"Who is acting very ignorant. I've seen the preliminary hearing information, Morgan. It's obvious your dad did this."

I clutch my stomach, feeling a wave of nausea hit me, and I shake my head. "He wouldn't."

George kneels beside me at the table, which makes everyone in the restaurant turn towards us as if he's asking me to marry him. We're in Denny's, people. I may not have huge criteria for a fiancé, but I am adamant that I would deserve a better proposal than in Denny's over a Swiss-mushroom burger that has just given me onion breath.

"He did it, Morgan. I've seen the wire transfers. I've seen the illegal laundering of money. It's not a mistake you're named on this. It was a way your father could launder more money."

I shake my head. "No, I don't believe that."

"Morgan, I have absolutely no reason to lie to you. None. Look into my eyes."

I search the deepness of his eyes, and I look at the happy giggles of Georgie as he roars and rips the feet off another dinosaur.

"Fathers don't allow their children to suffer. Normal fathers would give up everything to give their children more."

I force the lump in my throat away. I know what he says is true. I think about the letter from my mother, the harsh words from my father, and I know it's true. "But if I separate on the lawsuit, even if the grand jury allows me such a luxury, I'm only piling more on my father, and I can't do that. I'm the only one here to love him. If I'm not Jesus to him, who will be?"

"Morgan, you can't be a doormat and go to jail. Look at Georgie. Don't you want to know what your child might look like? Don't you want a chance to live your life?"

I nod. "I do, but not at the expense of my dad."

George's expression falls. "I understand."

But it's clear he doesn't. "I didn't profit from any of that money, George. They can't prove that I did. It will be fine."

"They can prove it, and they will unless you defend yourself and separate from your father."

I shake my head. "I can't do that."

"Let's go to the bathroom, Georgie." Mrs. Gentry takes her grandson by the hand, and they leave me alone with this incredible man I want to trust with my whole heart, but can't do at the risk of watching my father lose everything he worked for. I know the money is secondary to his reputation. This has to be killing him.

"Why are you working so hard for him, Morgan? When are you going to believe the truth that he has brought you into this mess?"

"I took advantage of it. I never questioned the money or what I was able to buy with it."

George gets back up and sits in the chair. "So what can I do?" He holds his hands out.

"You can pray, George. We've only seen the preliminary ruling. The actual charges have to come down from the grand jury, and I'll get my say tomorrow." Inside, of course, I don't feel nearly so confident, and when I see George and his family, I do know what I could be missing. To see how a normal family functions with love and laughter gives me pause like I hadn't imagined.

George has suffered, there's no getting around it, but he has also come out victorious. I can only hope for as much grace as God bestowed upon him.

I stand up, and I take his hand, "I hear you, George. I know you think I'm incredibly naïve, but I can't destroy my father to save myself. I just can't. He may not be the father that you are to Georgie, but I really do believe his motives were pure. He just got in over his head and was seduced by the money."

"You're making excuses for him."

I nod. "I probably am. Say good night to Georgie and your mother for me." I walk towards the door. George runs after me, and I turn to see him laying forty dollars and the bill at the cashier's desk.

"Morgan."

I walk outside under the cool fall night, and I pull my sweater around me tightly to ward off the damp. "You're incredible, do you know? I believe you, George, if it makes any difference. I really do, but something inside me says I deserve this. I lived off this money and it's time to pay the piper."

"Not the illegal stuff, don't you see that? The illegal stuff was off in an offshore account somewhere."

"George." I walk to him, stand before him and feel his breath, which clouds in the night's cold air. I'm face to face with him. He can't be any taller than me, and I suddenly feel so gawky and huge. I close my eyes, imagining what life could be like if I'd been born smarter, or into a family that played by normal rules. A family that didn't think fat was a plague, and poverty a disease.

His arms come around me, and he presses his lips against mine, and I feel the kiss through my entire frame.

This is what it feels like to be loved.

I pull the blue diamond off, easier now with the cold night shrinking my fingers, and I put the ring into his hand, closing his fingers around it.

"Diamonds are most certainly not a girl's best friend." I reach up and I kiss his cheek and put my hand on his neck as I say good-bye. Inside the restaurant I see Georgie, and I feel my eyes welling up again as I turn away.

"Morgan, the ring? What's this about?"

"Pick a better fiancée next time. That little boy in there deserves it."

I smile to myself as I walk toward the garage housing my car. Grand jury, here I come.

The loft is dark and eerie as I arrive home, but I'm floating on a platinum-lined cloud. To kiss a man like George— someone who is capable of loving a person past their accomplishments—was an incredible feeling, however brief. He's proof of grace. And while I might never see him again, the possibility is enough to keep me soaring upward. Although I've always known my father's ways weren't right, now I have proof positive of grace on earth, of action that I've heard spoken of for so many years in church. The knowledge that sometimes we don't get what we deserve, and life isn't all about living up to a perfect ideal. The beauty is often in the flaws.

Speaking of flaws, Nate is outside the door when I get home. "Is Lilly coming home tonight?"

"She's staying at Max's."

He whistles.

"Her husband's house. They got married."

He whistles again.

"Can you let me in?" he asks.

"Why?"

"Kim says her driver's license is in there."

"Kim?" I ask. "Would that be the Kim whose stuff you splattered all over the front steps?"

"Passionately." He wiggles his eyebrows. "I threw it passionately. She gave me an ultimatum. I don't like to be challenged. No man wants to hear his days as a playboy are over."

"Clearly."

"But she was right, so we're going to Reno tonight to get married. Do you want to come be a witness?"

"Doesn't anyone have a real wedding anymore?"

He shrugs. "I think it will help our relationship."

"Uh-huh," I say, unconvinced. "I wish you the best, but I've got court tomorrow afternoon. I'm afraid weddings are off-limits for the time being." Not to mention, if I showed up, it probably wouldn't happen. I have a knack for canceling weddings.

I open the door, and Nate goes for the refrigerator, where he pulls Kim's driver's license off the top. Of course, why wouldn't it be on the top of a friend's fridge?

"Good luck tomorrow, huh? No hard feelings." Nate holds his hand out to me, and I shake it.

"Thanks, Nate. You, too."

He takes off, and I'm left to the quiet roar of Lilly's loft. I guess it will be my loft soon. I take out the library of paperwork George left me with this afternoon, and see all the charges left to become formalized by a grand jury. I suppose we're lucky we got a preliminary hearing. A typical grand-jury indictment can come down without any chance to defend yourself. At least I'll get the opportunity, even if it's nothing more than a glimmer of hope.

I start to read all the words until my eyes are fuzzy, and there's a knock at the door. I gather up the pages, stuff them into a nearby box, and look outside the peep hole. I can't imagine who'd be here at this time of night.

It's Lilly and Max.

"Why did you knock? It's your house," I say as I open the door.

"We didn't want to scare you. I came home to get a few things." She snuggles into Max. "We're moving in together. Like a normal married couple."

"You two will never be a normal married couple," I laugh. "But I'm truly thrilled for you."

"At the end of the month, we're having a connection celebration at the hotel."

"What is a connection celebration?"

"Max's mother wants to make sure everyone knows we're already married so she's come up with the name so she can announce our wedding date beforehand in the paper."

"Connection celebration? It sounds like you're getting high-speed Internet service."

Max grins. "I think she thought it was better than my-young-stud-son-got-his-wife-pregnant-already celebration. It makes us sound less like farm animals this way."

"Not really," I quip.

"It's November 28 at the Red & White Ball. You and Poppy will be there, and I'm making your gowns. I'm wearing the one I made for you. Mrs. Schwartz thought it would be a perfect place to announce our nuptials, and I can wear the white gown without questions beforehand."

"The one that's been on the front of every newspaper in town, yet never made it down the aisle? That wedding dress."

"I can't have my design name associated with a—" She stops for a minute. "Well, you know, no offense, but a failure wedding dress."

I scratch my head. "No offense taken."

"Is it still here? I'm going to take it in."

"Salt in the wound, Lilly."

"And sew some boobs in it, okay?"

I laugh. "Okay. It's a gorgeous dress." I take it out of the closet, and allow my fingers to run over it one last time.

"You'll be a beautiful bride, Lilly."

"Hey, so will you, and I'll make you a better dress when your day comes, all right?"

"Oh my gosh, I'll probably end up marrying some loser who writes to me in prison because he saw my picture in the paper. We'll have conjugal visits, my baby will be born, and then taken away from me by child protective services while I scream through the bars."

"Would you quit? Don't be ridiculous." Lilly grabs my hand. "Where's the blue diamond?"

"I gave it to my lawyer."

Her forehead wrinkles in confusion. "Why would you give a ring like that to a lawyer?"

I look away, picturing his warmth and the sweet love I witnessed between him and Georgie. "Because he taught me to see the beauty in imperfection. I thought it only right he should possess a little perfection when the right woman comes along."

"You're going strange on me, girl."

"I'm going to take over the lease here, if that's all right."

"You're going to live here?"

"I have a little income that I'm still entitled to. I'll make the rent."

"It's not the rent I'm worried about. Have you ever really lived on your own?"

"I'll be fine, Lilly."

I start to tell her about Nate, but I don't want to ruin her moment. As she eyes the wedding gown, and makes the adjustments in her head, I watch Max following her with his eyes.

"You're letting him see the gown before you're in it?"

Lilly shrugs. "We're married already."

Max looks at the box filled with legal paperwork. "This all for tomorrow?"

I nod.

"Do you want us to be there with you?"

"They won't let you in anyway. There's no reason to come. Just pray for me, and my dad."

Lilly purses her lips. "I will. You call me the minute you hear anything."

"Nothing will happen tomorrow, Lilly. They'll decide they're charging us, and we'll wait years for a trial. This is only the beginning." I flop onto the futon. "I'm so glad I have a place to call home that's free of my father and Gwen. This is perfect for me," I pat the futon.

Lilly looks worried, and I have to admit, I have never in my life spent a night alone, other than in my dorm room, where I could just knock on a neighbor's door. Even Nate and Kim are gone, and this is me. I'm on my own, which I guess is what I said I wanted. A life with purpose. I was just hoping for more than staying out of jail as a goal.

chapter 34

efore I head to the courthouse, I offer to help Jenna get herself together for the girls to have their photo taken. I ring the doorbell, my suit carefully tucked away in plastic for fear the girls will decide to finger paint with jelly, and wait for several minutes before Jenna appears at the door. Although I spent the entire morning yesterday cleaning the house, there is literally not one sign that anyone's been here for more than six months.

"What happened?"

"Storm Keller happened. Aren't they effective?"

"Girls, you did not make this mess."

They nod proudly, as though they'll receive a reward for their efforts.

I sigh, taking them both by the hand. "Go get a shower, Jenna; this is your opportunity. Are their dresses for the pictures out?"

"Hanging on their door."

I climb the thin Victorian stairs, holding the hand of Anne (in front of me) and Amber (behind me) and when we get into their room, I draw a bath in the clawfoot tub for them both. As their wiggling bodies drain most of the water from the tub, and I wrestle them to get their hair washed, we end up giggling as they make soap bubble beards and clothes. I pull them both out of the tub, taking towels from the warming rack and wrapping them up in precious bundles.

"I am so not going to jail."

The little girls blink as though I've lost my mind, and their giggling stops. "I didn't have anything to do with this, Anne. Nothing, Amber, do you hear me?"

They both nod, incredulous that the game has stopped, and seeing their confused glances, I warm my expression immediately. "Because I have games to play, and puzzles to put together, and I have a family to be a part of."

I brush each girl's hair out, saturating it in some high-end version of "No More Tangles" that doesn't work nearly as well. It was my saving grace as a child. Once their hair is dried, I get them dressed for pictures in frilly frocks that render them the picture of sweet little angels with no sign of the terror within save their blue-eyed glimmers.

As I bring them downstairs, Jenna is dressed and ready to go. "You're going to be all right taking them to the photographers?"

"We'll be fine; it's in a place with plenty of parking."

"I'll stay here and get things cleaned up and then I'm off to the courthouse. But I'll see you in the morning."

"Perfect, we'll see you then." She gathers her girls and leaves me alone in the house to once again find the carpet under all the toys, and the places for kitchen utensils that have been windswept as play dough tools and battle accouterments in the living room—the formal living room.

My cell phone trills, and I note it's my father's cell number. "Hi, Daddy," I answer. "How are you feeling today?" I try to forget everything that took place between us the night before. If I'm going to move on—or in, as the case may be—I don't need a heart of darkness.

"Never better, princess. You ready to take on these Feds?"

"I am." I take a last look around the Keller home and its lived-in warmth, and I realize this is who God gave me for a father. Had I been presented with the opportunity to pick my own, I probably couldn't have done as well as God. My father may not be warmth personified, but he never allowed me to wallow in misery if he could make things better. Certainly, he used things to do it, but I can see now it's the only language he knew.

I get into my car, and I drive to the federal courthouse. A band of photojournalists snap my picture and I smile for them, widely. I climb the steps and enter the quiet hallway where I'm of about as much importance as the corbels on the ceiling—probably less.

Once inside the courtroom, the somber mood burdens my soul immediately. I look over the jurors—people who will decide my fate for the next couple of years—and they seem so severe. So ready to send me to my cell, and I can see my legs shaking as I sit in the chair. Monkey and Monkey (Lemur and Lemur) come and sit down across from me, and soon, to my surprise, my father is wheeled in wearing a freshly pressed suit I've never seen before. Leave it to Richard Malliard to have a tailor on call from the hospital.

"Dad, what are you doing here?"

"I wouldn't leave my little girl to these wolves alone," he whispers.

The charges against us are officially only criminal complaints. The grand jury has the power today to make indictments against us, and the list seems endless. I can honestly say after reading over the complaints last night that I've done nothing wrong, but as I look at the list of witnesses the prosecutor will call, I'm glad we won't be able to stay to hear the witnesses speak. I can see most of them avoiding my gaze.

I lean over to my father, afraid to speak, but needing some form of comfort. "Let's pray this is over today, Daddy."

He pats my leg. "It will be, Morgan. We're innocent."

I wish I had his confidence.

The first witnesses are called, and my father and I are excused from the room, though our lawyers stay. When I come back in the jury room, I try to decipher any expression, but there's none to be had.

My father is the picture. Clearly he has no worries, and he leans up and asks his accompanying nurse to get him a drink of water. If I didn't know him so well, it would invoke sympathy within me. Which it's clearly meant to do. I see his strained expression, and him clutch the nurse's arm as though it's taking every last ounce of his strength. "Water," I hear him croak again.

As he faces the jurors, he puts that plastic smile on—the one I know has absolutely no meaning of true affection behind it. It's troubling to see your parent's worst side, and for me, I suppose that one is so intermingled with his good side I can't discern one from the other. I imagine he's seen my bad side as well.

He won't look at me. He's withholding any emotion until I've proven my worth and testified accordingly, but as I search his face, I see the seething anger boiling under his plastered expression. He really feels as though he has a right to do whatever he wants. My heart sinks as I finally discover who he has always been. George was right.

The prosecutor turns to my father, and I watch his smile get bigger.

"How are you today, Mr. Malliard?" The prosecutor asks.

Bigger smile, "I'm fine, young man."

"We've heard from several witnesses that you and your daughter have taken in quite a bit of money."

He laughs. "That's what a successful business is supposed to do, is it not?"

As the questions become more difficult, I can see the strain on his face become more evident. The prosecutor has become less openly friendly and has started pointing out exact things my father did as general partner of the business.

Things like business trips to Caicos.

Tax returns that were lower than your average plumber's.

Extravagant business trips to Saudi Arabia, Aruba, and more.

And the wire transfers. Lord, the wire transfers. The money taking better trips than I ever thought possible. Clearly, that's the most damaging of it all, and I see the jurors shift as they hear about how many countries my father's money visited before it made it back to the United States—to us.

Through it all, my father doesn't flinch. When they're through with him, the prosecutor, a young man of about thirty-four or so fighting for the ideals of his country and justice in all things, turns to me. I've already been sworn in, so he begins to ask questions.

"You live a pretty good life?"

"I do," I admit. I figure he doesn't want the sob story about how my parents didn't hug me, so I go straight for what the world sees. Life in a penthouse, wearing elegant jewels to elite parties.

"Is this your signature?" I look closely at the paper he's thrust before me.

"No," I shake my head, more surprised than he is. "It isn't my signature."

"Objection," Monkey says.

"Objection to what?"

"She's been through a lot in the last few days. I'm certain her memory—"

"I know my own signature. It's not mine."

"This is your limited partnership agreement."

"I signed a lot of things. I'm not denying that. But that isn't my signature."

"Objection," my so-called-lawyer says again and I turn to him.

"What are you objecting about? That's not my signature. Are you my lawyer or aren't you?"

The judge knocks his gavel. "Mr. Lemur, is there a problem?"

"Permission to approach the bench, your honor." I got that from *Law and Order*.

He sighs. "Come ahead."

As I come to the bench, which is really just a raised table on a carpeted step, I say my fears out loud, "Your honor, that isn't my signature, and it's dated back when I was in college. I wasn't even living here in the city. I don't think my lawyer is acting in my best interest."

"Do you want to fire him?"

I look back at the desk where Lemur and Lemur are consulting with my father in deep conversation.

"Can I?"

"It's not the best time to be without a lawyer. You're lucky you're getting counsel at all before a grand-jury indictment."

"I'll take my chances."

"Recess." The judge calls. "Counsel, approach the bench. Ten minutes for everyone else."

As the judge tells my lawyers what I've just said, I see my father's expression darken and he looks at me the same way he used to look at my mother—as a boulder in his very clear path towards whatever he wants. I've tried so hard to believe the lie. The lie that he was the part he played—the perfect father who loved me unconditionally. My heart sinks as I realize that my wanting to believe in him was wasted emotion, and living in the fairy tale I always wanted to make happen.

The signature isn't mine, and neither is the life I thought I had.

My father beckons me over with his finger, but I look away. I feel my whole body as though it's in muck, and I have to force each step. I won't look at him. If I look at him, I'll feel the guilt. I will feel it's right to go down with the ship, but the truth is I never embarked on this ship in the first place. I was packed in a crate and taken along for the ride. I wish with my whole heart that George was here.

This is it. I may still go to jail, and I have just said good-bye to my family. If you don't play by Richard Maillard's rules, he takes his toys and goes home. I close my eyes as I walk down the makeshift aisle. I can't bear to look at him.

It's then that I feel the sharp sting in the back of my head. My surroundings suddenly become fuzzy and I see the ground rise up. I feel the darkness surround me . . .

"Morgan? Morgan."

"Here, let her sniff this."

When I wake up, I see Lilly and Poppy hovering over me. I'm in a hospital room. Poppy is shoving a sharp-smelling element from a jar in my face, and Lilly is trying to pull it away. "Quit it, Poppy; you're probably going to keep her out for a week with that stuff."

"What do you think they used in Victorian times? They used smelling salts. This is just the natural version."

"What if the doctor comes in here and sees you with that stuff? She's got a welt the size of Mt. Tamalpais on the back of that head."

I blink a few times, wondering if I'm imagining all this, but then I feel myself break into a grin as I realize my wonderful, bickering friends are here.

"I'm awake," I say, pushing the foul-smelling potion away. "What are you trying to do, kill me?" I start to sit up and feel the headache rush my entire noggin. "Oh," I grab my temples. "What the heck?"

They both look at each other, unwilling to tell me.

"Did someone hit me?"

"A brass paper weight, actually," Lilly says.

"I take it someone threw it."

Poppy nods.

"Is it who I think it is?"

They both nod again.

I grab my head with both of my hands. My family is gone. I know I never had the type of family that would tempt anyone, but it was all I knew. "I said I wanted to be free. I suppose I should be careful what I wish for."

Poppy takes my hand, and my two best friends, my real family, hover over me. "The good news is the grand jury dropped all charges against you. The foreman said anything you signed would be null and void due to the abuse."

"He's never hit me before," I say, stunned.

"He never had to, Miss Compliance." Lilly brushes my hair off my forehead. "You all right?"

"I want a hot-stone massage." I giggle, which makes me groan in pain. "I suppose I'm too poor for that, with the exception of the gift certificate you two got me."

"Your salary will continue to be paid until the lawsuit is over. Your dad was indicted on all counts."

"I can't believe it."

"Why not?"

"I just would have never thought him capable of cracking like that publicly. Our whole lives have been about the show, and when it really counted, he couldn't do it."

"I guess we all have our snapping point," Poppy says.

"I guess we do." I try to feel happy about being free of the indictment, but for the time being, I can only think about my father disappearing from my life. What's next?

chapter

35

The Red & White Ball is the height of luxury in San
Francisco, and as I dress in the dreamy scarlet gown
Lilly made for me, I realize tonight is the first time I will
have seen my father in two months. I suck in a deep breath
wondering what it will be like. I will forever be his Benedict
Arnold. His turncoat. How appropriate that I should be wearing red tonight.

I look into the full-length mirror that Lilly glued onto the
wall with some industrial product (I know because I tried to
tear it off to no avail) and I can see my nerves showing. I did
my own nails in a matching red, and they look homespun,
but that's the least of my problems.

My gown is a subtle shade of scarlet, sort of a fire-engine
red with a layer of chiffon over it to tone it down. It's got a
ruched bodice and free-flowing skirt that still clings, but the
chiffon gives it an ethereal feel that makes it look as if I'm
floating on air. The gown is strapless, but there's a matching
wrap and I pull it around me, clasping it with the fabric knot
Lilly created. Lilly is as good as any of the top designers I've
paid for in my lifetime.

As I look into the mirror I note there's not a single piece
of jewelry on me. Not a pair of simple earrings, not even a

necklace. I reach for my collarbone, feeling a bit naked to be entering a party wearing absolutely no gemstones and no sales pitch. My tenure as the daughter of San Francisco's Jeweler is over.

There's a knock at the door.

"You ready?" Nate and Kim are at the door, and they look like the picture of mainstream society. Kim is wearing the same dress, albeit with straps and a high back to cover her tattoos, and Nate is in a black tuxedo.

"I'm ready," I nod. I look back at the loft, a hobby of sorts that I've spent time cleaning and designing on my meager budget, and the stipend my father has been court-ordered to pay. It's not the stuff of San Francisco's top designers, but it's mine. Every last Cost Plus trinket and Target painting.

"Did you talk to Lilly today?" Kim asks. "Is she nervous?"

I smile to myself. "She'll be thankful when it's over, but this is good for her to mingle with a crowd that will pay the type of money she's ready to charge. This gown feels like a glove."

"Mine, too." Kim agrees. "She's amazing. I sewed them all in a week, but it's her measuring. She just knows exactly what darts to put in where and she puts them all on paper. The girl can do couture in a day. It's amazing."

Finally. Something Kim and I agree upon.

"The place is looking nice," Nate says to me. "You have a good eye. How's the new job working out?"

Besides being a part-time nanny, after the *Chronicle* ran my grand-jury indictment story and the legend of my father lobbing a brass paper weight up the backside of my head, the media suddenly grew much more understanding of my bad choices regarding men, and I suppose you could say I got a "get out of jail free" card.

Of course my nanny position came to an end when Jenna found someone full time who looked more like Mrs. Bush, Sr.

I loved the girls, and Jenna loved having me help her, but she kept me locked away as though any sighting of me would have constituted my complete evaporation. It wasn't working out, but I did find out that I love children, and I have a special affinity for them. I'm nothing like my mother, it turns out.

The mayor's office called after all the sympathy and my recovery, and I've started working as San Francisco's assistant chief of protocol. Which basically means when dignitaries come into town, I tell the city how they are to be treated based on their net worth. All right, perhaps that's a little pessimistic, but I help organize events for foreign dignitaries (meaning anyone from outside California). I'm a glorified concierge for people who would never be caught dead eating a Big Mac.

As we drive up to the War Memorial Opera House, the lovely French Renaissance building is glowing with the evening's activity. Tuxedos and women in wonderful shades of red are entering on the red carpet, and I feel my stomach twinge at the thought of being back here in a non-working capacity. Unless you count the protocol thing, which basically means I can't be caught eating without the proper utensil.

"Invitation, please," a man in a tuxedo asks as I get to the door, and he looks at the engraved masterpiece that was designed by the senior chief of protocol. "You're attending the Schwartz-Jacobs wedding?"

"I am."

"Right this way."

Nate, Kim, and I are ushered into a room off the main elegant entry. Inside are several socialites I recognize milling about with champagne. And there's Poppy, who looks absolutely stunning in her gown, but who is pouring some type of elixir into a guy's drink.

"Dr. Clayton," I say to her. "Tonight's not the night for health concerns." I pull the guy's drink away from him and grab a fresh one from a nearby waiter's tray. "Here, this will taste better."

The guy reaches for the drink and hustles off. He does look disappointed, though, and I imagine to be near someone who looks like Poppy does tonight he would have drunk any potion she gave him. He leaves the two of us alone, but he'd rather be drinking a lactobacillus latte, or whatever she gave him, and talking with Poppy.

"What are you doing?" I ask her, with a hand on my hip.

"He was complaining of sinus trouble. I thought he'd enjoy the party more if his lung meridians were open."

"Where do you store that stuff?"

She points to her tapestry bag sitting in the corner.

"You did not bring that ratty thing here tonight."

"It's got my stuff in it. I'm a doctor. I told them at the door it was my bag. They actually went through it, if you can believe that."

I let my head fall into my hands. "I can't believe they didn't strip-search you. Lilly had to get you a matching purse for tonight. She knows you better than to not make a matching bag."

"She did. It's inside my tapestry one. I couldn't fit anything in it. It's got room for, like, a lipstick and maybe a comb."

"That's what you're supposed to put in an evening bag with a compact. You are hopeless."

"But healthy." She smiles, and her gleaming white teeth (from a lack of caffeine habit) make me jealous. "This is my chance to share natural healing with Lilly's friends. Think about how much happier the elite would be with natural health."

"You look beautiful. No one would ever know you're anxious to fill them with enzymes. When do we get to see Lilly?"

"She's not here yet, her nana says."

Poppy looks at me, and we share a knowing glance. "You

don't think she'll bail?"

"No, no I don't think she'll bail. She's already married, and this is the chance for people to see that dress make it down the aisle. She wouldn't bail if only for her career."

"True. Doesn't she want us in back when she gets here?"

"Nana says no. Just to stand here, and she'll meet us when the wedding march starts. She just wants to get it over with, so the attention is off her as quickly as possible."

"That's so weird. Totally improper protocol." I'm shaking my head when I turn to see Georgie, dressed in a tiny tuxedo, and holding a lace pillow and I feel my entire being smile. "There's my date. Gotta run."

Georgie is the epitome of joy. He smiles morning, noon, and night, his delighted grin lighting up the room. I notice people around me whisper at a child being here and then I hear the horrible whisper behind me: "Down's Syndrome."

"Georgie." I bend down beside him. "How's my precious man?" I straighten his bow tie, and he stands with his shoulders back, clearly proud of his dapper appearance. "Don't you look handsome." He reaches for my hand, and I stand as I see his father enter frantically looking for him.

"George, you were told to stay by me."

Whispers of discontent surround me, and I know what they're saying. My love life is once again on display, but this time, I could care less about the talk. I stand between my two beloved Georges, taking each of their hands, and I am the belle of the ball. Lilly may be getting married, but tonight is mine alone.

"You look gorgeous," George says into my ear, and I feel a tickle from his lips.

"Are you ready for the wedding?" I ask.

"You mean the connection celebration," he laughs. "I don't want to get it wrong in front of the assistant chief of protocol.

Georgie is the ring bearer. Lilly thought it would be a good idea to announce to society that my current man comes with a precious bundle, and if the paper chooses to discuss it, they'll answer to me—and my boss, the chief of protocol.

"Did you bring the ring?" George asks.

I nod. He's given me back the blue diamond and told me I simply must return it to my father tonight as a symbol for leaving the past on the table. I thought it was a good idea until I stood here under these twinkling lights with a magical set of men as my escorts. Now, it seems like a complete waste. There is no going backward.

"I brought it. You know the papers will be filled with the wrongful spelling of your name on Monday."

"As long as it's linked with yours, I don't care, Morgan. Hopefully, they'll get in that I live with my mother."

"But you're unemployed now, so that sort of ruins it."

We laugh together.

"Hungry," Georgie says.

"I'll get him something to eat." I take the little boy's hand and we walk past the waiters with shrimp cocktail and liver pate crackers. He's looking upward, hoping each tray holds something more in line with hot dogs and chicken nuggets. I knew this would happen, so I take him to a corner and pull out some turkey jerky from my purse.

Poppy arrives to stand over me with her hand on her hip. "You're carrying dried meat and you have the nerve to chastise me."

"I'd carry the turkey himself for this little man."

Georgie tears off a piece of the soft jerky, and I watch to make sure he swallows it without choking. His beautiful blue almond-shaped eyes say thank you, and I take an apple juice box out of my purse.

"What else do you have in there?"

"Crayons, in case he gets bored, the 'learning lobster,' and a small abacus."

Poppy laughs, but being prepared for Georgie's needs is exactly the purpose my life needed. He challenges me to be the kind of person I always knew I could be, and very soon, I hope his father will ask me to do it permanently.

Without warning, the wedding march sounds, and I pull Georgie with me to the front of the room, where he plays with his tie and shows off for all the people oohing and ahhing at him. Max is there waiting for Lilly, and his smile is contagious. Although he's been married for three months now, his anticipation of Lilly's entrance is palpable. I watch them and look back at George. I never knew a simple look could cause such an earthquake of emotion within me.

Poppy stands beside me, with Georgie between us still primping for the audience, and Lilly enters the small but crowded room. I can tell she's looking directly at Max rather than thinking about being on display or his mother's thoughts. As I see her looking absolutely stunning in the gown I wore for some of my worst moments in history, it's lovely to see the gown as it was meant to be worn. And Lilly looks quite buxom in it. I'm not sure if it's the pregnancy taking effect or just some really well hidden pads sewn into her gown.

She walks elegantly down the aisle, and everyone mills around to catch a glimpse of her, gasping when they see her. As they are joined in marriage (or connection, as they're already married) in front of their families, I see George looking at me, and I feel his eyes burning into my quaking frame.

This is what it is to be loved. It is not based on my perfection. Life is so much more than that.

After the brief ceremony, the guests are released into the larger Red & White Ball. George escorts me and his son to the appetizer table, makes me a few bites to eat, and places a cracker into my mouth. I start to giggle when I catch sight of my father with Gwen. She is decked from head to toe in diamonds and rubies, and it's clear she doesn't come from the less-is-more school of thought. She's like the Ghost of Christmas Past, chains clanging as she walks.

My dad sees me, and then George, dons a disgusted look, and walks away from me.

"Georgie, stay here with your dad." I follow my father to the champagne table. "Daddy?"

"Don't call me that." He turns around, and I fear if he could hit me again, he would. Nothing has changed with him. There is no going back.

"I heard you were getting married next month. I just wanted to offer my congratulations. I'm sure you and Gwen will be very happy."

"Thank you," he says coolly. "Is that all?"

"I forgive you, Dad. I'm sorry I let you down, and I forgive you."

"You forgive me?" He laughs.

I look down at my dress. Where once I saw beauty and self-assurance, right now I feel only angst and a lack of confidence. In one moment, he has managed to bring up a lifetime of self-hatred.

I wander away slowly, and I see George's outstretched arms waiting for me. I fall into them and feel my tears start against his handsome tuxedo.

"Can we go?" I ask him.

"It's late for Georgie anyway. We should."

"Thank you for being here. You've gone above and beyond the call of duty as a lawyer." I take the handkerchief he hands me and dab my eyes.

"Do you really believe I ever wanted to be your lawyer?"

He kisses me again, this time harder and with more meaning than I thought possible. At that moment, he takes the blue diamond ring from my hand. "Finish it, Morgan. You've forgiven him. There's nothing more you can do other than show him you're free of these things."

I take the ring, and across the room I meet my father's hard gaze. Gwen walks away from him, sensing there's going to be trouble, I suppose. I walk back and hand him the three-carat flawless diamond. "Sometimes, Daddy, the beauty is in the flaws. It makes something completely one-of-a-kind."

He reaches for the ring and looks into the stone. "Perfect," he says, shaking his head. "Absolutely stunning and exquisite."

"Just like your daughter." George puts his arms around me and faces my father. I see Daddy's jaw twitch at the sight of the man he once fired, thinking like everything else in his life, he had waved his wand and the deed was done. He stuffs a shrimp in his mouth and turns away from us, dropping the blue diamond in his coat pocket.

"You ready to go?" I ask George.

"Let's go get a hamburger."

As I walk between the two men I have grown to love in only two months, I feel completely happy and free. In George, I know that I am capable of loving a man who actually wants the best for me. In Georgie, I know that my mother's sins do not haunt me, and that I am capable of loving a child unconditionally.

The three of us skip towards the door, giggling and allowing the paparazzi to snap pictures of yet one more Morgan Malliard societal sin.

You see, I just asked for one good fish. In His abundance, God gave me two.

Look for the continuing
adventures of the Spa Girls in

Calm, Cool,
& Adjusted

BOOK 3 OF THE

spa girls

COLLECTION

from award-winning author

kristin billerbeck

Coming Soon from Integrity Publishers

INTEGRITY®

PUBLISHERS

www.integritypublishers.com

Contemplating life, love and the pursuit of the perfect pedicure

The first novel in acclaimed author Kristin Billerbeck's chick-lit series introduces us to "The Spa Girls." Best friends since Johnny Depp wore scissors for hands, "The Spa Girls" live very separate lives, but stay in touch with regular—and sometimes emergency —visits to California's Spa Del Mar. There's diamond heiress Morgan Malliard, who's self-sacrificing to a fault; alternative healer Dr. Poppy Clayton, who can't meet a man without asking about his colon; and finally, up-and-coming fashion designer Lilly Jacobs, who thinks her bad hair is the root of all her troubles.

But it's going to take more than a facial and a massage to fix Lilly's problems this time. She's given herself just six months to succeed in her dream career. She's got abandonment issues from her childhood, a nagging grandmother, an unpredictable roommate, a vixen boss and mixed signals from three very different men who certainly aren't helping matters.

What does God have in store for Lilly and her friends? Lay back, kick up your feet and escape with the gals in *She's All That*.

Other Books by Kristin Billerbeck

She's All That

With This Ring, I'm Confused

She's Out of Control

What a Girl Wants

To Truly See

As American as Apple Pie: Four Romantic Novellas

San Francisco: Four Romances Blossom in the City by the Bay

Forever Friends: Four All-New Novellas Celebrating Friendship

Heirloom Brides: Four Romantic Novellas Linked by Family and Love

Blind Dates: Four Stories of Hearts United with a Little Help from Grandma

Fireside Christmas: Four New Inspirational Love Stories from Days Gone By

California: From the Golden State Come Four Modern Novels of Inspiring Love

Lessons of the Heart: Four Novellas in Which Modern Teachers Learn About Love

A Victorian Christmas Keepsake: Three Romantic Novellas About the Treasure of Love at Christmastime . . .